Message from a Mistress

Also by Niobia Bryant

Heated
Hot Like Fire
Make You Mine
Live and Learn
Show and Tell

Published by Kensington Publishing Corp.

Message from a Mistress

NIOBIA BRYANT

Dafina
BOOKS

KENSINGTON PUBLISHING CORP.

DAFINA BOOKS are published by

Kensington Publishing Corp.
119 West 40th Street
New York, NY 10018

Dafina and the Dafina logo Reg. U.S. Pat. & TM Off.

ISBN-13: 978-1-61664-068-2

Printed in the United States of America

I am a writer, born and bred.
I can't even fathom what else I would do besides
creating stories and telling tales.
When it comes to my writing
I dabble in many genres, my ideas are unlimited,
and the ink in my pen is infinite.

—Niobia Bryant

ACKNOWLEDGMENTS

Mama, I love and adore you so much. Words cannot express how much I miss you. My mother. My friend. My angel. I know that I am truly unstoppable now because I have you watching my back in the biggest way. You are / were / will always be the best mom ever because you were born to be a mother / nurturer / caregiver. So many people clung to you because of that. We were all blessed for having you in our lives. Completely.

Tony. My heart. Thank you for being my biggest supporter. My backbone. It's you and me against the world. What they gone do with us? Nada. I love you infinitely.

My big brother Caleb—you been fighting for me since we were kids and I would catch a charge for you. 4Real. Mama would be so proud of us right now. She did good, right? I love you, Bubba.

Kal-El. Auntie loves that baby. I didn't know I could have so much love for someone and I will sing "Auntie loves the baby" to you until you are grown. Yup.

Hajah, you are the sweetest little girl in the world and I cherish you because you have such a big heart for a little nine-year-old. You make me look forward to the summers.

Claudia. You're more than an agent. Stay the same, Mrs. Calm, Cool, and Collected. We both know the best way not to trip in some sexy heels—keep them off the floor. Ow!

To the Dafina team, especially Selena, thanks for everything. Being an editor is such hard and stressful work and I give you the utmost praise for knowing how to do a hundred different things at one time.

To my Twitter, MySpace, Facebook, Yahoo! Group, and Shelfari online family members, thank you so much for keeping me grounded in my love of books and writing. Interacting with you all inspires me to keep writing.

To Cydney Rax, thanks for the blurb. Really appreciate you doing that for me and also for all you do for all writers on Book-Remarks.com.

To all of those who grind so hard for books (reviewers, book clubs, independent bookstores, book vendors on the streets, etc.), thank you all for helping get the word out on what we all love: books.

Last but most definitely not least, I want to thank each and every person who has opened the pages of one of my books and spread the word that my books are definitely something to be enjoyed. Word of mouth beats any type of advertising and promoting. I appreciate y'all. 4Real.

—N.

Message
from a
Mistress

JESSA'S INTRO

Where do I begin? How do I tell the story? Our story. His and mine.

He was my lover and her husband. You would think that wasn't possible—like saying dry rain or cold heat—but it was true. She had the ring and the license . . . but I had him. From that first heated moment in their kitchen when his strong hands reached beneath my skirt to grab my soft, bare ass, I knew I had him.

I don't recall the specific moment when our lust turned to love. When our time spent together became about more than just fucking, more than just rushing through electrifying sex that left us both panting, sweaty, and in various stages of undress. We shifted so easily from sharing clandestine and wonderfully sneaky moments—even in their house while she was there—to him sneaking out of their home to be in my arms and in my bed.

I hated to lie alone at night surrounded by nothing but cool cotton sheets and plush down pillows while she had his hard and warm body to hold close.

I knew the time would come when I would want more from him than just his dick. I wanted his love, his time, his all . . . for me and only me.

She was my friend—true, but he was my lover, my love, and in this game there could only be one winner, as far as I was concerned.

Me.

CHAPTER 1

Jaime Hall enjoyed the feel of the steam pressed against her shoulders and her legs where she sat in the glass shower of their bedroom suite. The thick swirling vapors felt like a lover's gentle touch against her skin and those intimate parts of a woman's body. Her breasts. Her nipples. Her thighs. Her lips—both sets.

She relished it. She needed it.

Sadness weighed her shoulders down and soon she felt tears fill her oval-shaped eyes and race down her cheeks. Jaime brought her shaking hands up to hug herself close. "God, I can't take much more of my life," she whispered into the steam as her head dropped so low that her chin nearly touched her chest.

She heard a sudden noise in her bathroom. Her head jerked up as she immediately swallowed back any more of her tears and frantically wiped any traces of them from her face. The last thing she wanted was for him to see or hear her crying.

"Eric," Jaime called out to her husband of the last seven years.

No answer. Nothing to acknowledge her. Seconds later the bathroom door opened and then closed. Disappointment nudged the door to her heart shut as well. The body's automatic defense mechanisms were amazing.

Jaime rose from the bench, turned off the shower, and walked out of the stall. The vapors swirled around her nude curvaceous frame like fog as she stepped down onto the plush white carpeting that felt like mink against her pedicured feet. As she wiped a clear spot in the grand oval mirror over the pedestal sink, she came face-to-face with her unhappiness. She forced a smile and put on her usual mask, but even she could see it didn't reach her eyes.

She grabbed a towel and wrapped it around her frame. She raced out of her bathroom suite through their spacious cathedral ceiling master bedroom and out to the hall. As she raced down the curved staircase, her towel slipped and fell behind her on the stairs, but she didn't break stride.

Thank God she was home alone, because she wouldn't want anyone to see her stark naked and racing through the house like she was crazy.

"Eric!" she called out, striding through the circular foyer to the kitchen.

The house was quiet. She covered her exposed breasts with her arms as she looked out the kitchen windows over the driveway. The sun was just starting to rise. She just made out his tall and slender figure headed down the street toward their friends' home with his tackle box and fishing rods in hand.

He left to go deep-sea fishing and didn't even bother to tell her good-bye. *How much more can I take?* She turned and let her body slide down to the polished hardwood floor as tears racked her body and she could do nothing but wrap her arms around her knees and rock to make herself feel a little better.

———— ∞ ————

"Shit!" Renee Clinton swore as the gray acrid smoke rose from the frying pan with fury. She hurried to turn off the lit eye of the Viking stove before shifting the pan to one of the remaining five burners.

"Damn, damn, damn it all to hell."

Renee could only shake her head in shame at the blackness of the bacon she'd been frying. It was *beyond* crispy.

"Is something on fire, Ma?"

Renee looked over her shoulder as her fifteen-year-old daughter, Kieran, walked into the kitchen on dragging feet in her oversized fuzzy pajamas. "Just breakfast."

"*You* were cooking?" she asked in disbelief as she sat leaned her hip against the island in the center of the kitchen.

"I wanted to fix your father breakfast before he left to go fishing." Renee slid the halfway-decent-looking slices of bacon onto a clear glass plate.

"You never cook." Kieran moved across the kitchen to the pantry.

"I know how to cook," Renee protested as she ran a hand through her deeply wavy natural. "It's remembering that I have food on the stove that I have a problem with."

Kieran stepped out of the pantry digging into a box of cereal before throwing a handful of some sugary-sweet cereal she loved into her mouth. She moved over to stand beside her mother and looked down at the bacon with a frown. "Good thing Daddy loves you," she joked before turning to walk out of the kitchen.

"Yeah, good thing," Renee said hesitantly as she cracked eggs into a large red Le Creuset ceramic bowl and whisked them with a little extra ferocity.

She poured the eggs into a stainless steel pan and left them so that they would set before she scrambled them. She moved back to the end of the island where her briefcase was opened and instantly became absorbed into the facts and figures of the report she'd brought home to review.

At forty-three, Renee was the vice president of marketing for the CancerCure Foundation, one of the largest nonprofits serving cancer research and awareness in the country. It was her job and her passion to develop partnerships with major corporations for invaluable donations and increasing the national visibility of the foundation. She took her work very seriously—not just for the six-figure income she received, but because it intrigued and challenged her every day. It was very easy for her to get deeply absorbed in her work.

Renee picked up an oversized cup of gourmet coffee with one hand and the open report with the other. Her lips moved as she read. Her face showed her shifting feelings: interest, surprise, discontent. She leaned her hip against the island as she took a deep and satisfying sip of her drink.

"What the hell is burning?"

The words on the report disappeared as Renee closed her eyes and frowned as she thought, "Damn," at the sound of her husband, Jackson's, voice from behind her.

She dropped the report and snatched the burning pan from the stove in one continuous motion. "This just isn't my morning, Jackson," she told him, looking over her shoulder at her tall, solid husband of the last eighteen years.

His handsome square face shaped into a frown as he took in the papers and files on the island. There was no mistaking the immediate look of disapproval.

Renee hated the guilt she felt at that one look that spoke volumes about their marriage. "I thought I would cook—"

"*And* work?" he asked, moving past her to fill the thermos he held with coffee.

Renee swallowed her irritation. She looked down at the burnt bacon on the plate and the brown eggs in the pan and scraped them both into the garbage disposal. "I'm trying, Jackson," she stressed, her eyes angry and hurt.

He just snorted in derision.

Renee felt tension across her shoulders. She jumped a little as he moved close to her to press a cool kiss to her cheek. She closed her eyes, absorbing his scent as she raised a hand to stroke his bearded cheek. He felt familiar and strange all at once. It had been so long since they showed each other simple affection.

She tilted her head back to look up into those eyes that had intrigued her from the first time she saw him on the campus of Rutgers University. "I love you, Jackson," Renee whispered, hating the urgency in her voice as her eyes searched his.

For what seemed forever, his eyes searched hers as well. "We need to talk. We *have* to talk," he said, his voice husky and barely above a whisper.

A soft press of his lips down upon hers silenced any of her words or questions.

Moments later, he was gone and Renee felt chilled to the bone.

"You didn't have to get up so early with me, baby."

Aria Livewell shrugged as she followed her broad-shouldered husband, Kingston, down the stairs of their three-thousand-square-foot home in the family-oriented subdivision of Richmond Hills. A home meant to be filled with children. "It's no problem. You know me and the girls are hanging out today and I wanted to get some housework done before they picked me up."

Kingston sat his fishing equipment by the wooden double doors. "Think you four will be back on time? You know we're supposed to meet at the Clintons' tonight to fry up all the fish we'll catch today."

"Just three, actually. Jessa said she had *something else* to do today." Aria made a playful face and waved her hand dismissively.

Kingston put his broad hands beneath her short cotton

robe and pulled his beautiful mocha-skinned wife close to him. "If we whup our friends in bid whist tonight, I have one helluva surprise for you."

Kingston was *so* competitive.

She tilted her head up to lightly lick his dimpled chin as she pushed her hand into the back pocket of his vintage jeans to warmly grasp his firm, fleshy buttocks. "Can I get a hint?" she asked huskily with a teasing smile, the beat of her heart already quickening with anticipation.

"Damn, I love you," he said roughly, his eyes smoldering as he slid one hand up to her nape.

Aria moaned softly in pleasure at the first heated feel of her husband's lips. As she gasped slightly, he slid his tongue inside her mouth with well-practiced ease. She shivered. Her clit swelled to life. Her nipples hardened in a rush.

"Do we have time?" she asked in a heated whisper, barely hearing herself over her own furious heartbeat as Kingston undid her robe and planted moist and tantalizing kisses along her collarbone.

"We'll make time" breezed across her flesh.

As her robe slipped open and his familiar hands caressed her silky skin, Aria enjoyed their passion and wondered if the time would come when she didn't cherish and yearn for her husband's touch. His dick. His kisses. His love.

With his mouth, Kingston made a path to the deep valley of her breasts, bending his knees to take one swollen and taut dark nipple into his mouth. He sucked it deeply and then circled it with the tip of his clever tongue.

"Yes," Aria whimpered, flinging her head back.

Kingston turned them and pressed Aria's back to the towering front doors as he quickly undid his belt and zipper. His hands shook as he placed them on her plush hips and lifted her with ease until her pulsing and moist pussy lips lightly kissed the thick tip of his dick. "Why is your pussy so good?" he whispered against the pounding pulse of her throat.

Aria didn't answer, she just smiled wickedly—and a bit cockily—as she caused the swollen lips of her vagina to lightly kiss the smooth round head of his dick . . . twice.

Kingston dropped Aria down onto his erection, her pussy tightly surrounding and gripping him like a vise. "Damn," he swore, his buttocks tensing as he froze. He didn't want to cum. Not yet.

Aria pressed the small of her back to the door and began to work her hips in small circles, anxious to not just have his dick pressed against her walls but to feel his delicious strokes.

Kingston's jaw clenched. "Don't make me nut, baby." His voice was strained.

Aria raised her hands to tease her nipples with her slender fingers as she enjoyed the tight in-and-out motion of his penis when Kingston began to work his hips. She felt wild and free, uninhibited and sexy. "Umph. I'm gone cum, baby. Please make me cum," she whispered with fevered urgency as each of his deep thrusts caused her pussy juices to smack and echo in the foyer like applause.

Kingston's chest and loins exploded with heat as his primal need to feel as much of Aria's pussy as he could. He pushed deeper up inside her, drawing quick and uneven breaths as his heart thundered. His buttocks clenched and then relaxed as he touched every bit of her ridged walls with his solid inches. "Damn, Aria," he swore, planting adoring kisses along her collarbone as his dick filled her several times with warm shots of cum.

CHAPTER 2

Being a housewife was important to Jaime, but doing the actual labor of keeping a nearly four-thousand-square-foot house clean was a definite no-no. Especially when there were plenty of women who were willing to be paid a fair rate to do it for her. And once a week, while Eric was at work and completely out of the loop, Jaime had a professional maid service send someone else to come in and do all of the grunt work she disdained, leaving nothing but tidy work for her throughout the week. It was one of her mother's tips for a happy marriage that Jaime had actually found useful.

And the list of those tips was endless and had been drilled in her head since she was a preteen.

Too endless to count.

Too endless for her to truly care, although she played by every rule.

And I did them all . . . so why is my marriage in trouble? she thought, studying her reflection as she sat at her ornate dressing table.

She felt a gradient of stress across her shoulders and the back of her neck. The thought of a spa day with her good friends sounded all the more appealing to her.

Ding-dong.

Jaime thought the sound of that doorbell was an annoyance. She really was not in the mood for company of any kind. She just wanted some "me time" until she left for her midmorning appointment. More and more, the way her life was plated was becoming hard to swallow, and it was in those moments when she needed to be herself . . . like now.

Ding-dong.

Releasing a heavy breath, Jaime rose from the dressing table, her silk robe billowing out behind her as she turned to leave the room. *Who could it be?* she wondered as she descended the stairs.

Ding-dong.

She passed the large, framed oval mirror on the hall wall and doubled back. She'd forgotten that her hair was still tied up in her silk scarf, she was make-up free, and she wore nothing but her silk robe. Her own husband had never seen her without some sort of make-up on—another of her mother's marital rules.

She continued on to the door and looked out one of the ornate side windows as she pulled her robe closer around her slender frame. "Jesus, take the wheel," she drawled, deeply massaging the bridge of her nose before she placed a smile on her face and opened the door wide. "Morning, Mama. Hey there, Daddy," she greeted them, sounding more like a Southern belle than a city girl.

Her parents lived just thirty minutes away in another subdivision and that meant random drop-ins like this happened quite often.

"Good morning," they said in unison as they walked into the foyer and presented themselves for the customary air kiss to her mother's cheek and a big hug for her short, round, and completely loveable father.

"Do you normally answer the door in such attire?" Virginia asked as Jaime led them across the hardwood floors to the family room.

The question was filled with judgments . . . which was

normal when it came to Virginia Osten-Pine, the self-proclaimed wife, mother, socialite extraordinaire.

"No, I wasn't expecting company," Jaime said politely, catching her mother drag her finger across the top of the large leather ottoman serving as the coffee table.

Jaime's home was a showpiece. Pristine, stylishly decorated, and the envy of many of her neighbors. In fact, it had been showcased in the realty section of a small local newspaper. Most people walked in and paused at the first sight of it with its high ceilings, dozens of large windows, dramatic art pieces, and décor.

Not Virginia Osten-Pine, or rather, Mrs. Franklin Pine.

"What brings you to this side of town?" she asked.

"We just thought we would treat you kids to breakfast at our country club," Franklin said. "Where's Eric?"

Jaime turned to face him because not to do so would be rude and she knew her mother would've called her on it. "He went deep-sea fishing with Kingston and Jackson. They'll be gone all day, Daddy," she told him.

"Now, that sounds like a fun day out for the fellas," Franklin said, folding his hands atop his rotund belly.

"Yes, dear," Virginia said.

Jaime eyed her mother for a bit before she turned and continued up the stairs. She knew for a fact that her mother hated her father's passion for fishing, but Jaime would bet her last dollar that Virginia had never questioned her husband about it. She saved her opinions and judgments for anyone and everyone else *except* her husband.

Jaime couldn't recall one time her parents had argued. Ever.

Franklin spoke and Virginia obeyed. Chocolate-covered June and Ward Cleaver.

"So I'm going to . . . going to . . ." Jaime paused because if she said anything about a spa day she knew her mother might invite herself along. She loved her mother, but the woman could be so overpowering with her thoughts and opinions at times. Jaime had enough on her shoulders to bear without topping it off with her mother's crap. "I'll be cleaning all day and preparing a nice home-cooked meal for my husband."

"Well, you have time to go to breakfast with us," Virginia said.

Although Jaime didn't want to, she acquiesced. "Excuse me while I finish getting dressed," she told them, turning to climb the stairs and to be free.

She figured she could eat with her parents and then head straight to the spa. She shouldn't be too late. Her friends, unlike her parents, would understand.

Renee felt completely overwhelmed. A major marketing proposal was due on her boss's desk first thing Monday and she discovered she'd left important files at the office. Her seventeen-year-old son's room smelled of corn chips and puffy cheese doodles. The hampers were overflowing with dirty clothes, which equaled doing laundry to the fullest. The entire house could use a good deep-down cleaning—including eradicating the dirty dishes in the sink. Her kids wanted to go to Jackson's parents' and needed a ride. Side dishes for the fish fry/card party still had to be made. And she was looking forward to the spa day with her friends—she refused to cancel, especially after the "we need to talk" bomb Jackson had dropped in her lap before he left. She absolutely refused. Shit.

In the couple of hours since the men piled into Jackson's dual-cab pickup, Renee had tried not to think or imagine the worst. But it was hard. "We need to talk" were not the words a woman wanted to hear . . . especially when her marriage had been teetering on the edge of ruin. Nevertheless, she forced herself to believe that the conversation was all about making things better . . . and not worse.

Still, her original plans of focusing on her proposal until she left for the spa were out the window. The last thing she needed was for Jackson to come home to a dusty house reeking with dirty clothes.

Prioritize, Renee. Prioritize. Get your shit together.

She was a mother. A businesswoman. A multitasker. A problem solver.

"I can handle this," Renee told herself as she ignored the doubtful glance Kieran cast in her direction as she sat atop the island, now dressed in a cute T-shirt with a ruffled denim skirt.

She picked up her BlackBerry and dialed. "Darren, this is Renee. I hate to bother you on a Saturday but I need a big favor."

"Ask away, boss."

"Good. I need you to go into the office and pick up the files I left. I think they're in my chair, actually," she told him as she started dish water in the deep double sink.

"I know exactly the ones you're talking about."

"Good. Call me when you get them because I might not be home and I'll have to give you directions to where I am. Okay?"

"No problem, boss."

Renee sat the BlackBerry by her briefcase as she pointed to Kieran. "You. Dishes. Go," she ordered over her shoulder as she made her way out of the spacious white kitchen to the laundry room in the finished basement.

This hustle and bustle of trying to juggle her career and her family was the major point of contention in her marriage. Renee always looked and felt like she was one step in front of the eight ball. Nothing came easy anymore, but she saw it as a challenge while Jackson saw it as a hindrance.

"We need to talk. . . ."

She pushed that away, determined to find the balance and make everyone—including herself—happy. She planned to do everything on her recently revised to-do list—including blowing Jackson's mind with a great "talk" on bettering their marriage and then blowing his dick to top it all off right.

Renee hated to think back to the last time she'd sexed her husband. They had gone from sex at least once a day to barely once a week. And Jackson's sexual appetite was voracious. She shivered at the very thought of how they used to get down . . . absolutely *nothing* was taboo.

And she missed that. . . .

Shaking off a far too distant memory of a steamy night complete with scented body oil, handcuffs, and anal beads, Renee started a large load of whites and headed back up the stairs. She barely stopped when she reached the top to walk down the hall to the staircase leading to the top level.

She didn't try to fool herself into thinking that busy-work was keeping her mind distracted from that talk. As she neared her son's room at the top of the stairs, she heard the sounds of video games echoing against the wall. She knocked on the door twice before she opened it and walked in.

"Mornin', Ma," Aaron, her seventeen-year-old, greeted her.

Renee pinched her nose. "Aaron, this room makes no sense and it reeks. How can you lay up in this pig sty like this?" she asked, stepping over a pile of sweat-funky football gear to reach his full-sized bed. His room was disaster central. Clothes, dirty and clean, mingled on the carpeted floor.

"It's just self-expression, Ma," he said, never taking his eyes off the bright graphic images on the television screen.

"The ability and right to self-expression has a cost . . . and it's called a mortgage, which you don't pay," she drawled. "Go take a shower and then you have thirty minutes to get this room back to being habitable."

"Uh-huh."

Renee did a double take. "Now, Aaron," she told him in her best prison warden tone.

A second later he reached forward to turn the console off.

"It does smell pretty bad, huh?" he asked with a dimpled grin that truly made him the spitting image of his father.

Renee hugged his slender frame to her side and kissed his cheek.

"Ma," he complained as he made his way to his private bathroom.

Renee could only shake her head. She hated to admit that this was another example of how little time she spent at home anymore. In the past, Aaron wouldn't have even tried her by keeping his room this junky. She hardly had time to come in his room and check up on him anymore.

She pulled the football-motif comforter from his bed, planning on washing his linens. She froze and leaned in a little closer. The crusted white spots splattered on his sheets looked a lot like . . .

Evidence of Aaron's encounter with Mrs. Palm and her five daughters.

Renee gasped and made a horrid face as she hurried to put the cover back on the bed. She turned and flew from the room, trying to erase the image of her son—*her baby*—masturbating beneath the covers.

"That is Jackson territory," she told herself as she headed to the guest bathroom to wash her hands.

Renee had way too much on her plate to tackle Aaron's puberty. For now all she could do was shake her head.

Aria stretched her nude frame beneath the cool cotton sheets of her bed. After Kingston's sexy good-bye by the door, she'd headed straight back to bed to sleep off the mini adventure.

She smiled into her plush pillows before turning over onto her back and looking up at her reflection in their mirrored ceiling. It was so eighties but they both loved being able to see the motion of the other's body as they rode.

Aria flung the covers back and hitched her full breasts higher as she lightly stroked the top of her plump and bald pussy. Kingston loved when she got a Brazilian wax, and Aria always recommended it to her friends because there was nothing like a clever-tongued man licking circles on top and inside a woman's pussy.

Rolling off the bed, Aria grabbed lingerie from her nightstand drawer. She had to hustle. Her impromptu nut nap had eaten into her work time. Working from home as a relationship columnist and freelance writer was her life's dream . . . except when her procrastination kicked in and she was running late on a deadline. It was during those long hours into the night that Aria longed for a day job and a clock to punch.

Overall, Aria loved her life, especially when her career led her to the city. New York was so her vibe and pace. She didn't mind suburbia, but she craved the city. Still, she would have followed Kingston into the bowels of hell, and Richmond Hills was far from that.

The hospital where he worked as a surgeon wasn't far from their home, and NYC was just a thirty-minute commute. And he always pointed out that they were more at home in the 'burbs than they would be in New York.

Aria looked around their bedroom and she was amazed that this was her home. It was a long way from the Weequahic section of Newark.

Hell, her life as an Ivy League graduate, wife of a prominent doctor, and successful journalist was far removed from her upbringing. Her past. She felt and appreciated her blessings every single day, but she never forgot where she came from and those still there that she loved and cherished. Never.

Aria took a bath in their black Jacuzzi tub and for now dressed in terry cloth shorts and a cut-off wifebeater. Kingston loved when she wore things like this around the house. It never failed to get his attention—her husband would drop whatever he was doing to do her. Period.

She padded barefoot out of their room and down the hall to her office. Although it was morning, she flipped the switch to bathe the comfy but functional room with light. The chocolate and pink décor clearly spoke that this was her zone and her zone alone. Like Kingston had with his own office downstairs, Aria had decorated it just the way she wanted. They each had their own space within the unisex décor of their home.

She picked up her designer reading glasses and opened her laptop before she sat in her comfy brown leather chair behind her desk. She checked some e-mails, thought twice about updating her blog, In this Life, about her writing adventures, and then allowed herself to get lost in her research notes. She had to finish up her weekly column and finish an interview she had completed with Tyler Perry for *Essence*.

For the next hour, there was nothing but the steady click-click of her laptop keys as she worked.

Brrrnnnggg.

"Shit," Aria swore in immediate frustration, fighting the irrational urge to throw her laptop across the room.

When she was in a writing groove, she absolutely hated to be interrupted by someone calling. When a deadline was breathing down her neck, she wasn't in the mood for random phone calls about shit she considered unimportant to her life.

Brrrnnnggg.

Aria snatched up the hot pink cordless on the edge of her leather-topped desk. "Hello," she said, just short of snapping.

"Hey, girl, you busy?"

Aria leaned back in her chair at the sound of her cousin Lola's voice. "I'm working right now," she said, hoping she caught the hint.

"You got a job?" she shrieked like Aria gave her good news.

Aria rolled her eyes. Her family could not grasp the concept that she was not just at home watching the soaps and chilling like a villain. "Yes, it's called working for myself. I have a deadline, so unless this is an emergency there will be a dial tone coming in five, four, three, two . . ."

"Ooh, girl, you don't have to be rude."

Aria pulled the phone away from her face to stare at it incredulously before putting it back. "Yes, I do, because I told you I would be tied up with work when you called me last night to fill me in on the argument Grandma had with Uncle One-Eye over using old fish grease."

"Wasn't that a mess?" Lola said with a laugh. "You *know* I had to call and tell you about that."

Aria felt like she could literally strangle her flamboyant and loud first cousin, who usually was the comic relief in her life . . . when she wasn't busy working on a project. "Listen, Lola, when you're at Wendy's taking them orders, I don't get on the phone and call your job, effing up Wendy's hamburger flow, to tell you something."

Lola just laughed. "Aria, you a mess."

"Bye, Lola," Aria stressed.

"Call me, girl," she said in a singsong fashion.

Aria gladly ended the call, but as soon as she sat the phone back on its base it rang again. She dropped her head in her hands in frustration. This time she checked the caller ID. It was one of those 1-800 numbers.

"Ignore," she said pointedly, waving her hand dismissively.

She caught sight of the bifold frame she kept of Kingston on her desk. On one side was a photo of Aria and Kingston at an outdoor jazz concert, and the other side was a photo of a cuddly tear bear.

Kingston was so anxious to fill the frame and their lives with a baby. And the fact that he was so ready to be a family man made Aria love her loving, sexy, strong, and confident man all the more.

CHAPTER 3

For Jaime, image was everything, and in her world, the image was all about perfection. It was a must. The right look. The right hairstyle. The right clothes. The right associates and friends—love them or hate them. The right business contacts. The right thing to say. The right place to be. The right husband, house, and finances. This was all she knew. It was her comfort zone, and in her life she *must* find comfort wherever she could.

Jaime pulled her silver convertible Volvo C70 in front of the valet stand of the renovated 1930s Georgian cottage that served as the day spa Serenity. She double-checked her appearance in her Chanel compact. Her bone-straight jet-black hair—the best complement to her cinnamon bronzed skin—was evenly parted down the middle and lying better than Pocahontas's, thanks to a celebrity hairstylist who catered to East Coast celebrities.

Her MAC make-up perfectly in place on high cheek-bones that screamed of her father's African heritage and deep-set feline eyes that were all about her mother's Asian legacy. It was that mixed exotic look that first drew her husband to her. Once upon a time, she thought he would never be able to deny her anything because of her beauty. She thought her seat on his pedestal was unshakable. A constant. 'Til death.

She focused her vision on her reflection and tried to avoid the sadness filling her eyes. *I was so wrong.* She snapped the compact closed and dropped it into her oversized woven straw Coach tote. The diamonds of her two-carat wedding band twinkled brighter than the summer sun, but it was mocking her and so she quickly shifted her gaze away from it.

Literally shaking it off, Jaime slid on her Bottega Veneta shades and climbed from the vehicle, rivaling the sun in a bright lemon Nanette Lepore silk scoop-neck tank and matching flowing pants. If she felt as good as she looked, her walk of confidence into the building would've been more than just a front.

"Hello, Mrs. Hall. The ladies are waiting for you in the Heaven Room," Hannah, the tall and slim receptionist told her as soon as Jaime stepped in front of the solid mahogany desk of Serenity's foyer. "I have you all set up in changing room number one."

"Thank you, Hannah," she told the well-tanned and toned redhead as she passed the desk on the right to reach the changing rooms. Sure enough, a plush white robe and slippers sat folded and awaiting her on the suede chair. The warm décor, plush carpeting, and soft lighting certainly made her feel serene.

A spa day with her friends was just what she needed to forget that the shambles of her marriage was all her own doing. Guilt was a damn hard pill to swallow. Some drinks, pampering, and gossip with her friends would make her forget . . . hopefully.

Jaime hung up her clothes and slid her undergarments into one of the net bags supplied in the small closet. She sighed at the feel of the silk against her nude skin. Her nipples tingled and goose bumps raced across her flesh. Eric's emotional sabbatical from sex had her horny as hell. She tried to ignore the steady pulsing of her clit as she left the room and walked down the wide private hall in search of her friends.

"Hello, Mrs. Hall."

She smiled at the male attendant standing outside the double doors in his all-white attire. He was there to service any of their requests for the day. She gave him a nod and a fake smile as he opened the double doors leading into the private room. Her smile became genuine as she eyed Aria and Renee already comfortably seated in two of the four plush leather massage chairs situated in the center of the all-white room. Jaime knew without asking that they were having chocolate pedicures. She couldn't wait to join them.

Aria was young and pretty with the kind of laid-back, no fuss / no muss style that Jaime had long ago lost and sometimes yearned for. There was no denying that Aria and Kingston were in love. Jaime always fought hard not to let her jealousy of their marriage taunt her. She'd made the bed of her marriage and now she was lying in it.

Renee was the senior of their group, but looks would never reveal it. The woman was thick and solid with more curves than a roller-coaster ride. Forty looked damn good on her, and that eighty-hours-a-week corporate job wasn't putting a hurting on her either. *Just too bad Jackson doesn't appreciate her*, Jaime thought as she sat her purse on the floor and slid onto her leather club chair.

"Girl, your ass is gonna be late to your own funeral," Aria teased before taking a sip from some frosty red concoction in a crystal goblet.

"And looking good as ever, baby. Believe that," Jaime teased back, stepping up on the platform to take a seat beside Aria.

Renee snuggled down deeper in her chair and closed her eyes. "Better late than never."

Aria cocked a thick but well-shaped brow. "We talkin' 'bout Jaime or a period?"

"Shee-it . . . *both*." Renee opened one eye to peer at them as she laughed and reached for her BlackBerry.

"I know that's right," Jaime added as she accepted the slender suede menu the attendant offered her on a small silver tray. "I was hoping Jessa would show today because I had to ask her about Olivia's husband getting caught in the wine cellar . . . *with* a man . . . *without* a stitch of clothes."

"What?" Aria and Renee gasped in unison as they both leaned in close.

Jaime nodded. "Yup yup."

"Confirmed?" Aria asked, her bright eyes wide.

Jaime shook her head and studied her hands. "Can't confirm it. That's why I was hoping to see Jessa. She knows everything about everything."

Aria nodded in agreement. "That's true. Jessa always has the best gossip. Our girl does not play. Humph. Wendy Williams don't have shit on her."

"Who?" Renee and Jaime asked in unison with confusion on their faces.

"Never mind," Aria muttered, casting them both the side eye as she reached for her drink.

Jaime just shrugged and waved her hand dismissively. She was sure they had missed one of Aria's ghetto colloquialisms. "You have to admit that Jessa is easy to talk to, and that puts her ear to a lot of mouths telling their business in Richmond Hills."

"Call her," Renee suggested as she sat her BlackBerry down on her lap. "She was supposed to meet us here by now."

"I tried and she didn't answer." Jaime paused as the tall and muscular attendant came to quietly stand by them. Briefly, she eyed him and she couldn't help but appreciate his lean but athletic frame. Her clit throbbed to life. She pressed her thighs together just to get *any* type of feeling in her pussy. Even more than their sex of the past with wild and wicked strokes of his dick, she would take more than the one- or two-word responses to her constant attempts to talk to him. Reconnect with him. She was so sick of wondering if he would ever forgive her.

Jaime quickly placed her order for a mimosa, anxious to get right back to the juice. Anyone's business but her own was always interesting and . . . distracting. "I feel for Olivia. Can you imagine not only the embarrassment of your husband screwing a man, but walking in on them? Thank God I'm not her."

Renee placed her right elbow on the arm of the chair and held her chin in her hand. "I don't know what I would do if . . . if it were me. I mean, Jackson and I have problems, but I never figured infidelity was one of them."

Aria leaned forward and placed a "don't fuck with me" expression on her face. "Well, if I walked in on Kingston cheating on me, I would walk right on outta there and come back with nine reasons why both of they ass shoulda been more careful."

Jaime and Renee both laughed at their young friend as she used her hand to mimic a gun. Aria was a chameleon and could change her demeanor to meet the situation. It was mostly the dignified wife of a doctor, but at times the little girl raised in Newark and not taking any shit came out with much too much ease.

Jaime waved her hand dismissively again as the manicurist entered the room quietly and stooped to prepare the chocolate concoction for her feet. "Well, things couldn't be better between Eric and me. Marriage is tough, but thankfully we have a strong one and I feel blessed. I really do," she lied, hiding the truth behind a bright and continually fake smile as she slid her feet into the marble bowl.

Aria looked down to study her freshly polished toes as they walked down the short hall to their private room for coconut massages. As soon as they stepped inside, the sweet but subtle scent of the coconut milk that would be drizzled over their bodies was intoxicating. She allowed herself a deep inhale as they all removed their robes and laid their naked bodies down on their individual massage tables. The feel of the crisp cotton pressed against her skin made her sigh as her masseur covered her to the waist with another sheet.

Aria bit her bottom lip as she thought of Jaime's declaration of her terrific marriage during their mani-pedis. Something about it irked her. Something about their constant perfection always irked her. "Jaime. Question. If a marriage is good, does that mean a wife should sit and act like the other shoe might not fall?"

"Where's the trust in that?" Jaime asked.

Aria lifted her head from the table and looked over at Jaime on her left. "There's a thin line between trust and stupidity," she said as the masseur gently guided her head back down with one hand as he began the firm massage to her back, neck, and shoulders with heated stones. *God, this shit feel soooo good.*

"Well, without trust, the line between being married and being divorced is even thinner," Jaime shot back in a holier-than-thou tone.

"I think you're both right," Renee joined in from Aria's right.

Aria rolled her eyes. "I am married to a prominent, wealthy black doctor who is fine . . . matter of fact, fine as hell. Single women stay on the prowl for those endangered species," she said matter-of-factly, with her eyes closed as she fought to find the relaxation of the massage. "God forbid the wrong bitch with tits and ass for days puts him in a corner, his ass *just* might come out. Y'all feel me?"

"So you don't trust your husband around *any* single woman?"

That came floating over from her right.

Aria cocked a shaped eyebrow. "I don't trust him around *anything* that pees sitting down."

Jaime coughed as if to clear her throat. "What about Jessa?" she asked slyly.

Aria tensed at the question. "What about her?"

"She's got tits and ass for days. How you know she's not fucking your man?" Jaime asked calmly.

Now watch me fix her ass, Aria thought as the hot stones were pressed deeply into her lower back with just the right amount of firmness. "I guess the same way you know she ain't fucking yours," she said with equal calm.

Renee moaned in disapproval. "Ladies, Jessa Bell is our friend—our best friend—and she's not sleeping with *any* of our men."

Aria opened her eyes and playfully turned her nose up at Jaime, who in turn winked. "Jessa knows better."

Jaime nodded. "I was just playing."

"Aaaaah . . ." Renee let out a long, drawn-out sigh of pleasure that was more erotic than therapeutic.

Aria whipped her head over to eye her friend. Her sheet was down around the top of her buttocks as the tall and muscular masseur placed heated towels over her smooth back. "You all right over there?" she asked with a teasing tone.

The masseur's face remained stoic even as Renee began to giggle. "Girl, I'm *good*," she stressed with another soft smile.

Aria closed her eyes and tried to get focused on the goodness of her massage. This spa day, which she knew would cost her close to five hundred dollars, was a long way from her days back in Newark. That was a time when shit like a manicure wasn't on the radar of things to spend money on. Food, rent, light bills, bus fare were the first, the last, and the only priorities.

The big-time career as a freelance writer, the big car, and the husband with the big bank account and a big dick were all good, but sometimes she missed the heat and the unique beat of the hood. Sometimes, if she kept it real, Jaime and Renee were too white picket fence for her.

Aria felt out of place from the ladies' upper-middle-class upbringing and private-school educations. The same background as Kingston's. Sometimes, Aria felt like she wasn't good enough for her husband, his life, or his family and friends. Still, she made it her business not to embarrass him or remind him that she was just a poor kid on full scholarship at Columbia with a caseload of Salvation Army clothes when they met.

Aria knew that he loved her—or at least he loved what all he knew about her. She bit the gloss from her bottom lip as secrets she tried to keep buried nudged at her.

Even once the massage drew to an end thirty minutes later and she rose from the table to don her robe, Aria caught a glimpse of her reflection in one of the mirrors on the wall. Her eyes were filled with the secrecy of her past.

"I am so ready for my coconut and sugar body scrub," Jaime said as she swung her hair behind her back.

"Me too," Renee joined in as she stretched and then pulled her BlackBerry from the pocket of her robe.

Aria barely heard them as she studied her reflection.

The thick and smooth texture of her trendy Rihanna asymmetrical cut.

The slender, almost African beauty of her dark-skinned face with its just-barely-there make-up.

She thought of the clothes awaiting her in the changing room. The hip and stylish dark Rock & Republic jeans paired with a bright red Biba ruffled shirt of sheer silk—an outfit that retailed for more than one year's rent in the low-income projects where she was raised.

She wondered how much of the woman she was today was Aria Livewell the doctor's wife, living up to her surname, and how much was Aria Johnson, who was just a ghetto girl at heart.

―――――∞∞∞―――――

Their spa treatments were over. They had been massaged, exfoliated, and bathed to perfection. The scent of the coconut milk used throughout each treatment still subtly clung to their soft and supple skin. Now it was time for a light lunch at their favorite restaurant, the Terrace Room, to cap off their relaxing morning. Nothing went better with good friends and good food than a damn good conversation. Renee was more than game.

"I'm worried about my marriage," she admitted softly into the silence surrounding their table. She checked her BlackBerry for the umpteenthtime. Her job meant being accessible at all times. A day off—even the weekend—was never really a day off for her, it was just a day out of the office. She never knew when a possible promotional contact was going to return a call or initiate a call for a brilliant marketing idea.

Renee finally pulled her constantly vibrating BlackBerry from its case. "Go ahead, Darren," she said, absentmindedly fingering her utensils.

"Found the files."

"Yes! Where were they? No, you know what, it doesn't even matter. Can you bring them to the Terrace Room on Fairmount Avenue?" she asked, licking her lips as she tapped her fingers against the tabletop.

"On my way," Darren said without hesitation.

It was above and beyond the call of duty, and Renee appreciated her executive assistant all the more.

As she slid the device back inside the leather case snapped to her crisp Ralph Lauren black linen pants, she looked up and felt pitied at the look in her friends' eyes. The truth was the truth, and if she couldn't be honest with her friends, then who?

Renee had long since lost her mother to a massive heart attack. Her father now lived in Beverly Hills with his third wife, and their ties were invisible. She would never lay her marital problems on her children and, well, Jackson was a part of the problem. So who did that leave? Her friends.

"He gave me that 'we need to talk' bullshit before he left this morning," she admitted, filling the silence amongst them.

Aria reached over, and squeezed her hand leaving the faint scent of her Armani Diamonds perfume. "Maybe it's a talk to improve things. You always think the worst."

Renee raked her manicured fingers through her curls. "And you always see the glass as half full."

Jaime flung her weave over her left shoulder as she settled back in her chair to eye them. "We've been saying for years that you should encourage Jackson to go to counseling with you to deal with his issues."

Renee ignored the BlackBerry vibrating against her hip . . . again. For the first time in a long time, her focus was on her marriage. "I love him," she said fiercely. "I just don't understand the whole Ward Cleaver shit he's caught up on because I'm not June in the least. Well . . . not anymore."

As soon as she said the words, her eyes shifted to Jaime. "No offense to you and Jessa, I just love working."

Jaime just shrugged and waved her hand glibly. The diamonds of her numerous bracelets flashed. "None taken."

Jaime was a diva and loved it.

"I need to use the restroom, ladies," Renee said, already rising to her full five-foot-ten height.

She made a striking picture as she weaved her way through the tables to reach the privacy of the restroom. Her crisp white Calvin Klein tee gleamed against the deep cinnamon of her skin and emphasized the soft curve of her breasts. Her long strides were filled with confidence and were a testament to her weekly workout regimen in their state-of-the-art home gym. When exercise became the replacement for sex and happiness, a firm and fit body like hers *had* to develop.

Renee actually sent the call from her assistant to her voice mail as she opened the mahogany wooden door of the ladies' room. It swung closed behind her and she barely took in the warm plaid and floral French country décor as she leaned her hip against the counter and crossed her arms over her chest.

Fuck it, she needed a moment. Facing the end of a marriage—*her* marriage—wasn't easy . . . especially when both of her friends had the picture-perfect life she used to have.

Renee wanted her marriage.

She wanted her husband.

But she also wanted her career, and she couldn't have both. Period.

She gripped the edge of the counter. Her stomach felt like she'd swallowed sharpened nails.

"I love you, Jackson."

"We need to talk. We have to talk."

She tilted her head up and looked at herself in the mirror just as one lone tear raced down her cheek. She closed her eyes and released a breath heavy with her frustrations and fears.

Jackson wouldn't leave her. He'd better not.

She swiped away her tears and straightened her back while she studied her reflection in the mirror. The soft and curly tendrils of her inch-long hair fit her oval-shaped face, wide eyes, and full, pouty mouth. She'd never felt sexier . . . especially with her signature smoky eye make-up, extended lashes, and glossy lips.

Jackson didn't speak to her for a week after she first cut her long "good" hair. He used to love to play in it as she laid her head on his chest after steamy sex. But once she went back to work, she caught all kinds of hell trying to manage it before she had to leave home early enough for her thirty-minute commute to New York.

It took one hell of a freaky fuckfest to get him past the haircut drama.

She smiled naughtily at her reflection even as her eyes burned. A blow job and some handcuffs helped him right on down the road to forgiveness.

Would that type of "screw me 'til I'm sore" sex fix their problems now?

Renee walked into one of the wooden bathroom stalls. She made sure to flush the commode and then carefully wrap the seat with tissue before she dropped her pants and took a seat.

Her BlackBerry vibrated and she took it from its case. She frowned at the text message icon.

She was a grown-ass woman with teenagers and several e-mail accounts who didn't mess around with the text message trend. To hell with trying to keep up with all those abbreviations. LOL. KIT. BFF. How about LMTFAWT—leave me the fuck alone with text.

Renee opened the message with her elbows braced on her strong thighs.

LIFE HAS MANY FORKS IN THE
ROAD AND TODAY I'VE DECIDED TO
TRAVEL DOWN THE PATH LEADING
YOUR HUSBAND STRAIGHT TO MY
WAITING AND OPEN ARMS—

"What the fuck?" Renee gasped. She continued to scroll down and read some more as her heart slammed against her chest.

I CAN'T LIE AND SAY I HAVE
REGRETS. I LOVE HIM MORE THAN

YOU AND I NEED HIM MORE. YOU
SAW HIM FOR THE LAST TIME THIS
MORNING. TONIGHT HE COMES
HOME TO ME. HE'S MY MAN NOW.
THANKS FOR NOT BEING WOMAN
ENOUGH 4 HIM.

XOXO

Renee jumped to her feet and some of her pee ran down her thigh, wetting the waistband of her pants. Her stomach felt like someone had gut punched her. She clutched the BlackBerry with both hands as she read the message again.

And again.

And again.

And again.

"Oh . . . hell . . . no!" she shrieked, sounding more like Aria than herself.

She damn near dropped the BlackBerry into the commode as she snatched her pure silk panties and her pants up around her shapely hips. She barely registered that she didn't wipe.

Jackson was cheating on her?

Couldn't be.

Shouldn't be.

"Motherfucker . . . it *better* not be." She left the stall even as she dialed Jackson's cell phone number. She knew it was a waste with the fishing boat deep in the middle of the sea, but she tried anyway.

"The cellular customer you are trying to reach is currently unavailable."

She took a deep breath as she willed herself not to fall to the floor and cry like a baby. Somehow she found the strength to open the door and make her way back to her girls. Each step landed after the text message seemed to mock her.

Leading your husband straight to my arms.
Boom.
I love him more than you.
Boom.
I need him more.
Boom.
He's my man.

Well, right now she needed her friends more than she needed Jackson. She nearly dropped onto her seat as she roughly pushed her BlackBerry toward them atop the table. It hit against one of their glasses with a *ding*.

"How about some bitch just text me that she's running away with Jackson?" Renee snapped as she drummed her neatly manicured fingers on top of the wooden table.

We need to talk. We have to talk.

"Well, I'll be damned," Aria said in disbelief as she twirled Renee's phone to look down at the screen.

Renee looked from Aria to Jaime. The furrow between her waxed brows deepened as both women held up their cell phones with the same exact message displayed. "What?!"

"Oh, that's not the cherry on top of the sundae yet, baby," Jaime said with much attitude—definitely not normal for Ms. Suzie Sunshine. "Check your message again to see who it's from. You're not going to believe this mess."

Renee swooped up the BlackBerry and worked her thumb on the trackball to scroll to the top of the message. She gasped as she felt an angry fire begin to boil in her stomach.

Jessa Bell.

CHAPTER 4

The three friends could do nothing but look at each other, look at their phones, and look at each other again before looking away . . . at anything—*everything* but each other's eyes.

Jaime smoothed her perfectly straight hair as she struggled to maintain her composure. She wished like hell she had been alone when she got the text. She would have had time to compose herself and not squeal out in fright like a mouse caught in a trap. Being caught off guard had caused her to gush to Aria. She had forgotten one of the main rules her mother taught her. Never . . . *never* let them see you sweat.

Stay in control.

Stay on top.

Stay above criticism.

All the right words and the right look on her face did nothing for the way her nerves were immediately shot to hell as soon as she read that damned text message.

Jessa Bell and Eric?

She was his answer? His solution to their problems? His punishment? His payback?

Jaime slid her hand under the table as she gripped and released her hand into a fist atop her thigh.

Jessa Bell. Humph, more like Jezebel. Slut. Tramp. Whore.

No-good sneaky, conniving, lonely wench. She was *supposed* to be their friend.

Jaime froze. How could she have forgotten? Had the years that drifted by caused her memory to lapse as well?

Originally Jessa Bell had been *Eric's* friend. Not hers.

Eric had purchased his home in Richmond Hills several years before he married Jaime. His friendship with Jessa's husband had led to him befriending the beauty. In fact, it was Eric who had first introduced Jaime and Jessa. And for years after that Jaime had sworn that something was going on between them.

Was she finally—and unfortunately—about to find out she was right all this time?

Okay, breathe, Jaime, breathe. She tried but instead she just stuck the pure white tip of her thumbnail in her mouth as she imagined Eric, naked and sweaty, gliding his hard and dark dick inches in and out of Jessa—in their bed!

Jaime bit down so hard the acrylic on her nail split in two.

Okay, this wasn't about sex. This was way bigger than an affair. This bitch said that Eric was leaving her. Now *that* made her feel like she was slowly sinking underwater. Panic was setting in.

She began to visualize all the nice things in her life disappearing.

Her car.

Her shopping sprees.

Her work-free life. Uggh!

Her image. Sweet Mary, mother of Jesus. Her image.

In that moment she would have gladly wrapped her smooth hands around Eric's nuts and done an old-school Fat Joe and "lean back."

"So who is this about?" Renee asked, reaching up to try to swirl one of her short curls around her fingers.

Jaime knew she wished for her longer hair because Renee always twirled her hair in times of stress. "What?" she asked, her mind on this looming shift in her status. She didn't want to be the sexy divorcée on the prowl for her next husband . . . obviously like Jezebel—Jessa Bell. Whatthefuckever.

Renee scooped up all three cell phones. "We *all* got the message—"

"Yes!" Jaime exclaimed excitedly before she could contain herself as she clutched to hope like a crackhead holding on to his last hit.

Renee and Aria looked at her like she was crazy. Quiet as kept, she did feel a little bit of insanity nipping at the edges. *They don't even understand.*

What would she tell her parents? Her sorors? Oh Lord, Pastor Reynolds. What would she say to them all . . . *if* it was her?

"Is Jessa messing with our heads or was this trick sleeping with all three?" Aria asked, angrily fanning away the waiter who was about to approach their table.

"I wouldn't doubt it," Renee muttered as she held her BlackBerry tight enough to snap it in half.

"Yes, but she can't run away with all three." Jaime loved her girls, but she had to be honest and admit that she wished like hell that her husband wasn't the one. An affair she could forgive with ease, but leaving her?

That was out of the question.

———— ❧ ————

Renee's eyes fell on the elderly couple walking into the Terrace Room together. They held hands like they'd just started dating when Renee didn't doubt they'd been together for over fifty years.

She turned away from their happiness because her marriage wouldn't make it to half of that.

"We need to talk. We have to talk."

His words haunted and mocked her.

Jackson was leaving her for one of her best friends. She just knew it. Her emotions swung from pain and sadness to anger and frustration . . . and back again.

"It's me and you both know it," Renee admitted into the silence surrounding their table as she ignored her BlackBerry vibrating on top of the table in front of her. For the first time ever she felt like flinging it against the wall.

Jaime reached over and sympathetically squeezed her arm. "The writing *has* been on the wall. . . ."

Aria reached over and slapped Jaime's hand away. "We all got the message from the mistress, so we *all* are fair game, whether we like it or not."

Renee's first instinct had been to slap Jaime herself—right across the mouth. "Listen, I tried calling Jackson. No signal."

"Same here," Jaime said.

"Me too," Aria joined in as she used her stylus to tap on her iPhone.

Renee arched a brow. "Who are you calling?"

"That bitch Jessa."

Of course. Renee was so rattled by the whole situation, she didn't know why she didn't think of it herself. *Humph. Too busy feeling stupid. Betrayed. Broken down, busted, and disgusted.*

Little things came flying back to her in a rush.

Images. Memories. Clues that her ass missed because she was too busy to see the signs. Too busy trusting her husband and her friend.

Jessa and Jackson standing just a bit too close at a party.

Walking in the room just as Jessa was stepping away from Jackson.

Jessa smiling up at Jackson. Touching him innocently.

It was childish, but she hated how good their names sounded together like a mocking rhyme. Jessa and Jackson. Jackson and Jessa.

"It went to voice mail," Aria said, setting her phone back on the table. "So we have to sit all day until our husbands get back from some damn fishing trip to find out whose husband this bitch stole? Fucking ri-di-cu-lous."

Yes. Yes it was. Renee signaled for the waiter. "First. Please be on standby to call a taxi to drive me home because I don't plan to crash my Benz, and then bring me a bottle of Gran Patrón—the brown one."

"The Gran Patrón Burdeos Añejo," Jaime offered with ease. The high-end tequila aged in oak with a fruity flavor was right up her alley. To Jaime, the finer things in life had to come with a hefty price tag.

The waiter's eyes widened. "The entire bottle?" he asked.

Renee nodded. "And three shot glasses, salt, and lime."

She just wanted the image of tall, shapely, and beautiful Jessa Bell to disappear from her head. All of it. The Beyoncé hair. The Halle face. The J.Lo body. The sexpot Mariah voice.

"That woman was a walking *Fuck Me* sign and we *all* ignored it," Renee snapped, turning to see where the waiter was with her drink.

"Yes, but Jessa never gave us a hint she was this scandalous," Jaime offered. "We *all* trusted her. Outside of screwing one *or all* of our husbands undercover, she was always a good friend."

"No, she was always a good actress." Aria picked up her phone and her fingers started to fly as she typed. "See, this is the kind of shit that makes a woman get in her car and then slowly and deliberately run back and forth over her husband's body again and again . . . and again."

Renee watched as Jaime opened her purse and reached in for her monogrammed Louis Vuitton cigarette case. She fingered it. Opened and closed it several times. Fingered it some more and then slid it back into her purse. Watching Jaime struggle not to relapse on her new anticigarette policy was very telling. Her nerves were shot to hell too.

"Good morning, ladies."

Renee looked up at her assistant Darren standing by their table. "Morning, Darren," she said, accepting the small stack of colorful folders he handed her.

"My, my, my," Aria said. "Now I see why you work so damn hard, Boo-Boo."

"O-*kay*," Jaime added.

Renee looked at her friends and paused at the way they were looking up at Darren. She shook her head. Darren *was* an attractive man—not classically handsome at all, but his deeply chocolate complexion, six-foot-five, muscular build, strong angular features, and immaculate grooming would draw any woman's eye . . . especially in the crisp white polo and white pants he wore.

"Thanks, Darren," Renee said, her tone politely dismissing him.

Darren made eye contact with each woman. "Ladies, enjoy your lunch," he said, his voice as deep as the color of his skin.

"Thank you," they all said.

Renee rolled her eyes as Aria openly watched him walk away and then she caught Jaime sneaking a peek as well.

"Ladies, I think we have enough man drama going on. Don't you?" Renee snapped as their waiter set the bottle and three shot glasses on the table. She snatched the bottle up and couldn't care less that it was just noon.

Aria tucked her long bangs behind her ear. "Jessa and I had lunch a couple of weeks ago in the city and she was bragging about this new man in her life and how many times he makes her cum and all the beautiful gifts he gives her."

Renee poured a hefty amount of Patrón in her glass. "Who knew the heifer was talking about *my* husband."

Aria took the bottle from her and poured two more shots. "Or mine."

Jaime accepted the glass Aria handed her. "Or mine," she added softly, her voice barely above a whisper.

"When you walk down the aisle and you say the vows and have the house and the kids, you never imagine that your marriage—your life the way that you know it—is going to end this way." Renee looked down into the center of the liquid as she twirled her glass. "For that bitch to send a *text* message after all the years of friendship and trust we had with her. To play with somebody's life like that. Who was this woman we called a friend?"

Renee didn't fight the tear that raced from her eye and fell into the center of her Patrón.

"I knew her longer than both of you and she sent the message to me too." Aria swallowed the shot in one gulp and then winced like she'd swallowed fire.

Jaime sipped on her drink as she reached in her purse for the cigarette case again. "Maybe she's joking. Maybe she's just playing with us. Jessa likes to play games and jokes and pranks."

And that was true. Jessa loved to be the life of the party and the center of a joke. She liked to have fun and that's what made people want to be around her. Was this stupid and childish text her idea of a stupid and childish joke?

Aria pushed the cork back inside the neck of the hand-blown glass bottle as she signaled the waiter again, and in moments he was at her elbow. "We're ready for our car," she told him, easing the entire bottle of liquor and their shot glasses inside her camel leather Tanner Krolle tote.

Renee looked up at her in surprise. "Where are we going?"

"Phone games are Jessa's thing. It's time we switch it up." Aria rose to her feet and slid on her gold-rimmed aviator shades.

Jaime eased her own bag onto her shoulder and rose from her chair. "Meaning?" she asked.

Aria accepted the leather billfold with their bill and slid enough cash inside to cover it and a hefty tip. "I say we go to the bitch and get it all straight . . . face-to-face."

Renee loved, loved, loved when Aria let that "don't fuck with me" side of her come out. She snatched up her own designer tote and shades. "Let's ride, ladies."

───── ⤜⤛ ─────

The ladies didn't understand that Aria felt the most betrayed of all. Jessa Bell was her friend long before her marriage to Kingston and the house in Richmond Hills. In fact, they'd bought the house in the subdivision at Jessa's urging.

If Kingston was the culprit—and Aria had no qualms about thinking him not above the dirty deed—then when did the affair begin? Was that why he agreed to move to Richmond Hills? Was it a kick to him to have his wife and his mistress just houses away for his choosing?

Jessa was way badder than Lola because whatever Jessa wanted, Jessa got. Or better yet, whatever Aria wanted, Jessa got.

That was the gist of their friendship. Competition. One-upmanship. Bitch, I'm better than you and let me prove it. But she never thought Jessa would go that far. There's a big difference between higher grades and prettier shoes compared to someone's husband.

Was Kingston just one more item on the list of things Jessa can say she either stole from me or topped me on?

Her eyes shifted from looking outside the rear window of the cab to the back of the head of their driver. Malcolm.

Now that motherfucker was fine. Hella fine. Six feet, broad shoulders. Dreads pulled back with a leather tie. His white T-shirt strained to contain muscles—he could tear it to shreds with one huge breath. He was probably toting a dick big as a log.

Aria took another sip of her Patrón and felt it warm her

belly almost as much as her need for revenge was warming up her punnany. An image of her naked and sweating and tugging Malcolm's dreads back while she rode that motherfucker on a chair flashed hotly in her head.

It would serve Kingston right.

But then he was leaving, so why would he care?

She sighed.

"It's me, y'all. If this shit ain't a joke, then I know it's me," she said into her shot glass.

She felt Jaime's sympathetic hand and her eyes darted to her friend. "Well, they *do* hang out a lot. . . ."

It was Renee's turn to slap Jaime's desperate hand away.

Aria just rolled her eyes before she shifted her gaze back out of the tinted window. She felt like the happy days of her marriage flew by just like the picturesque scenery outside the window.

What about their plans for babies? Their retirement plans? Their lives?

Kingston might be tempted to fuck Jessa, but would he leave all that they had? All that they both worked so hard to attain? All that they still dreamt of accomplishing?

Just this morning he'd fucked her like there was not another woman alive who could wet his dick the way that she did and now, just hours later, the status of her marriage was up in the air. With one stupid text message, *everything* had changed.

Or were things already different and she was too blind to see what the fuck was going down right under her nose?

Aria felt frustration build up in her like a volcano about to blow. Seconds later the shot glass in her hand went flying to land with a hard thud against the back of the privacy glass.

Jaime gasped.

Renee applauded.

Malcolm slowed the taxi to a stop.

Aria dropped her head in her hands and cried.

"Is everything all right, ladies?" he asked in a voice that reminded Aria of making love on a fur rug in front of a fireplace. Just pure sex.

It was just what she needed to end her tears. *Thank God for waterproof mascara,* she thought as she smiled at him, quite confident she didn't resemble a fucking raccoon. "I'm sorry. It slipped," she lied, still swallowing back her tears.

As he looked over his shoulder his eyes locked on her.

Aria was a wife, but she was a woman first and a woman knew when a man wanted her. Lord knew at this moment and time in her life—her marriage—it felt good. Matter of fact, it felt bad, and *that* felt good.

"Excuse us, Marshall," Jaime said dismissively with a tight grin that was fake as hell.

"It's Malcolm—"

"Yeah, uh-huh. Shoo. Shoo."

Malcolm made a face and turned, ending Aria's smoky eye contact with him. Suddenly she felt relieved. She'd never cheated on Kingston. Up until today she never had a reason to. Besides, there still was a chance Jessa was joking—in which case Aria planned to give that bitch a real Brick City beat down—or Jessa's lover wasn't Kingston—in which case Aria still planned to give her that two-piece.

Aria shifted her eyes to Renee and it pained her to see the way her friend clutched the bottle of Patrón like she needed it.

She shifted them to Jaime, who was busy retouching her already flawless make-up in a gold Chanel mirror. As if looking beautiful when they faced Jessa was going to change a damned thing. Neither Renee's liquor, nor Jaime's make-up, nor her own tears were going to change shit.

"Either way, the bitch ain't shit," Aria said, slipping right into her comfort zone. "Joking or not. Fucking any of our men. The way I look at it, she stabbed one of us in the back, then she stabbed all of us in the back, because it shows what she is capable of, and I don't have any room for that in my life."

"I'm not going to lie and say I'm not ready to get to the bottom of all this," Renee said in a soft voice as she clutched the smooth rim of the bottle a little tighter.

Aria nodded as she watched the elaborate wrought-iron fence closing Richmond Hills off from any outsiders. In fact, the first row of houses didn't start for nearly a mile beyond the gate, so there were no worries about random cruisers scoping out the homes starting at half a million dollars. The taxi slowed at the glass-enclosed security booth and Aria lowered the window, knowing they would need to identify themselves to get inside their subdivision.

Sure enough, Lucky, the potbelly, red-faced security guard, walked back to the rear of the taxi. He stuck his head inside. "Hello, ladies," he greeted them warmly.

"Lucky, have you seen Ms. Bell yet?" Aria asked.

His face was instantly confused. "Ms. Bell? Well, remember she moved today—"

"She *moved,*" all three women said in unison with plenty of emphasis, obviously shocked as hell.

"You ladies being such good friends, I assumed you all knew she was moving today."

Renee popped the cork on the Patrón again.

Jaime's expression remained the same—like the supports of her marriage hadn't just taken a hurricane-type blow. Still, she reached in her purse for her cigarettes and lit up with shaky hands.

Aria snatched up her tote and dug around for her cell phone as Lucky stepped back and the gates slowly opened for the taxi to pull ahead. Her fingers flew across the touch screen keyboard. "Malcolm," she called out.

She looked up from the cell phone long enough to see his eyes on hers in the rearview mirror.

"How much will it cost me to have your services for the day?" she asked, rereading the message she'd just typed.

JESSA, ALL GAMES OVER. WHO
YOU FUCKING? WHICH OF THEM
MOTHERFUCKERS LOST THEIR
MIND AND DECIDED TO RUN OFF
WITH YOUR SILLY SILICONE FILLED
ASS? WOMAN UP, BITCH, KEEP IT
FUNKY. IF HE'S YOUR MAN, THEN
CLAIM HIM, HO.

"I would have to call in to my supervisor for a quote,"
he answered.

Aria hit Send before she looked up at him again. "Well,
you do that, because I may need your services, and it's
much more convenient for you to be around . . . just in
case."

Their eyes locked in the mirror.

"Yes, ma'am," he answered with a deference that made
her feel powerful. Lord knew a freakfest with a sexy
stranger was not the answer to the end of her marriage,
but it was one helluva step on her road to recovery.

The text message notification on her iPhone sounded
off.

Aria read it and shook her head as anger boiled in her.
"I asked that bitch to admit which one of those bastards is
running off with her," she told them.

Renee cried harder and her body shook, causing liquor
to slosh over the side of her glass to stain the front of her
T-shirt.

Jaime paused with her gloss-stained cigarette just a half
inch from her mouth. "And?"

Aria turned the phone so that they could read it for
themselves.

GUESS WHO . . .

JESSA

Today was the day we had hoped and planned for. Today all of my dreams finally would come true. Everything was in place and I couldn't wait.

With a smile that I knew was wicked, I dropped my cell phone onto the passenger seat of my bright red convertible Jaguar. Relished the feel of the air whipping against my face and the sun beaming down on my warm brown skin as I imagined the looks on their faces. My supposed friends. Humph. Fuck 'em.

Silicone ass? Worn out? What the fuck ever. I didn't get any complaints. In fact, he loved my beauty, worshipped my body, and fucked me strong every chance he got.

I'm no one's fool. I knew they tolerated me but they never really cared for me like they did each other. It was hard at times being the only single woman in the midst. Even Aria, my college friend, became more and more distant as she became closer to Renee and Jaime. Deep down I knew they all were afraid their husbands would not only take notice of a fine bitch like me, but take the lead and have me.

Well, one of these high-and-mighty bitches was right. The other two deserved to suffer just a little bit. But their pain would only be temporary. It was the one who would sleep alone in her marital bed for the first time of many times tonight who would know that I was the better woman. I was the woman her husband wanted. I was the woman he would have.

I shivered as I thought of him and I let one of my hands travel down my soft thighs as I spread them. I felt a thrill riding up the Garden State Parkway playing in the slick wet folds of this pussy he loved. I wished he had skipped that fucking fishing trip. Hell, I had all the snapper he needed right here.

I purred as I stroked my clit, but I fought the urge to make myself cum because tonight I wanted all of my energy to make love to him in our bed, in our new home in Saddle River—for the very first time as my man exclusively.

Damn, life was good as hell.

CHAPTER 5

The homes and streets of Richmond Hills were the perfect example of comfortable suburban living. Well-manicured lawns, perfectly maintained homes, and clean streets. Nary a sign of anything out of place. On the outside.

And that was just the way Jaime liked it.

Through her shades she looked out the smudged window at Renee and Jackson's spacious and pristine brick Colonial and eventually Aria and Kingston's beautiful Mediterranean three houses down. And then the timeless and classic European-styled structure she shared with Eric.

She fought the urge to shrink down lower in the backseat of the dilapidated yellow taxi as her neighbor Mrs. Thornwallow stepped out onto the porch. Jaime didn't mind using a car service, but she preferred those whose fleets included black Lincolns and not bright yellow banged-up and rusted Chevys.

As Aria instructed the driver to pull in front of Jessa's brick and stone French country–styled structure, Jaime fought the urge to light another cigarette. She craved the nicotine badly and she hadn't felt the urge in the last few months since she decided to stop. In fact, she was so cocky and defiant in her pledge not to smoke that she felt carrying around the pack meant nothing.

And now this *bullshit,* she thought, reaching in her purse for the cigarette case.

Jaime smoothed her hands over her flawless weave as she thought the proper thing to do was go home and dutifully wait for her husband to come home . . . if he was coming home. But in truth she didn't want to be alone. She couldn't. Fear was an awful thing to face with nothing around but the sound of mocking silence.

The taxi slowed to a stop in front of Jessa's home.

"It doesn't look like she's moved," Renee said, still clutching the bottle of Patrón as she climbed out of the back of the taxi.

Aria and Jaime shared a brief look before they too climbed out, both glad to stretch their limbs after the tight ride. "Don't move a muscle, Malcolm," Aria said.

Jaime looked between them as they shared another long look. Seeing trouble rising for her friend, Jaime slid her arm through Aria's and pulled her up the walk to join Renee. "Don't do something you'll regret," she advised her. *Trust me. I know.*

Aria shifted her eyes to her friend, but said nothing else on Malcolm. "If security says she moved, then she moved," she said as she pushed her bronzed gladiator sandals into Jessa's immaculate garden to peer through the window.

"What do you see, Aria?" Renee asked.

Jaime just prayed no one saw them spying. There wasn't much that went on in Richmond Hills that someone didn't see. And that thought instantly made Jaime tense. She turned slowly and eyed each of the neighboring houses.

"I wonder if any of them knew about this affair? How many have seen one or all of our husbands sneaking in her house?" Jaime asked in a voice that was filled with wonder. "How many of them knew?"

Jaime didn't even care that she was revealing her fears

and worries. People knowing that her husband had slept with her friend was a far more embarrassing sin to bear.

"It doesn't matter, the point of it is none of *us* saw it," Renee snapped. "She was our friend and we didn't have a clue."

But was that true? Jaime nearly bit off her MAC lip gloss. Had there been signs they missed . . . or even ignored?

"I'm going in," Aria said suddenly, tramping through the flower bed to head for the front door.

Renee held up her hand. "I am not breaking into this woman's house," she said sternly before releasing a loud hiccup.

Aria paused and turned to face them. "And wouldn't it have been nice if Jessa had said, 'I am not sleeping with my friend's husband'?" she asked sarcastically.

The three friends exchanged a look before they all turned and made their way through the landscaping to the tall double front doors. Aria punched the alarm's keypad. "Jessa gave me the alarm passcode a while ago when she was out of town and wanted me to watch her house," she explained as she reached in her purse and pulled out her keys. "Hopefully it and this spare key she gave me still works."

Jaime made a mental note to change her own password, because nobody was going all up and through her house when the mood hit.

Click.

Aria looked over her shoulder at them as she pushed the door open. "Welcome to the whorehouse," she said before pushing the door open wide.

Jaime paused for a long time before she followed Renee and Aria into the house. She was afraid that the old adage was true: Be careful what you look for, because you just might find it.

"Okay, so she did move," Renee said as she hitched her purse higher up on her shoulder and held the bottle of Patrón tighter. She knew the clutch was filled with desperation.

All of the furniture was gone.

All photos and personal items were noticeably gone.

Nothing but the curtains and blinds even hinted that someone had lived there that very morning.

This was a house that had been left behind.

And Renee just *knew* that like the house, she had been left behind as well.

"That bastard!" she swore as she followed Aria and Jaime up the wooden staircase.

"Well, the bitch always was a go-getta, and now that includes getting gone," Aria said sarcastically over her shoulder before she walked into Jessa's spacious bedroom. "It is time to look for something—anything—that gets us to the bottom of this."

Renee nodded as she tried to summon the same strength and will that helped her climb the corporate ladder. Even though she felt like a crumbling brick wall on the inside, she knew it was time to woman up. She released a heavy breath as she looked around the empty bedroom. She had been here before hundreds of times. . . .

Helping a friend dress for an event.

Tending to a friend who was sick in bed.

Running in to grab a dress or shoes to borrow from a friend's closet.

Memories that were tainted by thoughts of what else went down. The betrayal. The secrets.

If these walls could talk, she thought as she eyed the spot previously occupied by the king-sized bed. She tensed at a vivid image of Jessa naked and sweaty astride Jackson's dick as his hands clutched her wide hips and then slapped playfully at her buttocks. Renee winced. The vision of his glistening wet dick sliding up and down inside his whore made Renee physically ill, and her free hand clutched at her stomach.

"I have to get out of here," she whispered harshly as she ungraciously dropped the bottle of Patrón and flew from the den of sin before she brought up her lunch and every bit of the liquor she drank to numb the pain.

In the hallway she turned and pressed her forehead to the wall as she forced herself to breathe in and out slowly.

"We need to talk. We have to talk."

The words—his words—echoed mockingly in her head.

Renee turned and walked down the stairs. She paused at the bottom of the steps as she looked around at an architecturally beautiful house that was filled with dirty secrets.

Renee still clearly remembered the very first time she'd entered this house to welcome Jessa Bell to Richmond Hills. Back then she had tried to give Suzie Homemaker a run for her money. . . .

Renee settled the napkin over the basket of fresh chocolate chip cookies as she rang the doorbell. Having been one of the first families to move into the Richmond Hills subdivision nearly five years earlier, Renee felt like the godmother of the neighborhood. She made it her business to meet and greet every one of the homeowners that moved in after her and her husband. As she waited, she smoothed her ponytail and then her crisp white shirt and creased capris. She wanted to make a good impression on her new neighbor.

The door opened and Renee was a little taken aback by the voluptuous beauty in no more than her late twenties standing before her with a pageant-winning smile. She was young but self-assured. Renee knew that from the way the woman met her eyes. She was pretty and she knew it. In the jeans and fitted tee she wore that broadcast: MY EYES

*ARE NOT DOWN HERE, her endless curves were hard
to miss.*

*"Uh, hi, hello, I'm Renee Clinton. I live right up the
street," she said with a smile as she handed her the basket.
"I just wanted to welcome you and your husband to the
neighborhood."*

*She winked. "Well, Renee Clinton who lives right up the
street, I'm Jessa Bell, and I live right here," she joked with
a husky voice that evoked thoughts of a blues club, a jazzy
song playing and a microphone poised in front of her
mouth.*

*Renee genuinely smiled, instantly liking the younger
woman with the playful and disarming demeanor.*

*Jessa lifted the napkin and held the basket to her nose.
"Chocolate chip? Oooh. My favorite," she sighed as
she reached out to squeeze Renee's wrist. "How about we
take your cookies and my husband's ice cream and make
some magic?"*

*Renee laughed as Jessa stepped back into the foyer and
waved her right inside with a big, friendly smile. . . .*

And that day had been the first of many that Renee had
spent in Jessa's home. In the weeks that followed, she had
found Jessa to be funny, outgoing, lively, and spirited. Being
in her company had always meant a good time. Always.

Wrapping her arms around herself, Renee strolled back
into the sunken living room. Everywhere she looked, steamy
and naked visions of Jackson and Jessa mocked her horri-
bly.

On the floor in front of the fireplace.

On the sofa.

Against the wall.

Each vision was a pain in her heart. Even the remote
chance of a betrayal hurt. The idea of Jackson straying hurt,

but coupled with the mistress being one of her good friends? Devastating. Tripled with him leaving her for Jessa? Absolutely crushing.

"We need to talk. We have to talk."

Bzzzz.

Her hand immediately went to her hip for her BlackBerry. It was her office. Of course. Her face became pensive as she glanced away from the vibrating device in her hand.

Is that what pushed Jackson into Jessa's bed? she wondered. *Were all of his complaints and concerns about my workload far more serious than I took them?*

She took a deep breath as she answered the phone. "Hello. Listen, um, I have a family emergency that will need my full attention today," she said, not even giving them a chance to say anything. "I'm going to need you to just sit on everything until I get into the office tomorrow. If it's a crisis, then refer it to one of the other VPs."

"Yes, Mrs. Clinton."

Renee ended the call, thinking her stand to put her family before her career might be too little, too damn late.

Aria closed the closet door and moved over to the window. She eased back the curtain and looked down the street at her home. Everything about it seemed picture perfect. She thought everything about what was in it had been just as snapshot ready.

They had great sex. They talked about everything. They laughed about more. They didn't have money trouble. They spent lots of quality time together and apart.

Had she been wrong?

It can't be me. Not Kingston. He wouldn't, she thought.

Her eyes focused on her reflection in the window and the pain she saw in her eyes made her angry. The diamonds of her wedding band flashed and she moved her hand.

The flash of yellow caught her eye and she twisted her head a bit to look down at the sexy driver. Her eyebrow arched a bit as he climbed out of the taxi and stretched his tall and muscled limbs high above his head.

Aria's mouth opened in a mini-pant as he slid his hand under his shirt to massage his stomach. She caught a glimpse of rock-hard abs and her pussy literally thumped to life like it was calling out for him.

Thump-thump.

Stroke-me.

Thump-thump.

Lick-me.

Thump-thump.

Fuck-me.

Thump-thump.

Freak-me.

Thump-thump.

Save-me.

Thump-thump.

It would be so easy to forget all the drama within the heat of sex with a fine-ass, muscular-bodied, dreadlocked stranger.

Aria turned away from the window at Jaime's sigh. She eyed Miss Bougie as she brushed invisible dust from her clothes. "Nothing?" she asked, pushing aside thoughts of Malcolm naked and hard on the hood of his taxi.

She'd never cheated in her marriage. Never. And Aria had always been proud of that. She'd thought Kingston had never cheated and never would. That had made her proud in their marriage.

Now what?

She felt her hard shell crack as she released a shaky breath. "This is a bunch of bullshit. I could just really fuck Jessa up right now. I'm serious."

Jaime walked over to wrap her arm around Aria's shoulders. "Well, what about Kingston? It takes two to hustle, girl."

Aria rolled her eyes upward at the slick way she'd just tried to make her husband out to be Jessa's prize. "Jaime, if you don't get your bougie, delusional ass away from me, I swear . . ."

Jaime stepped away with a swiftness.

Aria brushed past her to grab her purse hanging on the doorknob before she left the room and jogged down the stairs. She stormed through the foyer, barely taking note of Renee searching the built-in wooden bar in the corner.

Malcolm looked up just as Aria swung the door open wide and strode down the steps and up the walk like she was headed to war. His eyes widened a bit as she neared him.

"How you doing, Malcolm?" she said with a sultry smile.

He eyed her from head to toe. "I'm straight. You?" he asked, a toothpick hanging from the corner of his mouth.

Aria reached up and took it from him to fling over his shoulder and the top of his taxi to the street. "I need you to do something for me. You think you can do something for me, Malcolm?" she asked, her heart pumping from the thrill of doing something she knew would hurt Kingston and from her world on the brink of being turned completely upside down.

"Depends on what it is," he answered with hot eyes.

Aria pulled from her past the skillful art of the pick-up as she tilted her head to the side in full flirt mode. "Yes or no?" she demanded softly, reaching out to lift his shirt and trace the grooves of rock-hard abdomen.

"Hell yeah."

"Aria!" Renee shouted from the doorway. "Step *away* from the dick."

Malcolm frowned deeply as he shifted his eyes from Aria

to over her shoulder. "You know what? You ladies tripping," he said.

"What if it *wasn't* Kingston, Aria?" Renee said as she walked up to them.

Aria closed her eyes and pinched the bridge of her nose. She was right. How would she feel if she gave this man—this stranger—her goodies and then Kingston came home and pulled her into his arms like he always did when he saw her? How could she live with herself if it wasn't him?

But what if it was?

Aria had never felt so frustrated in all her life.

"Here you go, sir. We won't be needing you any further today. Thank you," Renee said.

Aria opened her eyes just in time to see Renee hand Malcolm money. "I'm sorry," she said to him, not looking at him at all as she turned and made her way back up the walk and into the house.

Renee followed close behind her.

Jaime came down the stairs with the bottle of Patrón in her hands.

Aria eyed them both. She felt like their lives were on pause.

CHAPTER 6

Renee's thoughts were filled with the memories of the early years of her marriage. The good old days. Before the arguing. Before the constant conflict and the constant pull to see who had the upper hand (i.e. the "dick") in their marriage. When she *knew* nothing could stop them. It was them against the world and the world had better watch out. . . .

"*Happy anniversary, Mrs. Clinton.*"

Renee smiled in pleasure as she stretched her nude frame against the length of her husband's equally nude physique as his warm hands played in the luxurious lengths of her hair. "*Mmm. Happy anniversary to you as well, Mr. Clinton.*"

He reached down with his free hand and soundly slapped her round bottom. "*Damn, I love this ass. My ass,*" *he told her possessively before he gripped it like a football and then jiggled it.*

Renee giggled as she lifted her head from his chest just enough to twirl her tongue around his nipple, enjoying the feel of it hardening against her tongue. "*Hmm,*" *she moaned.*

His hand tightened in her hair as he pressed her mouth closer. "God, that feels good, Ne."

She smiled as she flickered her tongue against the chocolate bud. "I have loved being married to you these last nine years, Jackson," she whispered to him as she shifted her body to straddle his narrow hips.

Jackson shifted so that his dick now lay snuggled between her warm and moist lips. His own cocoon. His dick knew the intricacies of her pussy quite well. The rigid walls were molded to him, knowing how to grip him just the right way.

Renee sighed as she sat up and flipped the hair he loved over her shoulder before she lightly wiggled her shoulders, making her chocolate-tipped breasts sway back and forth—just the way she knew he loved.

"Which one?" she asked, working her hips to press her clit up and down the length of him. "Slow and hot? Or fast and freaky?"

Jackson shook his head against the downy pillows and wrapped one strong arm around her waist. "How about long and loving because you are my wife and I could stroke this dick deep inside of you all night?" he whispered against her neck as he rolled her body beneath his and settled between her open legs.

Renee smiled softly up to him. "All night long, huh?" she asked him softly as she languidly stroked his back and his square buttocks.

"I love your breasts." He moaned against her cleavage, the soft twin swells of breasts cupping his cheeks as he kissed her there.

"And?" she prompted as she spread her legs wide.

Jackson sucked one pointed and plump nipple deeply, reveling in the shivers that he felt race over his wife's body. "And I love your fat ass pussy."

Renee tilted her head back and released a husky laugh up into the heated air they created. "Whoot, there it is," *she sang playfully as she flexed her hips and spread her legs wider, causing the moist lips of her pussy to spread before his throbbing thick tip.*

"Damn, I love you, Renee," he swore fiercely, dipping his head to kiss her deeply as he plunged his dick inside her in a swift motion.

She gasped, some of the essence of her soul entering his mouth as she shivered from the feel of his hard dick sliding with ease along her rigid and wet walls.

Sweat covered their naked frames. Bed covers and sheets slipped to the floor. The sweet scent of sex funk clung to the air, mingling with their cries.

"Oh, God, give me that dick," she panted, reaching up to grab the headboard tightly as Jackson delivered strokes that seemed to touch her soul. "Harder, Jackson, harder."

And he obliged without the slightest hesitation until the soft hairs surrounding his dick tickled her pussy lips.

But it was when he slowed his furious pumps down to a slow grind that Renee melted. Completely lost it.

"Aww, damn," she cried out between pants.

"I love you, Renee," he whispered in between kisses all along her collarbone.

"Oh, I love you too. I love you too," she cried out, arching her back as her pussy walls spasmed against his dick.

"You cumming, ain't you?" he asked hotly against her sweat-dampened neck. "I feel that pussy cumming on this dick."

Renee just allowed herself to get lost in the waves that floated across her body starting at the very center of her core. In that moment as her man—her husband—stroked her walls, he also fed her soul. She felt so many emotions all at once. Emotions that intensified the high of her climax.

Love for her man.

Passion from her man.

Fear that he would ever leave her.

Anger that he would ever share that passion with some-one else.

Comfort being in his arms.

"Jackson, it's always gone be like this?" she asked, breath-less, just as his body froze with the thick tip of throbbing dick sitting nestled just inside her lips.

"Always," he swore, kissing a trail to her mouth to suck her tongue deeply as he thrust his hips and filled her with all eleven inches of his hard and curving dick.

Renee clung to him, desperate and sweaty, as he cried out wildly into her mouth when his dick swelled against her walls and he filled her time and time again with explo-sive spasms of his seed until the sounds of their sex rivaled the light smacking of their feverish kisses. . . .

Renee shivered at the hot memory and then she shivered in anger thinking that her husband of the last eighteen years had shared his dick with another woman. Jackson had al-ways been hell in bed, and when they said their vows she just knew that all that had been for her and her alone.

And she swore that she had been his equal. His freak when he wanted. She had done it all and had it all done to her with everything in between.

Had it been too much? Not enough?

Or had her career and equality with him in the work-force been too much? Had that sent him into another woman's bed? Had she made him feel like the man that he swore she tried to devalue him as?

But then the thought struck her that this was more than an affair. An affair she could forgive. This was about more than worrying if Jessa's pussy was better than hers. This was about the possible end of her marriage.

And that was not something Renee was ready to accept. Not yet.

Aria eyed Renee, who was lost in thought. In the last couple of hours since the message from the mistress, her own mind had wandered time and time again, trying to piece together the puzzle. "Renee, un-ass those shot glasses. And, Jaime, let me get that Patrón," Aria told them as she moved across the living room to plop down on one of the swivel stools attached to the bar. "Might as well get fucked up while we sit here like three fools waiting to find out which of our marriages is over."

"That's not funny, Aria," Jaime insisted as she walked over and set the bottle of liquor on the bar.

"I bet *she's* just laughing her ass off," Renee said bitterly as she walked over to the bar and dug the shot glasses out to place them atop the bar in a straight line before she sat down on the stool next to Aria.

Aria eyed Jaime and the cigarette she'd just lit. "So if we pretend our friend didn't just drop a bombshell in all of our laps then it will go away, Jaime?" she asked.

Jaime placed the cigarette to her lips and cut her eyes over to watch Aria through the stream of silver smoke she released through pursed lips. "Who says *I'm* pretending?" she asked calmly. "I thought about it, and I'm sorry, ladies, but there is no way it can be Eric. Absolutely no way."

Aria arched her perfectly shaped brow. "I can tell you who says you're full of shit. Me," she countered.

"Hey!" Renee exclaimed, loudly tapping her hand on the top of the bar. "We can't turn on each other."

Aria slid off the bar stool and walked out of the room.

"Where are you going, Aria?" Renee called behind her, sounding every bit of the mother.

"To see if that bitch missed and left something behind to use as a chaser," Aria called over her shoulder as she strutted from the room and down the tiled hall leading to Jessa's kitchen.

She paused in the doorway, taking in the noticeable lack of all personal items on the countertops and walls. She shook her head. It was true she hadn't been to Jessa's in a week or so, but it was obvious that a busy beaver had been busy packing her little heart away. Plotting. Scheming. Damn.

Aria leaned against the beautiful wooden island in the center of the kitchen. "Damn," she swore again.

She felt like a fool when she remembered how Jessa had been the one to convince her to talk to Kingston about moving into Richmond Hills. . . .

<hr>

"*Oh, Kingston, I love this house!*" *Aria exclaimed as she stood back from the box of dishes she was unpacking in their kitchen.*

"*Me too. You did real good, baby,*" *Kingston said, squeezing her side as he walked by her to pick up another of the boxes they had to unpack.*

Aria eyed his strong and muscular arms in appreciation as he lifted the large box easily. "*Well, Jessa was the one who told me about the house. I can't wait for you to finally meet her,*" *she told him.* "*We were thick as thieves—and almost as cutthroat with each other—in college. But one thing about it—we were competitive, but when the shit hit the fan with somebody else trying to step, we always had each other's back.*"

"*Love-hate, huh?*" *he asked as he pulled the stack of paper-wrapped plates out of the box and sat them on the island.*

"*Like sisters with some serious sibling rivalry,*" *Aria assured him.* "*I cannot wait to show off my handsome, smart, sexy doctor husband.*"

"*Glad I can be of help in the pettiness,*" *he drawled.*

"I'm happy to see her ... it's just that I don't know if we're going to fall back into the whole one-up we used to do. I just want to be ready."

Kingston nodded, but Aria could tell he really didn't understand.

"I'm glad that you accepted the position at UMDNJ and we were able to move from Pennsylvania."

Kingston cut his eye over at her. "Me too, because that phone bill was getting as high as our rent for the apartment."

Aria frowned playfully as she picked up a dishcloth and unceremoniously tossed it into his face. He came around the island and wrapped his arms around her waist to pick her body up against the length of his. "You want me to put you in time-out?" he asked with a broad smile that was more white, straight teeth than anything.

Aria brought her hands up to his shoulders as she looked down into his handsome face. "Are you going in time-out with me?" she asked huskily as she brought her legs up to wrap tightly around his waist while she massaged the muscles of his shoulders.

Kingston's playful expression changed. "Oh, it's like that?" he asked thickly.

Aria dipped down to stroke her tongue across his mouth. "Oh, it's like that," she confirmed.

Kingston sat her down on the edge of the island before he nearly pulled the white tube top she wore down around her waist. With a hungry grunt that was purely primal, he pressed her down until her upper body was sandwiched between the island and his own body. With snakelike motions of his tongue, he tasted one fat nipple and then the other.

"Oooh!" Aria moaned, arching her back.

"Oh, y'all wrong."

Aria and Kingston jumped apart in surprise.

"Jessa!" Aria squealed as she rushed to cover her small but plump breasts with her tube top.

Jessa leaned in the open doorway in white linen slacks and a ruffled white shirt that was feminine, chic, and cool—so like Jessa—while Aria felt like a twelve-year-old in her cut-offs and tube top.

Aria scrambled down off the island to run across the room and into her friend's open and waiting arms. "Jessa!"

"I see you're still dressing like you're in college," Jessa joked in that husky voice.

Kingston walked up to slide his hand into the back pocket of Aria's frayed cut-off jeans. "She knows these turn me on," he told her.

"Jessa, this is the love of my life and the changer of my last name, Kingston," Aria said with pride as she kissed his smooth cheek. She wanted to show off her handsome doctor husband to her frenemy

Jessa held out her hand. "Nice to meet you, Mr. Livewell. I hope for Aria's sake that you live up to your surname."

Kingston wrapped his hand around hers. "Nice to meet you, Jessa, and you'll have to ask your friend about that."

Jessa nodded in agreement as she slid both of her hands into the pockets of her slacks. "Well, I hope you know you just met a new friend, Kingston."

"Well, any friend of Aria's is a friend of mine," he told her with a friendly smile.

"Where's Marc? I want to meet him," Aria asked, looking over Jessa's smooth shoulder out the door.

"He's at work, but we're taking you and two more couples from the subdivision out to dinner tonight. A little welcome to the neighborhood party. You will love Renee and Jaime."

Aria waved her at the kitchen. "Good, I don't think we'll be done unpacking the kitchen for me to cook."

"I had an appointment this morning but let me zip home and change so I can help you unpack."

"Well . . . I was wondering if you were going to help a sistah out."

Jessa smiled up at Kingston. "You see her trying to test our friendship?" she asked.

Kingston held up his hands. "My mama didn't raise a fool. I'm staying out of that," he said before turning to finish unpacking plates.

"I like him," Jessa mouthed with a nod and a wink before she turned and breezed back out of the kitchen door.

Aria frowned at the memory, hating that now she wondered if that was the moment her husband and Jessa had sparked their interest in one another. When they shook hands had the current of electrical chemistry gone off?

Who made the first move?

When?

Where?

In my house?

In my . . . bed?

All through college Jessa and Aria's friendship was based on competition—grades, clothes, boyfriends. All of it. The whole nine.

But never had Aria thought Jessa wanted to top her badly enough to steal her husband away.

Was Kingston even fishing? Maybe he had already left. Maybe he was already in Jessa's new house—*their* house.

Aria felt breathless as tears welled up in her eyes. She blinked them away as she pursed her lips and released a deep—and hopefully—cleansing breath. She banged her fist against the top of the island.

"Okay, I need that drink," she muttered aloud, opening the door to the Sub-Zero. It was empty and as clean as when it came off the showroom floor.

Aria made her way back to the living room and snatched up her drink from the bar. She downed it in one gulp but she hardly felt the fire it burned down her throat and in the pit of her stomach. She was numb.

———— ∞∞∞ ————

Jaime accepted the shot of tequila that Renee handed her, but she hardly took a sip. Alcohol was not the solution to the drama unfolding in their lives, but she wasn't going to stop her friends if they needed it.

Alcohol did not equal answers. And Jaime needed answers. Reaching in her purse for her cell phone, she slid off the stool and walked away from the bar as she dialed the security desk.

"Security."

Jaime eased her hair behind her ear. "Lucky, this is Mrs. Hall. Listen, did Jessa leave a forwarding address? I misplaced it when she gave it to me and I wanted to send her some flowers to welcome her to her new home," Jaime lied with ease as she stood by the front window.

"But I thought you ladies didn't know she moved?" Lucky asked.

Jaime's eyes glinted. Now this buffoon want to get some sense? "Lucky, she asked us not to say anything about moving and I guess we thought *you* didn't know, you know," she said lightly, wanting to strangle his ass.

"Trust me, Mrs. Hall, I know everything about Richmond Hills," he said cockily.

Jaime bit her lips to keep from yelling: "So did you know that bitch was screwing my damn husband?" But she didn't. She composed herself. "Lucky, the address?"

"Well, actually she didn't leave a forwarding, but I do know the moving truck went to Saddle River because they stopped here for directions to the interstate."

Jaime's shoulders dropped in disappointment. "Okay, all right. Okay. Um. Thanks, Lucky. Thank you."

She ended the call, taking a moment to compose herself before she turned around. She walked back over to her friends as emotions she fought hard not to expose nearly strangled her. She fought hard to maintain her composure as Aria and Renee gnawed at the drama like a starving dog would a bone.

"You know, we joked a lot about Jessa, but I never thought she would do something like this," Aria admitted.

Jaime nodded. "Jessa definitely should be ashamed of herself. You just don't do this to friends and marriages and homes. It's not right."

"Who was this woman we let into our lives?" Renee asked in agreement.

Aria took a sip of her Patrón and winced. "She fooled the hell out of my ass," she spat.

"No, baby, she fooled us all," Renee said in anger.

Silently, Jaime wondered if both Jessa and her husband had pulled the wool over her eyes. . . .

Jaime loved Eric endlessly. From the moment she said yes to his romantic moonlit proposal, she knew she would be with him forever and a day in marital bliss. Everything about their courtship had been a dream for her. He had been a perfect part of her perfect plan for her life.

They'd met when he brought his mother to their church for an afternoon worship service. He just happened to sit beside her, and Jaime had found the short and slender man attractive. The attraction was mutual because he returned to their church that following Sunday—without his mother—and asked her out for a date after service.

Jaime smiled as she recalled how nervous he had seemed

on their first date at a soul food restaurant. But even that had drawn her to him. That and the fact that he was a handsome, well-mannered, college-educated, churchgoing, home-owning, business-owning man. When she expressed to him her desire to remain a virgin until she wed, he completely understood and even expressed that he respected her decision. What more could she ask for?

And for one year they were nearly inseparable as they slid with ease from dating into a relationship. It seemed only right that he propose one year to the day after their first date. They wed in a beautiful church ceremony one year after that with all of their family, sorors, fraternity brothers, and well-wishers in attendance on a beautiful sunny day.

Complete fairy tale for Jaime.

Everything had been perfect. Everything.

Until the night of their honeymoon.

She had been so anxious to finally get beyond heated kisses and lots of groping to make love with her husband. And what better locale than a beautiful hotel suite on a secluded beach in Jamaica.

Seeing Eric naked for the first time, Jaime realized the one downside of not being intimate with a man before the wedding. She had no idea what she was getting—for the rest of her married life. And she had to admit that the sight of his slender dick had made her pause. Then, as she lay there beneath him with her eyes to the ceiling, she wished she was lost in passion and not washed over in confusion. She wasn't even sure if she had cum before he shuddered, pumped twice, and was done.

So far it was a fail on size and delivery.

As he slept away his satisfaction and left her completely starved, Jaime dressed and went down to the bar. She bought a drink and bummed a cigarette—her first but not last smoke.

Jaime had been hoping for that spectacular explosion of fireworks and passion that her friends told her about. But where was it?

When she returned from her honeymoon, all of her friends and sorors wanted to know about it. And so began Jaime's life of lies and pretenses as she looked them all dead in the eye and flat-out lied, even embellishing and adding details she could only wish Eric had in his sexual repertoire.

She almost fooled herself as well as she fooled them all. She only hoped things would get better and they would find their groove.

They didn't.

Jaime sighed as she looked around their bedroom. Satin sheets and rose petals were on the queen-sized bed. A bottle of champagne, a bowl with plump, juicy strawberries, and a can of whipped cream sat on a tray in the middle of the bed. A medley of Luther Vandross, O'Jays, Isley Brothers, Maxwell, and other sultry slow jams was playing on the surround system running throughout their house. Scented candles were everywhere.

She smoothed the silk over the bright red crotchless teddy she wore with a serious pair of five-inch "fuck me" pumps. Her make-up was heavy. Her perfume was heavier.

She followed all the instructions in the dozen different self-help books she'd bought on reviving the passion in your marriage. She had a few more tricks she planned to deliver as well.

Jaime was ready for a better sex life to match every other aspect of their marriage. Eric spoiled her endlessly—except in the bedroom. Enough was dang-on enough.

Picking up the cordless phone, she called Eric's cell phone.

"Hey, baby."

"Where are you?" she asked as she sat down on the leather bench at the foot of the bed.

"I had to stop at Jessa's."

Jaime sat up straighter. "For what, honey?" she asked, keeping her tone calm and polite like a lady even though she felt like cussing like a sailor.

"She needed me to put up some shelves she bought today," he told her.

"Well, I have something I need you to do at home," she told him, rising to her feet and almost stumbling in her heels as she tried to pace the hardwood floors.

"As soon as I do this, I'm coming straight home."

Jaime hung up on him and then flung the phone. It ricocheted off the bed and knocked over the champagne bottle and whipped cream can like dominoes.

"Okay, I am sick of Jessa Bell," she snapped, kicking off the heels because she was sure she was no longer in the mood to fuck.

When Jaime moved into Eric's spacious home in Richmond Hills and finally met his best friend/neighbor, Jessa Bell, she had taken an instant dislike to the woman. He had mentioned her before, but Jaime hadn't been expecting a tall, beautiful woman with golden skin and hair.

Her immediate thought as she eyed the woman whose body made an hourglass look like a pencil: "Oh, heck no. What man with a working dick can be friends with this woman and not want her?"

But then the fact that she appeared to be happily married herself had quelled some of Jaime's suspicions.

But then it seemed that any time her husband, Marc, went out of town for business, Jessa was forever calling Eric to help her with things around her house. Fix this. Mow that. Lift this. Move that.

Well, Jaime wasn't at all sure just what Eric was fixing, mowing, lifting, and moving when he was at Jessa's. She understood that the woman's husband had passed, and Eric swore that he saw Jessa as nothing more than a good friend, but Jaime was no fool.

She bit the bright red gloss from her lips as she paced the floor. When she happened to look up and catch a glimpse of herself in the dresser mirror, she actually jumped in surprise. The hair. The make-up. The teddy. She looked like one of those video girls.

Shaking her head to clear it, Jaime thought about what to do about Jessa. And then it came to her. She raced about the room blowing out the gazillion candles before she dressed in one of those velour sweatsuits and cleaned some of the make-up from her face.

Jaime zoomed down the stairs and out the house to walk the short distance to Jessa's. Her back stiffened to see her husband's Lexus parked in her drive, but she forged ahead, knocking on the door.

It opened.

She barely spared Jessa a glance as she eyed Eric on the floor surrounded by all the components of a shelving unit. He looked confused but smiled at seeing her. "Hey, baby."

"Hi, Jessa," she said, shifting her eyes back to the beauty.

"Hey, Jaime, come on in. I had to borrow Eric again. I wanted to surprise Marc with this shelving unit for his birthday," she said in that soft and husky voice of hers.

"Yes, Eric is Mr. Fix-it," Jaime said with a big fake smile as she looked at her husband. "Actually, I thought I would come over and help since I was home doing nothing."

"Come right on in. The more hands the better," Jessa said, stepping back to wave Jaime over.

Jaime didn't usually fool up with Jessa, but she had suddenly decided that perhaps it was good to keep friends close, but it was even better to keep enemies closer.

In time Jaime went from hanging out with Jessa to watch her to just enjoying the woman's company. Her suspicions had faded away and they had become close. Jaime had truly considered the woman a reliable friend.

But now in the light of this betrayal—be it of Renee, Aria, or herself—Jaime wished she had stuck to her original judgment of the woman and kept a close eye on her with her husband.

CHAPTER 7

When you look for shit, you find shit.

After nearly an hour of searching Jessa's house, Aria now believed that was not always the case. Nothing. Not one clue. Not one hint.

And so the torture and the waiting continued.

She walked out of the study and followed the sound of her friends' voices to the foyer.

"Maybe they met at hotels or something," Renee said, running her hands through her hair. "Maybe they never fucked . . . here."

"Maybes . . . what-ifs . . . coulda, woulda, shoulda . . . *shit!*" Aria threw her hands up in the air before she walked over to the bar and grabbed their purses to then walk back and hand to them. "Let's just get out of here."

"I agree," Jaime said, turning to give the house one last look.

Aria breezed through them to rush out of the front door, and once she stepped outside, she breathed deeply of the smell of suburbia—where more drama swelled behind closed doors and facades.

Jaime and Renee walked out of the house. Aria used her key to lock the door. "I shoulda fucked Malcolm," she told them as she gave the house one last long look before she turned to face them. "At least by now I would be some-where knocked the fuck out and sex funky."

"Who the hell is Malcolm?" Jaime asked as she popped several pieces of gum into her mouth.

"The cabbie," Renee offered.

"Oh, please." Jaime blew air through her teeth and waved her hand dismissively. "Besides, having an affair is so be-neath you, Aria."

They all fell silent. No one moved. A car went slowly driving up the street and they all lifted their hands to wave briefly.

"It's so funny that life goes on but ours is stuck in this stupid-ass limbo," Renee said as she looked at the neigh-boring houses, at women on their knees gardening and husbands mowing lawns. Children playing. People leaving and arriving home. "I feel like time is stuck at the exact moment we got that stupid-ass message."

"I'm so sick of this shit," Aria admitted, her strong stance weakening as the effects of the liquor made her emotional.

"Aww, baby," Renee cooed as she pulled her younger friend into her arms and held her tightly as she rocked her.

"It's me. I know it's me," Aria said in a whisper as she stared down the street at her house as a telling memory came to her. She wondered how the hell she had ignored her instincts. . . .

Aria smiled into her goblet of sangria as she stepped out of the kitchen out onto her deck. Their spacious lawn was filled with nearly a hundred friends and neighbors enjoy-ing good music, good drinks, good barbecue. The bartender was set up in the corner. The deejay was in an opposite corner serving up good music. Kingston's father was at the grill putting some fire to ribs, chicken, pork chops, and quail. Tables ran along the side filled buffet style with all types of side dishes. People talked, danced, mingled, ate, and just were having a good time under the welcoming cool of night and the large fans stationed in the four corners of the yard.

She shook her head thinking what a different set it would have been back in her hometown—just as fun, but different as hell.

Every summer since they moved into Richmond Hills three years ago, Aria and Kingston had thrown a huge three-day barbecue that everyone looked forward to. It was the jam.

She swayed to the sounds of Frankie Beverly & Maze's "We Are One" as she took a look around to make sure everyone was happy. "Awww," she sighed at Renee and Jackson in the center of the dance floor holding each other close as they swayed to the music. She was particularly pleased because she knew her friend's recent entrance into the workforce had led to tension. Jackson wanted a stay-at-home wife and Renee thought she would go crazy if she had to continue staying at home—especially with her youngest child in school all day.

Her eyes sought and found Jaime and Eric. She wasn't at all surprised to see them sitting together in a cozy corner with their heads bent as they talked. Aria fought the urge to mock throw up because they were the most sickening affectionate couple she had ever met. Everything about them was just perfect, and that usually gave Aria a perfect damn headache. She laughed a little as she pictured them smiling through their whole fuck session.

She saw Marc over by the grill, but her eyes searched the crowd for Jessa and she didn't see her anywhere. Aria frowned a bit. Maybe she went to the restroom, Aria thought.

"Ooh, that's my song," Aria exclaimed when Al Green's "Let's Stay Together" came on. She threw her drink up in the air as she searched for Kingston to dance with her.

When she didn't see him she turned and walked back inside the house. "Kingston, where you at, baby?" she called out, setting her glass on the island.

Aria went into her living room. "Kingston," she called out again.

Lights flashed against the wall as a car turned into the driveway. Thinking more guests had arrived, Aria glanced out the window. She saw her own vehicle. The door opened and when the car light came on, she saw Jessa in the passenger seat. "They must have made a store run," she said.

But she paused when they climbed out of the vehicle with nothing. No packages. Not nary a nothing in sight that could have been purchased at a store.

Aria stood back from the window a bit and watched as they stopped to talk and laugh. Jessa's hand lightly landed on Kingston's arm and Aria cocked a brow. When Jessa walked around to the back of the house, Kingston turned to watch her leave before he turned and cut across their lawn to enter the house through the front door.

No, Aria, don't trip, she told herself as she turned on her heels to face the door, surprised at her own thoughts of something foul going on between her friend and her husband.

Kingston walked in looking like her loyal and faithful husband in his orange polo and khaki cargo shorts. He paused in surprise to see her standing there. "Hey, baby," he said, walking over to pull her into his embrace.

Aria hated that she smelled him for some hint of Jessa. "Where you been?" she asked. "Our song is playing."

"Awww, you was looking for Big Poppa, huh?" he teased as he used his hands to jiggle her buttocks in the strapless sundress she wore.

Aria leaned back to look up into his eyes even as her heart pounded crazy as hell in her chest. "Where you been?" she asked again, bringing her hands up to massage his shoulders the way that he loved.

"Your mama sent me for some cards," he told her, re-

leasing one of her ass cheeks to reach in his side pocket for two decks of cards.

"You know Mama loves to play pitty-pat," she told him, only feeling a little less suspicious.

"Damn, you smell good, baby," he whispered against her neck as he planted soft kisses in the soft hollow above her collarbone.

Aria shivered but she wasn't even trying to get played, she didn't care if the feel of his mouth was making her moist.

"Baby, you should check on Jessa too," he said in between kisses.

Aria stiffened as her pussy juices dried up. "Why?"

"She was just sitting up front by herself looking down," he told her. "Maybe something's up with her and Marc, so I made her ride with me to the store."

Aria brought her hands up to his face and leaned back to look up at her husband, her lover, her friend, her confidant. She started to third degree his ass about their car ride, but she passed. There was more than one way to skin a cat. She was a journalist, and she'd learned early that sometimes to get to the truth it was best not to ask direct questions. Sometimes you found other ways to get to the bottom of shit.

She kissed him deeply as she kept her eyes locked with his. She flickered her tongue against the tip of his before she sucked it intensely into her own mouth with a moan.

"Damn," Kingston swore, his hands working her dress up around her waist.

But she brushed his hands away as she reached between them to undo his button and zipper. With her eyes still locked with his, she roughly jerked his shorts and boxers down around his muscled thighs. She squatted before him and took his semihard dick in her hand.

"Baby, someone could walk in," he said, not sounding remotely concerned.

"So?"

Kingston held his hands up in surrender as he leaned sideways a bit to look down at her.

Aria smelled him without him knowing. The curly hairs of his crotch smelled lightly of sweat and his cologne. Not pussy. Not soap used to clean off the scent of pussy. She ran her tongue along the length of his hard pitch-black inches before she circled her tongue around the caramel-colored tip that was thick and smooth. No taste of pussy or soap.

Humph.

Closing her eyes, she took all of his hardening dick into her mouth until the smooth tip kissed her tonsils. His body tensed and she felt his knees weaken as his hands clutched her hair in his fist.

Aria sucked her husband's dick like she was trying to give him life and then take it away by draining him of every bit of cum his nuts could muster. She knew his dick in and out. Soon she felt the pulse of his dick against her tongue as he cried out with each spasm of cum exploding into her mouth. He fell back into an armchair and Aria moved with him on her knees to stay with the dick, still sucking him deeply and swallowing his seed as he cried out in a chorus of sopranolike high notes, shivering and weak.

It was a reward and a reminder.

She was that bitch who didn't leave room for another bitch to take care of her man/her dick.

Period.

Renee was stunned by the weakness she felt in Aria's body. In their friendship, everyone had her role. Renee was the Mama Surrogate, Jaime was Mrs. Bourgeoisie, Jessa had been the Life of the Party/Queen of Gossip Control, and

Aria had been the Hard Ass who didn't take shit off no one.

To feel her friend completely shaken by Jessa's bullshit made Renee just as angry as the thought that it was indeed her. Renee was not a fighter, but in that moment she knew if she laid eyes on Jessa Bell the Jezebel, she could wear her ass out easily.

Because of the drama, because of the hurt still to come for one of them, because she felt like a fool. She'd invited the spider into her lair. . . .

Renee strode out of the building with her car keys already in hand. She deactivated the alarm of her SUV and then opened the door to slide into the driver's seat as she tossed her briefcase on the leather passenger seat. She felt completely overwhelmed but she was determined to get her shit together with a quickness.

Easier said than done.

She leaned back in her chair and eyed the phone. She felt dread to call her husband even to tell him she was on the way home. She didn't feel like arguing again. She didn't have time to argue. But rest assured, they would argue.

That's all we seem to do lately, she thought as she massaged the bridge of her nose with her hand.

Knock-knock.

Renee looked over at her assistant, Darren, tapping on her driver-side window. Turning the key in the ignition, she lowered the window with the power button. "Yes, Darren?" she asked, looking up at the young man whose skin was as dark as chocolate.

"You left the CD with all of your press releases, and I know you said you were going to work on them tonight," he said, handing the plastic case to her.

"Thanks, Darren. I'm trying to rush home and I for-

got," she told him as she took it from him. "What would I do without my assistant?"

He smiled in pleasure. Darren was a college senior with well-expressed desires to get into nonprofit work with the use of his business degree. He was young, eager, ready to learn, and beyond ready to work.

Sometimes Renee wondered if he was gunning for her job.

"Thanks again, Darren," she told him.

"Have a safe ride, Mrs. Clinton," he said, stepping back from her SUV.

Renee gave him one last smile and wave before she pulled out of her reserved parking spot.

As soon as she settled in her seat for her twenty-minute drive home, Renee wondered what the atmosphere would be like when she got there. She was truly afraid for her marriage.

Jackson wouldn't or couldn't understand that once the children were in school all day, sitting around the house all day washing clothes and cleaning was slowly driving her ass insane.

She was a college-educated woman who wanted to use the brain God gave her. She wanted to put on her shoes, get the fuck out of the kitchen, and not have any more babies.

Renee found charity work of attending social events, posing for pictures, and writing big checks to be superficial. After a photo-op trip to CancerCure, Renee had truly taken an interest in the foundation and the work they did for cancer research and awareness across the country. She stopped putting in frivolous hours wearing pretty suits and big hats to luncheons with her Women's League and started volunteering directly at CancerCure.

Now she was the vice president of marketing. When the opportunity arose to apply for the position she couldn't pass it up. Combining a chance to use her skill, vision, and degree with such a worthy cause? She had to apply and then accept when they offered it to her.

She had to.

Jackson hadn't spoken to her for weeks after she told him she was going to work full-time.

She wondered how long he would stay mad because she was going to be late to the business dinner at their house tonight. CancerCure had a huge benefit concert planned for next week with some of the top artists in the country, and it was her job to get with the various teams and work out last-minute details. Her bosses wanted everything done today and Renee knew she wouldn't be done by three to get home in time to supervise the caterers.

Thankfully Jessa had stepped in for her and was at the house getting everything prepared so that all Renee had to do was take a shower, twist her shoulder-length hair up into a sexy topknot, and change into the dress she'd already picked out.

Renee was grateful for Jessa's help. Aria was busy working on a freelance story and Jaime was busy tending to a sick Eric.

As she pulled through the gates of Richmond Hills, Renee actually felt herself getting excited about the dinner party. She was determined to play the hostess and have a good time while ensuring her husband's party was flawless.

And tonight after everyone was gone, Renee planned for them to fuck away their drama. She would bathe him, suck him to the edge of an explosive nut, and then ride his dick backwards until his mouth was twisted.

Renee parked on the street in front of the house behind the catering van, not bothering with the garage because it was easier to fit four or five cars in the garage and driveway than on the street. Luckily none of the guests had arrived yet. "Good," she said aloud as she grabbed her cell phone and hurried out of her car to walk up the asphalt walkway leading to the side of the house. She paused and then backed up as she looked through the front window into her living room.

Jessa was snuggled on one end of the leather love seat sipping from a goblet of wine while Jackson was beside her doing the same. Something about the scene was intimate to Renee. Intimate and a bit disconcerting.

Renee tried to laugh off the sudden sting of jealousy and suspicion as she switched gears and walked across the lawn and through the front door into the house. She peeked through the small oval glass at the top of the door as she purposefully made as much noise as possible opening the door.

Through the mirror she saw Jackson rise to his feet and move away from where he'd just sat with Jessa.

"Say what say who?" Renee said as she walked in.

"Hey, Renee," Jessa said, greeting her with a warm smile.

"Hey, Jessa." Renee's eyes shifted to find Jackson standing by the bar topping his glass off with his favorite cognac. She walked over to him, placing her hand on his back. "Hey, baby."

He said nothing and moved away from her touch to take a deep sip of his drink.

That stung like salt poured in an open wound.

"Well, since you're home, I'm going to head out to get dressed," Jessa said, rising to walk over to Renee.

Renee accepted the goblet Jessa gave her. "Thanks again, Jessa. I really appreciate it," she told her friend, even as she felt like she'd interrupted them.

"There really was nothing to do. You had everything planned out perfectly," she stressed with a wink at Renee as she squeezed her hand. "The caterers own the kitchen. The samples I had of the food are delicious. I set the table and dropped the kids at your mother's."

Renee drank down the rest of the wine in one swallow. She felt horrible for her thoughts of Jessa betraying her.

The woman was helping her out, and her repayment was thoughts that she was fucking her husband? Renee felt ashamed of herself as Jessa slipped out the door.

"Jackson, I'm sorry that I couldn't be here—"

He stared at her over the rim of his glass. "Couldn't or wouldn't?" he said coldly.

Cold enough to make Renee shiver. "Jackson, why do you have to keep fighting about this?" she asked.

He walked over to her. "And you're comfortable about turning to another woman to step in to do my wifely duties?"

Renee frowned. "Wifely duties? Look here, Ward Cleaver, you tripping—"

She swallowed the rest of her words as one of the servers stepped into the living room. "Sorry, I was looking for Mrs. Clinton," the short and plump man said.

"How can I help you?" Renee asked, walking over to him.

He looked confused. "The . . . um . . . other Mrs. Clinton?"

Renee ignored Jackson's sarcastic bark of laughter. "She's a friend helping me out until I got home. I'm Mrs. Clinton. The one and only."

She gave her husband one last look over her shoulder before she followed the server into the kitchen. He was standing by the bar staring at her. "I love you, Jackson," she mouthed to him with a plea in her eyes.

And after a moment he simply nodded.

For now it was enough.

———— ∞∞∞ ————

Needing a diversion, Jaime reached in her bag and pulled out her shades, slipping them into place.

Brrrnnnggg.

Aria and Renee both looked over at her as her cell phone

loudly rang from her purse. She calmly removed it from her purse and checked the caller ID. "It's my mother," she told them.

Jaime frowned deeply in displeasure as Aria waved her hands dismissively. "Hello, Mother," she said into the phone as she turned, giving Renee and Aria her designer-covered back.

"Jaime, since we missed Eric at breakfast, your father and I wanted you and Eric to come over for dinner tonight. We're having the Hamptons and Reverend Greggs and his wife over as well."

Jaime looked heavenward as she flipped her weave away from her face and pressed the phone closer to her ear. "We have other plans, and you taught me well not to cancel an event when I have already sent back my RSVP," she lied with ease.

Her mother sighed in obvious disappointment. "I don't remember you saying you had something to attend this evening. What is it, a dinner party?" she asked.

Virginia Osten-Pine could work for the FBI with her natural ability to snoop out a lie. The woman kept Jaime on her toes trying to keep up the facade of her marriage. The truth? Humph. Virginia couldn't handle the truth. *I have a date with my destiny, Mother. It's very likely my husband may be leaving me for one of my best friends. Now how do you like them apples?*

Like everyone in their world, Virginia and Franklin had no idea their daughter's marriage was a sham. They had no clue of the coldness of their home when there were no watchful eyes. They had no clue that she was lonely. They had no clue that she was the first to stray or that she had long ago suspected her husband of sleeping with *their* friend. . . .

Brrrnnnggg.

Brrrnnnggg.

Jaime rolled over in her sleep at the jarring sound of the phone ringing in the middle of the night. And then it hit her. The phone was ringing in the middle of the night and that never boded well. Never.

Sitting up, she turned on the lamp and then grabbed the black cordless from its base on her nightstand. "Hello," she said, her heart already pounding as Eric shifted and just snored a little louder beside her.

"Jaime, get over here. Jessa needs us."

No other words were needed. Jaime hung up the phone and rolled out of their plush down-filled bed in one movement. She scrambled out of her sheer nightgown and pulled on one of her sports unitards. Quickly she zoomed into the bathroom to remove her silk hair scarf and brush down her wrapped hair. Wash her face. Brush her teeth. Rinse her mouth. She was ready.

Jaime walked back to the bed. "Eric," she called out softly.

A louder, more drawn-out snore was her answer.

After sliding her feet into step-in shoes, Jaime reached over and shook his shoulder.

He frowned as he awakened and looked up at her. "Huh?"

"Renee just called and Jessa needs us," she told him, not even waiting for a response before she turned and left the room.

Only two weeks ago, Jessa had buried her husband of just five years after a fatal motorcycle incident. It had torn up Jaime's heart to see Jessa crying and so obviously lost without her husband, especially when it was Jessa who usually led the fun and good-time brigade. Over the last week they had all kept her under their watchful eye, and the only thing Jaime knew in that moment was Jessa needed them.

As she stepped out onto her porch she looked up the street and saw Aria walking out of her house as well.

Jaime waited for her. "What's going on?" she asked as they hurried up the sidewalk to Jessa's brightly lit house.

"I don't know," Aria said, her hair still wrapped with a cloth. Crust still in the corner of her eye. Drool still dried in a path from her mouth to her chin.

Jaime frowned but said nothing. She just knew she wouldn't be caught dead walking the streets like that.

Aria eyed her from head to toe. "Were you up exercising?" she asked as they turned up the walk leading to Jessa's front door.

"No."

Jaime didn't miss the way Aria shook her head.

The front door opened and Renee ushered them inside. "I was up late working on a proposal for my new job and I happen to glance outside and she was sitting in the gazebo."

"At this time of the night?" Aria asked as they climbed the stairs together.

"Exactly."

Renee led the way into the bedroom. It clung with sadness and depression as Jessa lay on her side of the bed stiffly, as if she was afraid to roll over and discover that her husband was not there. And would not ever be there again.

She looked up at them with puffy, red-rimmed eyes that were filled with pain as they came to stand by her bedside. "I can't do this, y'all. I can't. . . ."

"Awww." Jaime sighed, sitting down to rub Jessa's back. "Listen, I can't imagine how you feel. I can't imagine at all, but I want you to know that you are one of the strongest people I know, and even though it doesn't seem like it now, you will get through, Jessa. We will help you get through this."

Aria and Renee climbed onto the bed beside Jessa. As

they allowed a mourning friend to cry, they found tears
swelling in their own eyes.

"I thank God for y'all. What would I do without you?"
Jessa asked softly.

"Well, you'll never find out, girlfriend," Aria assured her.

What a bunch of crap, Jaime thought.

Jaime bit the lip gloss from her lips. "Humph. When Marc
died, we were so good to her, neglecting our own husbands
to be her friend. Not a neighbor. Not an associate. A friend.
What would I do without you, she asked," Jaime recalled
sarcastically to herself. "Looks like she figured it out for
herself, huh?"

Bitch.

CHAPTER 8

Ding. Ding. Ding.

"*Excuse me, everyone. Excuse me.*"

The seven people gathered around the large round table in the Spanish restaurant quieted their chatter. They all focused their attention on Marc standing with his glass of sangria in one hand and a dinner fork in the other.

"*Oh, Lord, here comes a speech,*" *Jackson joked before taking a swig of his bottle of light beer.*

"*Baby, you're just mad Marc beat you to it,*" *Renee quipped, reaching over to lightly squeeze his upper arm.*

Marc just laughed good-naturedly, looking like his usual charming and handsome self in a crisp black silk shirt and dark denims that seemed beyond black with his fair complexion. "A night like this, surrounded by good food, good drink, and most importantly, good friends, deserves a toast."

"*That's right, baby,*" *Jessa said in husky tones as she looked up at Marc adoringly.*

"*I just want to thank you all for coming out with me and Jessa tonight to celebrate my promotion,*" *Marc began. "Jessa and I couldn't think of any better people to surround ourselves with. You all are the epitome of good friends."*

Everyone lifted their glass in a toast as they all looked toward Marc with warmth.

"*And to my wife. You have proven to me that there is*

*nothing but truth in the statement that behind every suc-
cessful man there stands a good woman," Marc said, staring down into her upturned face. "I love and appreciate you
for anything and everything you have done to make my
life complete."*

*Jessa rose to her feet in a strapless red dress and wrapped
her arms around Marc's neck to kiss him passionately. His
hands went to her waist before sliding around her completely to hold her body closely to his as they both moaned
in pleasure.*

*"Hey, get a room, you two," Kingston said jokingly as
their kiss lengthened.*

"O-kay," Aria drawled playfully right along with him.

*Jessa laughed huskily as she leaned back in her hus-
band's tight embrace and looked up at him. "We almost
put on a show, huh?" she teased Marc.*

He winked at her as they took their seats.

*"Well, congratulations, Marc. I'm sure I speak for every-
one when I tell you how proud of you we are," Eric said,
raising his glass. "Cheers."*

Everyone did the same. "Cheers."

Two waiters came with trays carrying their dinners.

*"I am starving. I skipped lunch today," Renee said as
her steaming bowl of paella was set before her.*

*Jackson side-eyed her before digging into his own plate
of paella. "Okay, Mrs. Corporate America, Rome was not
built in one day," he said to her, a hint of sarcasm evident
in his voice.*

*Renee paused. "Actually, I missed lunch to attend the
parent-teacher conference for our child. You know . . .
the one you couldn't make it to, Mr. Corporate America,"
she returned smoothly.*

*"Okay, you two, down there," Jaime said, with a ner-
vous smile.*

*When it came to discussing Renee's career, the couple
could go from happy to hell in no time at all.*

"Oh, no, no, no we're cool," Renee said before tasting her food. "Just making sure he understands that I do what he does plus more."

"I guess if you could screw my dick off and let that swing between your legs you'd really be a superwoman," Jackson returned coldly.

"Jackson, man, I do not need that image, and I'm eating stuffed sausages," Kingston quipped, trying to lighten the mood.

It worked.

Everyone laughed.

"You're right," Jackson said with a nod as he looked to his friend. "My apologies."

"No worries, Jackson," Marc said genuinely.

Aria covered her husband's hand with her own. "I married Kingston for his sense of humor," she quipped. "Among other things."

"I thought we agreed not to discuss . . . things?" Eric asked.

Everyone groaned and laughed, but the mood had definitely switched back to one of a laid-back atmosphere of easygoing conversation.

"I just want to say that nights like these, when the eight of us are together, are the best," Jessa said in her husky tone as she eyed her friends. "I can only hope that we all have many more good times ahead of us."

Aria shook herself to free her thoughts of the memory of one of many couples nights they all shared together. Card parties. Cookouts. Just nights sitting on someone's deck or porch talking or joking. Joint vacations. The whole nine. Their lives—all of their lives—had become intertwined.

She turned and looked up at Jessa's house. "The secrets

that house holds. If those walls could talk," she said aloud, more to herself than anyone as she shook her head.

She felt Renee and Jaime walk up to stand beside her on the sidewalk.

"Jessa betrayed one of us, and one of our husbands also betrayed Marc. I mean, we all were friends—especially Eric," Aria said, still thinking out loud.

"What do you mean, especially Eric?" Jaime asked with attitude.

Aria leaned back from the hostility she saw in Jaime's eyes. "We all got the text, so every last one of our husbands is suspect. Don't you think?" she snapped back.

"I think the only husband you need to focus on is Kingston," Jaime countered.

"That's cool, but don't you overlook your husband either, Boo."

Jaime crossed her arms over her chest and eyed Aria up and down. "You know what? Let's get to the real, Aria. Friend or not, you have a problem with me."

"I sure do when you're on your Pollyanna perfection crap." Aria threw her hands up in the air. "One day reality is going to set in on your ass and you might go crazy."

Jaime didn't say anything at first as she maintained her calm and simply smoothed her hand over her hair as she eyed Aria. "You don't know anything about my marriage," she said in a cool voice.

Aria stomped her feet and pointed her finger accusingly at Jaime. "Oh, my God, you just did it. You just took a sec to put on that Calm, Cool, Collected bullshit when you know damn well your ass is mad as hell on the inside, you nut."

"You really need to get more of that hood out of you." Jaime sighed dismissively.

Aria made a fist and stepped forward.

"No, Aria!" Renee screamed, stepping between them. "I

let this go on long enough. Why are you two turning on each other?"

"I don't need this bullshit." Aria turned to walk away.

"No, what you need is etiquette training," Jaime called out over Renee's shoulder.

Aria froze. Paused. Turned. Locked eyes with Jaime. "So you think Eric is better than Kingston? There's no chance in hell it's your husband. There's no way in hell it's your marriage being destroyed. You think you're above being cheated. Does your pussy shoot sparks or some shit? What the fuck make you so special, Polly-fucking-Anna?"

Renee turned to face Aria. "Aria, don't," she warned with a stern eye.

Jaime cocked her head to the side and eyed Aria up and down. "If it makes me Pollyanna because I'm not immediately taking the word of someone else above my husband's, then so be it."

"You are so full of shit, Jaime," Aria said, walking up.

"Don't take your anger out on me because you think your best friend stole your husband."

Whap!

Aria's hand stung from reaching beyond Renee and slapping the hell out of Jaime. She didn't plan it. She didn't mean to. She didn't even realize what she was going to do until her hand landed across Jaime's face. "Jaime, I'm sor—"

Whap!

Aria gasped and her mouth fell open after Jaime soundly slapped her back.

Renee pushed her hands into both of their chests. "Are you two kidding me right now?" she roared. "Calm your asses down."

Aria wanted so badly to crawl right over Renee and beat Jaime's ass like she stole something precious.

"This is all Jessa's doing, so why in the hell are you two turning on each other like this?" Renee asked, looking between the two of them. "If anything, we need each other more than ever. Come on, ladies, put on your big-girl panties. Come on, pull 'em up."

That old Aria from the Bricks wanted to wear Jaime's ass out, but the Aria she was today was mindful of the scene they were making on the streets of the upper-middle-class subdivision. "I shouldn't have hit you first and for *that,* I apologize, Jaime."

Jaime nodded even as she continued to rub her reddening cheek. "And I apologize for that slick comment . . . but not for slapping you back."

Aria actually smiled. "I didn't know you had it in you, Bougie," she joked.

Jaime smiled. "I didn't either," she admitted.

"Now that you two done found some sense," Renee began as she turned back to face Jessa's house, "do you think Jessa told one of our neighbors where she moved to? I mean someone has to know, right?"

Aria shook her head. "I doubt it. She would've been scared someone was going to tell us," she said, bending down to pick up the purse she dropped when she was about to spot Jaime's eye. In truth, she still thought Jaime was full of shit, but more than giving her a big dose of reality, right now she knew their focus had to be on bigger and worse things.

But God, it felt good to slap the hell out of her, she thought, *even if Jaime did get some get-back.*

"I was just thinking about when we went to the Fiesta the night Marc got promoted," Aria told them.

"You're right about what you said, though," Renee said. "We all were friends. I mean, what would Marc say right now? How could they do something so low-down?"

"Because they are low-down," Jaime added. "Creeping with the widow of your friend? There are some lines you just don't cross."

"Maybe they really love each other," Aria said, pain at the thought of that radiating across her chest.

Both Jaime and Renee turned their heads to look at her.

"What?" Aria asked. "If Jessa is being straight up, not only did one of the men cheat with her, he is leaving to be with her."

"Trust me, I *know* Eric is not leaving me," Jaime said. "We've been through—"

Aria cut her eyes at Renee as Jaime shut her mouth and swallowed back the rest of her words. *Been through what, Pollyanna?* she wondered, fighting the urge to voice her thoughts. *Humph.*

She saw the worried look on Renee's face and knew she was thinking of that conversation Jackson wanted to have. "Hey, regardless of who it is, we have to remember that Jessa might be doing us a favor taking a dog off our hands. Let *her* fight those fleas. Life is all about a cycle, and people always get it as good as they gave it. Trust and believe that."

Renee wanted—needed—to talk to her husband and/or Jessa Bell. Period. That was all to it. The combination of the alcohol and her emotions was wearing her down. "Does anyone know the company where they chartered the boat or the harbor they left out of?" she asked.

"Shee-it. I wish, because the way I feel, I would charter another boat and go and get they ass out of the sea, baby. Believe that," Aria said.

Jaime shook her head. "I never thought to ask for that information."

Renee felt like she needed another drink, but the effects of the liquor she already had were kicking in. She felt relaxed and mellow and weepy. She felt a surge of tears but blinked them away. "They're in the sea but I feel like our asses are the ones up a creek without a paddle."

"Listen, there's nothing we can do until the men show up. Why are we letting this foolishness stop our lives, especially when we have no clue who should be upset?" Jaime tried to reason.

"So what do you suggest, Jaime, that we all go home and pretend or hope it's not us?" Aria asked.

Renee felt her head spin and she forced herself to stand still while she got her bearings. "Well, it's not going to make me that much more happy to find out that Jessa betrayed either one of you and not me. This woman was all of our friends, and as far as I'm concerned, it could have been me just as well as you—and that *pisses* me off that she would do this to any of us."

"I didn't say I didn't care or that I hope it's not me," Jaime stressed. "I'm just saying that this is what Jessa wanted or she wouldn't have sent the text to all of us. She wanted us all to second-guess our marriages and ourselves."

"True," Aria agreed.

Renee walked to sit on Jessa's front stoop. She dropped her head between her knees. "What made me think I could handle Patrón?" she moaned.

"Sit still. I'm going to make you a cup of coffee," Jaime offered, turning to walk the short distance to her house.

"You okay, Renee?" Aria asked.

Renee lifted her head and nodded before she wiped her face with her hands. "Just a little tipsy, but with all this shit going on, I wish I was tore up," she admitted with pure honesty.

"No, they ain't worth that. The last thing Kieran and Aaron need is a drunk for a mama," Aria told her, squatting down beside her to rub her back.

Renee turned to look up the street at her own home. "I can't lose my family, Aria. I won't. I can't," she said in a whisper. "Jackson and I have been together since college. I grew up with this man, you know? I learned how to cook and to fuck and to keep house and all of that with him. What am I without him?" Renee admitted her fears to her friend and herself.

⬦

Jaime dropped her keys and purse on the marble counter of her kitchen before she grabbed a bottle of Starbucks mocha Frappuccino from the fridge and poured it into a cup to heat in their steel microwave. The stuff was liquid crack and just what Renee needed to sober up.

She pushed her hair behind her ears, exposing her three-carat diamond studs, as she fought not to let her emotions push her to strike out in anger like Aria or drink like Renee.

Truth was, she had always held out hope that ultimately Eric loved her, because he could have easily divorced her and kicked her out without it costing him a red cent—and truly she still was waiting for that moment to come.

But she still felt like he had to have some love for her because he never left and he never asked her to leave. She swore there had to be some authenticity to the affection and devotion he bestowed upon her in public. Surely he wasn't faking all of that. . . .

⬦

"How do I look, Eric?" Jaime asked him as he strode into their bedroom suite.

He didn't break his stride to the dresser or even look in her direction. He didn't say one word as he began to search the drawers for something.

Jaime walked up to him and lightly touched his shoulder. "Eric, I said how do I look?" she said with insistence.

He turned and stared at her stoically, still saying nothing.

Jaime stepped back from him. "Eric, we're having a dinner party—"

He brushed past her and left the room, leaving nothing but his cold dismissal to surround her.

Ding-dong.

Jaime blinked away the tears she felt building and double-checked her appearance in the mirror. Although her hair was perfectly glossy and straight as it flowed like Pocahontas's down her back, her MAC make-up flawlessly applied, and the deep purple satin sheath she wore fitted impeccably, Jaime knew it was all a facade.

Ding-dong.

Taking a deep breath, she left the room and made her way downstairs. Eric was already standing at the door, waiting for her to reach his side so that they could greet their guests together.

He opened the door and they both placed on perfectly lying smiles as their first guests arrived. His parents, Mr. and Mrs. Hall, stepped inside the foyer.

Jaime's smile became genuine as her mother-in-law removed her coat and double kissed Jaime's cheek. "Something smells good."

"Jaime made her homemade lasagna and a Sock it To Me cake, Ma," Eric said, taking their coats.

"Hello, son, and there's my beautiful daughter-in-law," Harrison Hall said, tall and distinguished and every bit the image of a judge.

"Hi, Dad," Jaime said, accepting a warm hug from him.

Eric slid his arm around her waist and it felt foreign to her.

"I tell her all the time how lucky I am to have her, Dad," Eric said with warmth before leaning down to kiss the corner of Jaime's mouth.

Jaime leaned into him and placed her hand on his chest. "I'm the lucky one," she said, looking up into his eyes.

"Don't they make a beautiful couple," his mother sighed. "And their babies are going to be something."

"Soon, Ma," Eric said, easing his arm around to massage Jaime's stomach.

Jaime thought of her body filled with their child, and love exploded in her heart for him.

Ding-dong.

His parents moved on into the living room.

"We would have beautiful children, Eric," she said, resting her head on his shoulder.

He gently shook her off. "Please. You actually think I would fuck you without a condom?" he said brutally.

Jaime felt pain fill her eyes and she looked away from him, wanting badly to move away from him. But his arm locked like steel around her waist as he opened the door and greeted more spectators to the show they were putting on. . . .

Beep. Beep. Beep.

The sound of the microwave brought her out of her memories. As she searched for the lid to the cup, Jaime knew that as much as she could hope was that the true facade was Eric pretending to hate her. But no one was that good an actor.

She carried the coffee outside and down the street to where Aria and Renee were still sitting on Jessa's steps. "Drink this," she said, handing it to Renee.

"Thanks, Jaime. I need it."

"I'm gonna head back home," Jaime told them, really just wanting to be alone with her thoughts.

"I guess we should too," Aria agreed. "For one, I'm going to play Inspector Gadget and see if I can find some clues on whether I need to whup up on Kingston."

Renee sipped the coffee and nodded. "I think we all should do that. And please, if one of us finds something, let's promise to call the other two," she said, rising to her feet.

Jaime nodded. "I will."

"For sure, Renee. For sure."

JESSA

Our new home. Well, almost our new home, truth be told. My Realtor was the shit because we were leasing this house until my home in Richmond Hills was sold. That would free up the capital to purchase our dream home. I loved it and I would love being in it with him even more. As I walked through each room of the three-thousand-square-foot house, I couldn't wait to start making memories together. A smile of pure pleasure and satisfaction covered my face. Our day was finally here.

I checked my watch. It was just 2:00 P.M. He'd promised they would be back from the fishing trip around seven or eight and he was coming straight home. To me. His one and only love.

I took a deep and satisfying sip of wine. All of the furniture had been brought in and set up by the movers. The boxes were neatly stacked in their appropriate rooms for us to unpack tomorrow . . . together.

Regrets? I had none. After Marc's death I thought I would never love again, but I found life in his arms. I found how to breathe again. I found how to be again. He did that for me. No one could understand that. No one. I couldn't give up this chance to be happy. I couldn't give up this chance to be loved. Cherished. Adored.

I threw my friends away, but I'd make more.

I gave up my house that was paid for via Marc's insurance, but now I had another one. Bigger and better too.

I loved a man who was supposed to be faithful to another, but he would never betray me. Our bond was too special. Besides, no man had ever cheated on me. None. This I knew.

I had to tell people what I'd done—stealing one of my friends' husbands—and there would be scorn but we would get through it together.

His family would have to adjust to the new Mrs., but in time they would. They had no choice.

This was no fling. This was the start of everything for us.

Mrs. Brokenhearted would get her divorce papers sometime this week, and when everything was legally square, I would marry the man I loved, who loved and adored me endlessly.

Reaching in the pocket of my linen slacks, I pulled out my cell phone and flipped it open. As I dialed the number of the secret cell phone he kept just for us to talk, I made a note to have him shut the other one off.

I'd be damned if I sat back with her calling him and begging him to come home—yes, he was that good.

I shivered at the memory of the sex we'd shared.

"Hello, lover. I'm home. The movers are gone and I'm all alone thinking of you, waiting on you, needing that dick." I laughed huskily into the phone. "Tonight I will cater to you. I will pamper you. I will suck and then fuck you. Hurry home, baby. I don't want to start playing in this pussy without you here to watch me."

With a smile, I snapped the phone closed and held my glass up in the air. "Here's to my happiness."

CHAPTER 9

Aria paused at the door to her house before she used her key to open the heavy front door. As soon as she stepped into the foyer and closed the door behind her, she felt weak and slumped back against it. She closed her eyes and tried to fight through a wave of emotions that threatened to strangle her.

Her purse, cell phone, and keys dropped to the floor. She didn't care. She was barely keeping herself from falling the hell out.

"Come on, Aria. Get it together, bitch," she warned herself as she pushed off the door and forced herself to stiffen her spine.

Jaime and Renee had headed home.

And there she was. Alone. Angry. Aggravated. Afraid.

Releasing a heavy breath, Aria kicked off her heels and then headed down the hall to Kingston's office. She opened the door and stood in the doorway, looking at the one room in the house that was Kingston's and Kingston's alone.

She hesitated. Aria had never snooped before. She never really felt she had a reason.

Until now.

She crossed her arms over her chest and leaned back against the door frame. She honestly didn't want to be that wife that had to sniff drawers and play detective, trying to catch her man doing dirt.

Until now.

Aria walked up the hall with her head hung low, but then she turned on her heel and headed straight into the office to his desk. She dropped into the plush leather seat, her eyes falling on their five-by-seven wedding photo sitting at the edge of the desk calendar. The photographer had caught that small and very intimate moment just before their lips connected as they stared lovingly into one another's eyes.

Of all their photos, Kingston had always said that this particular one was his favorite. "I see your love for me," he would say. Aria leaned forward to pick it up, smoothing her finger against his profile with a soft smile.

Brrrrnnnngggg.

Aria damn near dropped the photo in her scramble to pick up the cordless phone. "Hello?" she breathed more than spoke into the phone as she leaned forward to set the photo back in its spot.

"What you doing?" her mother, Heather Goines, said into the phone, her tone already playful.

Aria felt relief flood over her. "Oh, my God, Mama, guess what?"

"What's the matter?" she said.

Aria let out a deep sigh and then told everything to her mother, leaving out nothing. Not even Malcolm.

Heather let out a sigh longer than her daughter's. "Boy, you just heaped a bunch of crap on my plate. First off, are you okay?"

"I'm just trying to wrap my mind around all this, Mama," she admitted as she dropped her head in her hand.

"Well, you gave it to me and you know how I go . . . I gots to give it back the way I see. You ready?"

And that's why Aria loved her mother beyond words. Nothing but realness.

"First off, Jessa need her ass whupped and good, but

right now she is so irrelevant because the commitment was made by y'all's husbands and not her. Believe it or not, this ain't about that scandalous bitch. This is about y'all's marriages because if not her, it could have been somebody else. A faithful man remains faithful regardless of the woman. You understand that, Aria?"

Aria's eyes shot back to their wedding photo. The truth of her mother's words was hard to swallow. "Yes."

"Now here is the million-dollar question for your ass, Aria. Forget Jessa. Do you think your husband is cheating on you?"

Aria paused.

"Don't think about it. Just answer with your gut reaction?"

"Before that dumb message I would have said no . . . but I would also say I don't put nothing past no man."

"So do you think Kingston has left you?"

Aria's eyes flooded with tears and she reached out blindly to slam their wedding photo face down onto the desk. "Yes," she admitted softly as her throat tightened right along with her chest.

"Oh, hell no. Aria Monique Livewell, are you crying? I know damn well this ain't the same Aria that gave me hell in her teens."

Aria's back stiffened. "Mama, this ain't easy. Shit."

"Oh, it's real easy and real simple too," Mrs. Goines said. "Either he's a no-good dog and don't deserve one tear shed over his corpse, far less because some other woman got to try and keep him chained, or it's not him and you crying for nothing. See? Easy. Simple."

Aria said nothing as her tears dried up. Her mama had that effect on people.

"And screwing some stranger is not going to give you anything but a wet ass and maybe a disease a shot can't clear up. You hear me?"

Okay, sometimes Mama is too real. Damn.

"Now why don't you come on down to the hood with your family? We frying fish in the backyard and playing cards."

"I'll pass. I need to think some, so I'm gonna chill out here until Kingston gets home."

"Suit yourself, but if you need me to catch Uncle One-Eye up to your house, I will."

"*No!*" Aria laughed. "No, no, no. I'm good. Let Uncle One-Eye stay retired from driving. There's a reason why his name is One-Eye, so leave the Nova parked, Mama."

"Shee-it, that one-eye jigga be driving his ass off. You don't know?"

"And I don't want to know," Aria said dryly.

Heather just laughed.

After a few more minutes of her mother trying to distract her with endless family gossip, Aria finally begged off the phone with a promise to call her as soon as she knew who was the ultimate victim of Jessa's betrayal.

Aria hung up the phone and her eyes spotted a heart sketched onto Kingston's calendar and in the center was her name. Aria. It was like saying she was the one who filled up his heart, and until that morning, Aria didn't have much doubt that she did.

They made love, fucked, and freaked each other out damn near every night—only illness, extreme fatigue, or her monthly kept them from each other.

Kingston never pulled one of those dip moves and not come home every single night to sleep in her arms.

Their marriage wasn't perfect like Eric and Jaime's, but they were stable and in love.

So why was she letting one stupid text message tear away at the foundation of her marriage?

Because of secrets.

She had some of her own that weighed down on her conscience and made her wonder why she should expect total honesty from her husband when she was not giving him the same thing. . . .

———————— ◦∞◦ ————————

Aria mouthed the words as she reread the last few lines she had typed onto her laptop computer. She stretched her limbs from her spot snuggled into the corner of her favorite armchair. It was two in the morning. Kingston was in bed. The entire house was quiet and dark. She was writing away and loving it.

She smiled and twisted her hair atop her head as she remembered being a ghetto girl who loved to read and had big dreams of growing up to be a writer. After earning her journalism degree from Columbia, Aria did that. She worked her way up the ladder as research assistant, editorial assistant, and contributing writer on several well-known magazines and then she entered the arena of freelance writing—and it was there that she felt she flourished. Perhaps it was the freedom of not having a nine-to-five, but her creative spirit soared when she struck out on her own. Her articles and celebrity interviews had appeared in some of the top magazines in the country. Throughout her career, she worked hard to establish herself as a professional and creative writer with vision and a fresh outlook.

And now with her new column for Lady *magazine she was really enjoying the combination of making money and exploring the written word.*

The fine hairs on the back of her neck and her arms stood on end. Aria shifted her eyes up from her computer to find Kingston leaning in the doorway of her office just off their bedroom.

He was naked and she allowed her eyes to explore his body, wondering if she would ever not enjoy the sight of him—especially naked.

"Hey, you," she said. "Why are you up?"

"I missed you in bed," he told her as he strolled across the room with his dick swinging back and forth like a bat across the top of his thighs.

"Awww, my baby," she told him as she removed the glasses she only used to read and work on the computer.

He sat down on the floor by her chair and pulled her legs over his shoulder to remove the Hello Kitty socks from her feet. Aria's head fell back against the chair. "Oh, goodness, that feels so good," she sighed. "God blessed you with those hands, Dr. Livewell."

Kingston chuckled. "That's what my patients say all the time," he teased.

Aria froze and tried to snatch her feet from his grasp, but he held her ankles as he laughed. His work as a plastic surgeon was a point of contention for them. "Just playing, baby," he told her, bending down to suck her toes.

Aria's anger dissipated like nothing.

"You almost done working?" he asked.

Aria shrugged. "Why?"

Kingston turned around and rose to his knees to take the laptop from her lap and set it on the floor. He swung her legs around and pressed them open. Her nightshirt inched up her thighs, exposing that she'd skipped putting on panties. "Time for play," he told her as he leaned forward to lick her mouth hotly.

Aria frowned. "Kingston, baby, I'm sweaty and funky and . . ."

"And about to be fucked by your husband," he finished for her as he kissed away her protests.

Aria gasped as he grabbed her thighs and jerked her down to the edge of the chair.

He leaned back to stare down at her pussy in the light from the computer screen. "Pure pussy," he told her, taking his dick in his hand to tap against her clit and lips.

"*Pure good pussy,*" Aria told him cockily as he pushed just the tip inside her lips to tease her core.

Aria set her feet down on the arms of the chair as Kingston rolled his hips and slowly fucked just the top of her pussy with the thick tip of his dick. His tip slipped in and out of her, causing her lips to smack like kisses. "*Just a little light fuck,*" he told her thickly. "*I'm not even gonna get my whole dick wet.*"

Aria was too busy shivering to care how much dick he slid in her.

He stopped and looked down at her. "*Let's make a baby,*" he said suddenly.

Aria's eyes popped open and she froze. "*Say what? Say who?*" she said, pushed out of her sex-daze state.

Kingston reached down and held her chin. "*Let's make a baby, Aria. It's time.*"

Aria smiled, trying to keep the panic she felt from her eyes as she looked at her husband, the man she loved.

"*I want you to have my baby. I want to watch him or her grow inside you. I want to be there to cut the cord. The whole nine, Aria. I know I said we could wait, but dammit, I'm ready,*" he told her with intensity.

Aria's heart swelled with love . . . and with pain because she couldn't fulfill his dreams and his wishes. But she couldn't tell him that. She wouldn't. She reached up to tease his nipples with her fingertips and she worked her strong pussy muscles to open and close around his dick. "*Make love to me, Kingston. Please,*" she begged, jerking her nightshirt up to tease her own nipples just the way she knew he loved.

And she felt sweet relief when he swore and started that vicious stroke inside her, going against his word as he went deep and wet every inch of his dick.

As her husband made savage love to her, Aria wished she could enjoy it but her mind was stuck on how she *hated to disappoint him. She could only pray that his sudden wish for a child had been more about the heat of the moment than anything.*

He dug his hands beneath her bottom and held her ass up as his strokes deepened and he shuddered with his release. "Aria," he moaned.

She kissed his shoulder and worked her hips to pull down on his dick and drain the line.

Afterward she held her husband closely as he stood and swept her up into his arms to carry her into their bedroom. As they snuggled close in their favorite spoon position, Kingston said, "We're not done talking about a baby, Aria."

She just stroked the arms that he settled over her waist. Long into the night she lay there with her eyes open, hoping, wishing she didn't have to disappoint the only man she truly believed had ever loved her.

That had been over a year ago and somehow she had convinced Kingston that they should wait, using every excuse she could think of, from their careers to their hefty mortgage and everything in between. She was stalling because Aria didn't have the heart or the clit to tell her husband that she couldn't have children.

Aria reached over and picked up their wedding photo. Kingston was right; the love they had for each other was evident in the photo. The man had no clue of the true woman he married. Her past—the past she was ashamed of—threatened to step into the light and destroy her present. . . .

Aria grooved her fourteen-year-old body to the music booming against the walls of the club. When she noticed the crowd of men in the corner watching her, she started to grind and wind her hips even more until a snake couldn't compete with her—especially in the tight baby tee she wore tied beneath her full-grown breasts. Flat stomach. Wide enough hips. Tight jeans cut low on her hips, showing the vee of her hot pink thong.

She knew she was the shit.

"Heeey! Go, Aria. Go, Aria. Twirk it, work it like you got no fear," her eighteen-year-old cousin Jontae cheered her on. "Go, Aria. Go, Aria. Pop it. Drop it. You the shit in here."

Aria loved it. She was having a ball. And the fact that her mama thought she was spending the night at a friend's house—and not up in a club courtesy of her fake ID—made the night even more fun. Fuck it.

Jontae was her uncle Freddie's daughter from South Carolina and she was spending the summer with her father and teaching Aria all type of things she'd never even dreamed about.

She felt a hand on her stomach as someone brushed up against her from behind. She looked over her shoulder to find a tall, sexy nigga the color of chocolate grinding her from behind.

She bent right on over and started bouncing and ticking her ass against him. The crowd building around them cheered so loud that the music was drowned out a little bit. No matter which way she worked her body he was right there on it, matching her grind for damn grind.

Cute and could dance and had a long dick that she felt pressed up against her ass?

She turned and wrapped her arms around his. "Shit, let's go get a room," she whispered in his ear as he brought his hands up to squeeze her ass.

"Nah, I got my brother with me," he told her, nudging his head toward a light-skinned cutie standing on the edge of the crowd, sipping a drink and watching them.

She turned and pressed her back to him as she kept her eyes locked on his brother, who was just as fine. Damn. His eyes dipped down to watch the back-and-forth motion of her hips. "He can come too," she said.

He stopped moving behind her. "Word?" he asked in surprise. "Let's bounce."

She shrugged and did just that, waving good-bye to Jontae, who was dancing in the middle of the floor, fanning herself as she followed the 2 Fine Crew as they squeezed their way through the crowd.

Two hours later, Aria stopped pretending to be asleep between the naked bodies of the two men. Both snored like crazy and that was just fine with her. She eased over the dark one and hurried to grab her clothing, ignoring the semen dripping down her leg as she rushed into her clothes.

With her eyes on them, she picked up their pants and ran their pockets, taking every bit of cash and the two sacks of weed she found. With one last glance to make sure they were still knocked off from weed and sex, she eased out of the motel room.

Aria raced down the stairs and paused just long enough to spot Jontae's hooptie—a sky blue hatchback Ford Escort that smoked whenever she drove over fifty miles an hour. Jontae flashed her lights and Aria took off in her cherry red high-top Reebok Classics.

Jontae squealed off as soon as Aria slammed the door shut. "What we got?" she asked in her thick-ass down South accent.

Aria reached up to turn on the light. "Um, 'bout two hundred dollars and some weed," she told her.

"You?"

"Just fifty. That lame-dick nigga couldn't fuck either."

Aria laughed.

"Now we can't bring no more niggas back to this motel 'cause they might be looking for us." Jontae pulled to a stop at a red light and the car backfired. They both laughed when several people ducked down to the street, afraid it was gunfire. "Stick with me, cuz, it's gone be one helluva summer."

And it had been that.

They ran that "fuck and pluck" scheme all over Jersey that summer and one more summer after that. Aria had lost count of the men and a large part of her life that summer with all the weed, liquor, and lying she pulled.

Many things she wanted to forget. Had to forget. Even now she felt an actual terror at Kingston knowing things she fought hard to keep from him. Things she kept from a lot of people . . . except her best friend. . . .

Aria accepted the glass of wine Jessa gave her as they lounged on the floor in front of the fireplace in Jessa's living room. She reached down to pick up one of the many photos scattered on the floor. "Girl, look at how long my hair was," Aria exclaimed as she looked at the snapshot of herself in her twenties in a pair of tight jeans and a Columbia University sweatshirt. Her hair was six inches longer and her waist five inches smaller. "Don't show this to Jaime, she'll freak if she knew I cut off hair she pays good money for."

Jessa laughed in that husky voice of hers. "Has anyone ever seen her real hair?" she asked, picking up another photo from the floor as the fire crackled before them.

Aria rolled her eyes and waved her hand. "Probably just her hairdresser, and I wouldn't be surprised if she had to sign a confidentiality agreement."

They shared another laugh as Aria picked up another photo. Her eyes darkened as she studied it. "This is my first year at Columbia," she said softly, pursing her lips to let out a long breath as emotions caused her eyes to flood with memories. "To think if I didn't turn my life around, I don't know where I would be."

Jessa frowned. "Oh, good Lord, this isn't the whole I made it out of Newark thing, because you were hardly in Beirut or some shit, Aria," Jessa drawled.

Aria smiled but it couldn't defeat the sadness in her eyes. "I've done some things that I ain't proud of, Jessa," she admitted in a soft voice.

"Haven't we all, girl?"

Aria shifted her eyes to her, feeling the effects of the alcohol. "Tricking? Running scams? Threesomes and foursomes? Shoplifting? Smoking weed and drinking? You did all that too?" she asked, her low voice mocking and filled with a tinge of the anger that she had for herself.

Jessa sat back on her haunches as her mouth fell open a bit. "Whoa," she said, obviously stunned by Aria's admission.

Aria laughed bitterly before she swallowed down the rest of her wine in one gulp. She thought—hoped—the liquor would numb the pain she felt. It didn't. "If I knew that being so stupid would still affect my life today . . ."

Jessa moved over to Aria on her knees, to wrap her arms around her shoulders. "Oh, Aria. That's all in the past, girl. A shady past, but your past."

Aria shook her head as she leaned forward to grab the wine bottle. "If only life was that simple and cute," she snapped before taking a swig of the wine straight from the bottle as all the emotions she had about her past resurfaced.

"See, when you fifteen, fast, and fucking, having abortions left and fucking right, life has a way of punishing you because now . . . now I can't have any babies." Her voice broke. "Now you tell me that ain't a bitch."

Jessa was rarely speechless, so Aria knew she had stunned her.

Aria stared into the fire. A solitary tear that was the manifestation of ten years' worth of her guilt raced down her cheek.

———◦◦◦◦———

Aria closed her eyes and shook her head in shame, wondering if a secret revealed to someone she thought was a friend had been used by an enemy to weaken her marriage instead.

CHAPTER 10

Jaime had never ever been the wild one.

Growing up, all through high school and college, she had been the good one. The safe one. The predictable one. But over the years she had discovered that at times she wanted to be bad. Naughty. Indulgent.

And when she allowed herself to dwell in that place just 5 percent of the time in her life, it made being the good one bearable the other 95 percent of the time.

Jaime parked her nondescript rental car near the rear entrance of the equally nondescript building. The loud thump of the music seemed to make the building shake. She didn't bother to focus on the pale peach paint that was peeling and revealing the putrid green paint beneath it.

Although she doubted any of her circle of friends would see her, Jaime still slid on her shades as she climbed out of the car and entered the building through the heavy metal door. For a second there was nothing but darkness and music. She waited for her eyes to adjust.

The sounds of Jamie Foxx's "Blame It" echoed around her as she made her way past the security booth to the front of one of the three large circular stages lit by colorful lights.

Club Trick was the spot for male dancers for their Thursdays ladies' night, but Jaime didn't like to share—or try to come up with an excuse to not be at home with her hus-band—so the early five o'clock show was for her.

Less crowd equaled more dick to peruse. Although Jaime really was here for one dick and one dick alone. She shiv-ered in anticipation and her clit swelled with life between her clean-shaven pussy lips as she strode to a swivel seat right at the base of the stage.

Usher's "U Got It Bad" filled the surround system, and on the stage the dreadlocked, muscled dancer with a dozen black tattoos switched from making his dick pop in a neon sock contraption to ease down to the floor in a snakelike motion.

Jaime crossed and uncrossed her legs while she watched his smooth hard ass as he ground the floor like he was putting in major work in someone's pussy. Her nipples tin-gled and her clit felt like it would explode between her thighs. She was transfixed. Completely mesmerized. Hot. Bothered.

Her demeanor was not that of the women waving and yelling as he gyrated, but she didn't dare assume she was better than them. She just handled hers differently. She reached in her purse and pulled out a fifty dollar bill to calmly hold up in the air.

Pleasure left the attention of an oversized woman with bright orange hair to dance his way over to her. He dropped on his knees, straddling her body in her chair as he popped his hips so that his dick flip-flopped against the valley of her breasts. His hips worked in a clockwise and counter-clockwise motion that was in tune with the music. The rock-hard ridges of his abdomen were defined and glisten-ing with some oil beneath the colorful strobe lights.

Jaime felt so breathless and so bad as she pushed the fifty dollar bill into the front of his sock. He grabbed her hand and eased it down until her hand brushed against his dick.

She jumped back a bit at the smooth and hard feel of it.

"Don't be scared," he said to her loudly to counter the music.

It was one of the rare moments when they'd spoken during their five-year dance, and the sound of his voice thrilled her just as much as the sight and smell of him.

Jaime was first introduced to Pleasure at a bachelorette party while a senior in college. And something—no, everything—about the six-foot-nine caramel-dipped walking piece of pure hot sex had turned her. When he left them all a card with his contact info, Jaime had snuggled it away . . . first.

Constant wet dreams for three weeks after had led her to pull out that card and find the club where he worked. That first night she watched him perform, Jaime had almost cum on herself. The little virgin with the sheltered life in suburbia was hooked.

And once a month for the last few years she allowed herself to indulge in the sinful goodness that was Pleasure. Just an hour or so watching him titillate a bunch of horny women with erotic gyrations and the print of what had to be a ruler-sized dick. In time he came to recognize her, and she knew that he knew he had her hooked.

But she never crossed the line. She never told anyone either, including Eric—although Jaime was sure that when she got home on those Thursday nights and released all her pent-up sex drive on him, he was more than happy, whether he knew why or not.

Pleasure jumped down off the stage, still straddling her as he placed one hand behind his head and the other one eased down his abdomen as he ground his hips.

Jaime's eyes were transfixed on the up-and-down motion of his dick and she swallowed over a lump in her throat. He straddled her lap and she didn't even care if some of his body oil ruined her Tahari skirt.

"You know what you need? A private dance," he whispered near her ear. "You game?"

Her pussy was soaked at that point.

"I'm married," she said as he moved closer to grind his dick against her stomach.

"I don't give a fuck."

And in that moment, neither did she.

Usher faded into Ginuwine's "So Anxious"—and that she was. He stood and took her hand to pull her to her feet and lead her around the stage and past a heavy black curtain into a small room lit only with a red light, with nothing in it but a few club chairs and a small stage. The sound of Ginuwine followed them into the room as he pressed her into one of the black leather club chairs and then climbed onto the small stage.

Suddenly the lights began to flicker in a wicked strobe effect as he worked his hips and slowly worked the sock/thong contraption off.

"What exactly happens during a private dance?" she asked as he jumped down to straddle her hips before he bent backwards to lean against the stage.

Jaime wanted to fan herself as his dick stood up straight, pointing to the ceiling before the wide tip curved to the right. And it was a beautiful piece of work. Dark and smooth, with wide veins that ran along the side up to the tip.

She licked her lips, surprised that she wanted so very badly to just bend forward and take it into her mouth. Eric wouldn't let her give him head . . . and sometimes she wanted to, but she hadn't worked up the nerve to talk about it with him.

Pleasure licked his lips as he wrapped his hand around the base of his dick before he massaged the length of it.

Jaime knew she shouldn't be in the strip club, and certainly not in a private room with a stripper named Pleasure whose dick was twice the size of her husband's. Her mind and body were focused on him and just him as he jacked his dick.

"Touch it," he ordered thickly as he moved to stand be-

fore her. "Come on, you been coming to my shows for years. You know you wanna touch it. Go ahead, I won't tell."

Jaime hesitated for just a moment just before she wrapped her hand around it tightly and stroked him. She felt a rush as he shivered and pressed his hips forward.

"That's right. Beat that motherfucker," he told her hotly.

Sex with Eric was just like her life. Normal. Predictable. Sometimes so very boring. She couldn't remember the last time the man she loved made her cum, while she was near an explosion just from watching Pleasure dance.

He brought his hands up to stroke her nipples through her silk shirt, and Jaime nearly fainted from the pure electricity shimmering over her body.

"You need to be fucked, don't you?" he asked, dropping to his knees to press her legs open wide. He moaned as he sniffed the air. "Damn, that pussy smell good."

Jaime fainted back against the chair and shivered while her clit ached and she felt the seat of her silk La Perla panties cling wetly to her lips. She closed her eyes and pushed her chest higher with her tingling nipples pointed to the ceiling as his strong and warm hands massaged her inner thighs.

She gasped as one of his fingers pulled her panties aside and dipped deeply within her. The cry she released was one of anguish and pleasure.

It was wrong. So wrong. But it felt so good. And so very, very bad.

"Your husband ain't taking care of this pussy, is he?" Pleasure asked, his heated words blowing against her clit before he pushed her legs wide to run his tongue up her pussy to circle and then flicker against her clit.

Jaime felt bolts of electricity hit her as she nearly passed out.

Eric had never tasted her there. No man had.

"Do it again," she begged in a hoarse voice.

And he did. Again and again until she was shivering and sweating like a fiend.

She barely heard the tear of foil as she reached to tease her own nipples—another first. She felt his lubricated latex-covered dick strike her thigh as he bent forward to move her hands and suck her nipples through her shirt.

"Yes," she sighed as his hands easily lifted her hips to hitch her skirt up around her waist. He tore away her panties with one strong pull, and Jaime didn't care.

She wanted him inside her. She needed him inside her.

"You want me to fuck the shit out of you, don't you?" he whispered to her.

"Yes. Please," she begged without shame as she squirmed her hips in anticipation.

"What's my name?"

"Pleasure."

"And what do I give?"

"Pleasure."

He laughed huskily as he pushed deep inside her with one swift thrust.

Jaime felt the pressure of him against her walls. She felt the heat of him deep inside her. "Fuck me," she ordered, hardly believing her words or her actions.

"My pleasure," he told her thickly as he stroked deep and fast inside her before switching up to a slow grind.

Her pussy walls throbbed against the length of him as her juices drizzled around his dick and down to wet the cleavage of her buttocks.

She brought her hands up to twist in his dreadlocks, feeling bold. Feeling free.

"Say you my nasty bitch," he ordered.

"I'm your nasty bitch."

And she was.

In the midst of the heat Jaime lost track of time as that man fucked her as if his whole life depended on it. From the back. In her back. On her back. She lost count of how many times he made her cum as he twisted and turned her body inside out until she was just as naked as he and not caring if the people in the outer club could hear her moans and cries.

"Have you been pleasured?" he asked her as he fucked her from behind with his hand twisting her weave in his tight grasp as he rode her like she'd stolen something.

"Yes," she cried out, nearly weak and faint from pure satisfaction as she dropped her head to the floor.

He stiffened and she felt his dick throbbing against her walls. "This dick 'bout to cum," he told her.

He grunted and pumped inside her fast and furious, like he was trying to win a race, before he snatched his dick out. She heard the snap of him removing the rubber and then the steady smacking of him jacking his dick before she felt the warm and wet drizzle of his nut on her ass and back.

"Damn. Whoo. Damn it. Shit," he swore between hoarse cries.

Jaime slumped to the floor, not caring that her sweat caused her to stick to the wood or linoleum.

"That's two hundred dollars."

Jaime's eyes popped open. The lights were on and he was already back in his thong contraption standing over her, holding her purse out to her. Shame flooded her in the light of the aftermath. She grabbed the purse and hurried to pay him.

"Um, thank you. I guess," she said, rising to her feet to rush into her clothes and shove her torn panties inside her purse.

"You're more than welcome. Call me sometime," he told her before he stepped forward to press a kiss to her forehead and then walked through the curtain like he hadn't just fucked the hell out of her.

Jaime spotted her cell phone on the floor beside the club

chair and she bent to pick it up, ignoring the soreness and
wetness between her thighs. She pushed it inside her purse
and scurried out of the room and out of the club, feeling as
if all eyes were on her.

Embarrassment and shame were her fuel.

Nearly six months had passed and Jaime felt herself flush
with humiliation at that night. Her little flirtations with
being bad had led her skidding straight across the line into
the ultimate betrayal of her husband, her values, and her
upbringing. The man had completely freaked her out and
then totally fucked her up by leaving her sex funky and
sweaty on the dirty floor of the back room.

And then charged her for the privilege. Jaime was done
with being bad, and even gave up her one indulgence . . .
smoking.

Jaime shook her head at her own foolishness as she
walked throughout her house, taking in her prized posses-
sions. Everything about her home was a reflection of everything about her life. Perfectly designed. Skillfully organized.
Beautifully presented.

She paused as she walked down the long hall to the
guest room. For a long time she just stood there and stared
at the door. It was more than a piece of wood shutting off
the room from onlookers. Since the night her husband
moved into the bedroom, that door had shut her out from
his life. His world.

Ever since the night he found out about her infidelity,
everything about their marriage changed. Everything.

She reached out and touched the wood, knowing that
she'd caused the door and his heart to be locked to her. . . .

Jaime shook from her head to her feet during her entire ride home from the strip club. She had to grip the wheel tighter to keep her hands from trembling. And there seemed to be nothing she could do for her fast-racing heart.

"Oh, my God, I just had a one-night stand with a stripper," she thought as she pulled to a red light. With a little shriek she leaned forward and banged her head lightly against the steering wheel.

The pleasure. The passion. The excitement.

All of it was gone. Forgotten. Resented.

Someone laid on the horn behind her and Jaime jumped and sped ahead, zooming her car under the green light. The sun was just beginning to set and traffic was heavy as people made their way back home from their jobs after a long workday.

Jaime cringed as she thought of her contribution to Pleasure's workday. She said a prayer asking forgiveness from the Lord, Eric, and herself.

When she pulled through the open gates of Richmond Hills, her thoughts were on getting home and getting showered before Eric got in from work. She just wanted to feel normal and so she was prepared to act normal. Her dinner of lasagna and Caesar salad was already ready and waiting to be warmed. She would kiss her husband as soon as he walked through the door. They would eat dinner together and then watch a little television before they went to bed. Just like always.

She would pray on her sin. She would make it up to Eric somehow. She would be the best wife and the best lover. And above all, she would stay the hell away from that strip club and Pleasure.

Rushing, Jaime parked her car on the street in front of their home and raced up the walk and into their house. She felt odd being without panties and she wanted to wash— scrub—away the scent of her scandalous sex from her body and her soul.

Whoom!
The front door slammed closed behind her and what little was left of the sunlight cast the house in shadows. Jaime flipped the switch to bathe the living room in light as she set her purse and keys on the table in the foyer.

"Welcome home, wife."

Jaime whirled and she released a small but audible gasp to find Eric sitting in one of the four chocolate leather club chairs before the stone fireplace. Shoving back her surprise, Jaime smiled. "Hey, you're home early," *she said, hearing the nervousness in her own tone as she eyed him. But the round, boyishly handsome face and even the stance of his five-foot-eleven frame was different. His face was cold and his body was rigidly stiff. He looked like Eric, but then he didn't as well. Off. Very odd.*

"Something wrong, Eric?" *she asked as she turned and made her way toward the staircase, afraid that he would come close and smell the scent of Pleasure and sex. Or grab her ass and detect that she wore no panties.*

Click.

"You want me to fuck the shit out of you, don't you?"

Jaime froze on the steps as her knees nearly gave out beneath her at the muffled sound of Pleasure's voice.

"Yes. Please."

"What's my name?"

"Pleasure."

"And what do I give?"

"Pleasure."

Jaime turned and her eyes fell on the cell phone he held up in the air. Her heart pounded and she fell back against the wall in weakness as she dared to shift her eyes to meet his. Instantly she became lost in the anger and the pain that swirled in the brown depths.

"Fuck me."

"My pleasure."

Jaime felt the world was shifting beneath her feet. Panic

was nearly choking her. Guilt flooded her. Fear had her frozen. "Eric—"

"Shut up," he roared, flinging the cell phone across the room to crash into the wall.

She flinched.

Eric stood, and in three angry strides he was standing before her, completely enraged. "That's quite a voice mail you left me, wife," he bit out, his eyes red rimmed and puffy.

She knew her touch-screen phone had gotten jostled somehow and called Eric's cell phone, leaving him a message that revealed her infidelity.

He reached out and grabbed her neck tightly and his other arm held her arms at her side. "I had no idea I married a slut, a no-good whore who would beg another man to fuck her like a trick."

Jaime felt fear for her life as her eyes stayed locked on his, trying to plead with him. "It wasn't like that, Eric," she managed to say before his hand tightened and she struggled for air.

He banged her head against the wall. "I hate you, Jaime. Do you understand me? I hate your guts. I don't give a shit about you anymore. Do you understand me?"

Tears filled her eyes and raced down her cheek. "Eric . . . please . . . I can't . . . breathe."

He released her neck only to roughly shove his hand down between her legs. His face hardened and his eyes were a storm of emotions as he raked his fingers across her lips. "You walk in this house without panties on, still wet from fucking some other man?" he asked her in a tight and angry voice that was low in his throat.

Jaime felt this moment was her worst nightmare. She thought of the consequences of her tryst and couldn't help but wonder if death was an option. "I'm sorry, Eric. I'm so sorry," she begged in a whisper. "I love you."

He laughed bitterly before he raised his hand to roughly

*smear her moist pussy juices all over her mouth and face.
"You love me? Huh. You . . . love . . . me. Then I'd hate to
be married to a bitch that hated me."*

*For a long time, Jaime held her breath as he just stood
there staring at her like he never really knew her—and in
that moment Jaime was filled with shame and so many regrets.*

⧉

That night Eric had moved into one of the guest bedrooms
and out of her life. And from then on the charade began.
In public they were the perfect couple, but behind closed
doors he was cold and hateful and punishing. He barely
spoke to her. He ignored her most of the time. And when
he did come to her room for sex, he was degrading and
rough, calling her "slut" and "whore" while he fucked her
like the slut and whore he thought she was.

And Jaime took it all because of her guilt and her shame—
and because she wanted to weather the storm she'd created until her marriage got back on track.

Jaime released a heavy breath and turned away from the
door to walk to his home office. She sat at the desk and
turned on the computer. As she waited for her bank's Web
site to load, she winced as Eric's degrading words came
back to her in floating whispers.

"Suck my dick, you no-good bitch."

"Suck my cum, whore."

"Turn over. I wanna fuck you in your ass, slut."

Jaime closed her eyes just as one tear raced down her
cheek. She couldn't believe the humiliation Eric put her
through on those rare nights. She suffered it all because
she knew she'd hurt him deeply—particularly when he questioned her and questioned her until she revealed everything
about her "relationship" with Pleasure. Everything.

And it made everything worse.

Jaime was no fool. She never knew just what was going to become of her marriage, but she knew she had to look out for herself. Eric had severely tightened the purse strings, and she knew the proof of her affair could ruin her chances for alimony. Her whole life had been Eric. She'd never worked or put her college degree to use. If he left her, her life would never be the same.

Jaime logged into her online banking account. She released a sigh of relief to see the balance had not changed. Nearly eight thousand dollars—every dollar and red cent painstakingly siphoned from Eric's account over the last five months.

Eric didn't know about the account. At least she didn't think he did before today.

As far as she knew, there was one person who knew about her affair. Jessa Bell. Eric had told her.

As far as she knew, there was just one other person who knew about her secret account. Jessa Bell. Jaime had left a bank statement in a purse she'd let Jessa borrow.

Jessa swore she would keep her secret, but of course now Jaime wasn't sure about anything. But to be sure, she was going to close the account Monday and move her stash to a new bank or put it in a safe-deposit box.

It was her safety net. She wanted her marriage. She wanted her husband. She wanted things to be the way they used to be.

But . . . *if* Eric left her, she refused to be brokenhearted *and* broke. Period.

CHAPTER 11

Renee got busy cleaning as soon as she had strolled through the door of their home and changed into a T-shirt and sweats. For the next two hours, she cleaned like she hadn't had the will, time, or gumption in months. Cleaning was a great distraction from her life.

But then, as she paused in cleaning her marble countertops, she thought maybe losing focus on her married life had led to this dilemma. . . .

Renee excitedly studied her reflection in the full-length mirror of her walk-in closet that was the size of a small room. The Tracy Reese cocktail dress was way beyond the limit she set for herself, but she had to have it once she saw the onyx appliqué lace creation. It fit her tall and toned shape well. She loved it.

"Just the dress to win a major award," she told her reflection as she looked down at her Louboutin satin stilettos.

The bedroom door opened and Renee struck a seductive pose as Jackson strolled into the room. He paused at the sight of her, smiling so deeply that his dimples were clearly defined. "Wow, you look beautiful, Renee, but you're a little overdressed for a school dance recital."

Renee's smile faltered. "No, no, no, you're a little under-dressed for my award banquet tonight," she said lightly.

Jackson sat down on the foot of their bed and kicked off his Gucci loafers while he undid his silk tie. His smile faded and the face of her handsome husband was replaced with that of the brooding stranger she was beginning to get used to. "So you're going to miss our daughter's dance recital tonight?" he asked in a cold voice that was already filled with resentment.

Renee walked over to stand before him, her footsteps silenced by the plushness of their carpeting. "Jackson, I thought we discussed this. Winning this award is a very big accomplishment for me and I want you there with me," she stressed softly, reaching down to stroke his strong cheek.

Jackson leaned back to avoid her touch. "As a parent, my first concern is for my child, so I will be attending her recital and I would advise you to do the same."

Renee licked some of the MAC lip gloss from her full lips. "Jackson, Kieran has a recital once a month, and I talked to her. She understands why we will miss this one recital, Jackson."

He looked up at her. "How many times will your career matter more than this family, Renee?"

"I've been a good wife and a phenomenal mother all these years, Jackson, and now I want to be a fantastic career woman. And this award tonight is justification that I'm doing pretty damn good at it." Renee grabbed his chin and jerked his face up so that her pained eyes met his angry ones. "So I am still a good wife, and still a phenomenal mother, and now a brilliant career woman. I am all of those things. And my husband, whom I have supported every moment we've been together since college, should help me up the ladder and not try to drag me down it."

Jackson stood and breezed past her. "I don't support your career and you know it, so why pretend, Renee? Why fake it?" he asked.

Renee stiffened her spine. "Why not go to the recital and
then you and the kids join me at the banquet, Jackson?"
she offered, wanting the peace in her family back.

He looked at her over his shoulder for a long time before he nodded and turned to walk into the bathroom.

Renee took a deep sip of her third Long Island iced tea as
she eyed her star-shaped award sitting on the bar. It sym-
bolized her hard work and, dedication, and recognition on
a national level for her marketing abilities.

And Jackson couldn't care less.

The hardest thing she'd ever done was get through her
acceptance speech without showing everyone in attendance
that she was extremely hurt to look out and see the empty
seat where her husband should've been.

He'd lied to her. He never brought the kids, and when
she called he flat-out told her he never had any intention of
showing up.

Renee sighed as she sat at the bar of the hotel's lounge.
She jumped in surprise when a hand lightly touched her bare
arm. She looked up to find her assistant, Darren, standing
there. "I thought you had left," she told him before picking
up her glass.

"I was about to leave and I saw your car still parked in
the deck, so I came back to check on you," he said, easing
onto a stool beside her.

"Just enjoying a drink and toasting to myself, since no
one else gives a shit," she muttered into her glass.

"Well, I'm proud of you and I want to be you when I
finish growing up. The male version, of course."

Renee side-eyed him. Darren's enthusiasm for the job
was always contagious and Renee had no doubt that the
majority of his ass kissing was completely genuine. "Well,
considering you don't have to get sidetracked by expecta-

tions of full-time motherhood and wifely duties, you'll get there a lot sooner than me," she drawled before tipping her head back and finishing her drink.

Darren said nothing and Renee was glad. She motioned for the bartender and ordered another Long Island iced tea.

Renee side-eyed him. "Are you old enough to drink?" she asked dryly.

He shook his head. "So, boss, can I ask why, on a night like tonight, you are here celebrating alone?"

"Long, drawn-out story," was all that she said.

"Well, I want you to know that I understand and I admire the work that you do," Darren told her.

"Thank you. Appreciate it." Renee lifted her glass.

"I know a good way we could top off the night," he said.

Renee frowned a little before she turned her head to look over at him. "Careful, little boy, that sounds like an indecent proposal," she said, her voice slurring a bit.

"It was."

Renee locked eyes with Darren. Her inferior. Her assistant. Someone not too much older than her own children. He was so completely her type with his tall and dark sexiness. And in truth, Renee had long appreciated in silence just how sexy he was. His broad and square shoulders, his narrow waist . . . even down to the scent of his cologne.

Her clit swelled to life. "No strings?" she asked.

"Absolutely. No one will know but you, me, and the sheets."

Renee rose unsteadily to her feet.

Blame it on the alcohol, she thought as Darren followed her to the elevator.

⌘

Renee had never felt so uncomfortable in all her life. Ever. Darren wetly kissed her neck as he ground his soft penis against her thigh like he was trying to squash a roach or mash potatoes.

Renee was tipsy but Darren's lame and lackluster approach to sex was sobering her up. She was sure the condom he put on was going to slip off because there was no way it would stay on that semi.

He worked his way down to her breasts and Renee cringed at the feel of the wetness of his tongue on her nipples. She shivered in revulsion. Goodness, who doesn't know how to suck a damn titty?

"Ow!" she yelped when he bit down on it.

"Sorry," he mumbled and then proceeded to sop it down with spit again like that would make it better.

Renee brought her hands up to his shoulders and immediately noticed that he was missing the strength and breadth of Jackson's broad shoulders. He was missing a lot of what Jackson had.

Her eyes popped open when he lifted her leg roughly and tried to pack his semi inside her pussy—which was as dry as a desert.

Worst fuck—or almost fuck—ever.

"Okay, Darren?" she said, tapping his shoulder. "Let's stop. Puh-leeze."

She didn't want to hurt his feelings, but damn, he sucked in bed and his dick wouldn't get hard. She had to bite her lips to keep from telling him so.

He dropped her leg and rolled off her to the other side of the bed to lie on his back.

She lay in the bed with the sheet tucked tightly around her naked frame, as stiff as a corpse. The weird thing was Darren lay beside her in the same damn position. She felt like two Popsicle sticks.

"Ummmm," she began, not sure what she wanted to do—or to say.

"No words necessary. It was awful," he supplied.

"Oh, God, yes, it was," she gushed, bringing her hands

up to cover her face. "I don't know if it was alcohol . . . or our age difference . . . or the fact that I only get hot for my husband . . . or . . . or . . ."

"I'm gay."

Renee frowned. Deeply. "Oh."

Darren started to laugh.

Renee joined him. "Oh, thank God."

"I just wanted to help you out . . . and help myself."

Renee sat up, being sure to keep the sheet up around her armpits to cover her nudity. "Explain, please."

"Just one last try at the whole straight thing. If I can't get my dick hard in a bed with a woman with your titties, then being straight is a major fail."

"First, thanks for the compliments on my double Ds, and secondly, I so agree with you, and thirdly, male or female, please ease up on the nipple bite and the wetness and you're not half bad," she told him before she climbed out of the bed, keeping the covers snug around her body.

Darren flung the covers back and pulled the unused condom from his dick. "I was trying something for the first time, cut me some slack," he drawled.

Renee hurried into her clothes. "Listen, Darren, I had a little too much to drink and a lot of emotional crap dumped on me tonight, and I am actually glad that your dick doesn't like me because I would have regretted this."

"It's forgotten," he assured her.

"Thanks."

"I better head home," Renee said, slipping her feet into her shoes.

Darren rose with her. "Can you drive okay or do you want me to take you home or call a cab?" he asked.

"I'm going to call one of my friends to come and get me, but why don't you stay in the room, it's all paid for," she told him, reaching in her purse for her cell phone. Nearly ten o'clock and not one missed call? Fuck you, Jackson. Fuck you all the way, Negro.

She dialed Jessa's number since she was the only one who lived alone and she didn't want to pull Aria or Jaime from their marital bed. "Jessa, please come and pick me up from the Hilton on Belmont," she said as soon as Jessa answered the phone.

"On my way."

Without question. That was Jessa. Always there when needed. Always coming when called.

"Thanks, Mrs. Clinton," Darren said as he walked her to the door of the hotel suite in his red bikini briefs. "See you Monday."

"Night, Darren," she told him before making her way to the elevator.

She knew she had to sit Jackson down and find a compromise—a happy middle ground—for their marriage. One gay dick was the only thing that had saved her from cheating. Never had she crossed the lines outside of her marriage, but Jackson had hurt her so deeply and she couldn't help but wonder if it was going to get worse before it got better. The good moments that used to dominate their lives together were now few and far between.

Renee leaned heavily back against the wall and closed her eyes. She didn't even want to go home to Jackson. In that moment she wasn't sure if she didn't hate him. And that was a scary thought, because maybe he felt the same about her.

Renee shook her head and swiped the tears away, wishing she had invited her girls to the banquet. She just felt like someone should have been there for her.

When the elevator door opened, Renee slowly made her way to the lobby as she yawned. The alcohol went from making her foolish to making her sleepy. She dropped her head in her hand.

"Hey, girl. Wake up."

Renee's eyes popped open to find Jessa looking down at her. She wiped the drool from the side of her mouth and sat up straight. "Hey, girl, thanks for coming," she said.

Jessa frowned and covered her nose with her hand. "Damn, Renee, your mouth smells like shit. What the hell were you drinking?"

Renee laughed as she got to her feet. "I had a rough night, so hush, girl."

They climbed into Jessa's car parked in front of the hotel.

"How was the banquet?" Jessa asked as she started the car and accelerated forward.

"It was nice, but it was the random collision with a gay dick that really topped off the night like a cherry on a sundae," Renee drawled, searching in her bag for a mint because her mouth tasted worse than it smelled.

"Huh?"

"Jackson's hardheaded, stubborn-mule ass didn't come to the banquet and fed me a guilt trip about missing our daughter's dance recital," Renee told her. "In a recap. Me. Emotional. Lots of drinks. Cute enough assistant who think my shit doesn't stink. Hotel suite. Really bad foreplay. Really bad. A nonfunctioning dick. My self-esteem drops. Assistant reveals he is gay. Me. Asleep in lobby like a drunk. Breath smelling like puffy cheese doodles and cow shit. Ta-dah."

"Oh, my God, you were going to cheat on Jackson?" Jessa asked in total shock.

Renee slipped a dust-covered Certs into her mouth. She sang Jamie Foxx's "Blame It". "And it was awful. Oh, my God, my nipples are raw and my clit is bruised—and not in a good way."

"So you and Jackson really need to get y'alls act together," Jessa said.

"Yes, because I think I'm going to lose my husband— my family—if I don't give up working."

"Honey, there's always shades of gray. Find the middle ground, because you both deserve to be happy in your marriage."

Renee nodded even though her thoughts were that happy hadn't dwelled in her marriage in a long time.

"So you couldn't convert him, huh?" Jessa teased.

Renee was glad for the diversion. "Listen, my name is Renee Clinton, not Miracle Worker."

The ladies laughed as Jessa sped them toward Richmond Hills.

Renee sat back on her haunches wondering if her friend had relayed the story of her award banquet night to Jackson. Had that been the impetus for Jackson climbing between Jessa's legs, or was it just plainly the state of their marriage?

"Now I wish Darren could've gotten it up," she muttered and then regretted it.

Screwing Darren wouldn't have changed anything about the situation.

Brrrnnnggg.

Renee jumped up from the floor and snatched up the cordless phone. "Jackson—"

"No, Ma, it's me."

Disappointment settled around Renee's shoulders at the sound of her son's voice. "Oh, hey, Aaron, what's up?" she asked, forcing normalcy into her voice.

"Is Dad back from fishing yet?"

Renee closed her eyes and held the phone away from her mouth as she released a heavy breath. That one innocent question from her seventeen-year-old son just kicked things up a notch. If Jackson was the culprit—the fly in Jessa Bell's web—then he was not only turning his back on their marriage but their family. Unlike Aria and Jaime, she knew she had much more at stake. Much more to lose. *Damn you, Jessa Bell,* she thought. *And damn you too, Jackson, if you're leaving me for her. If you're leaving us for her.*

"No, your dad's not home yet, can I help?" she asked, wondering if their father was ever coming home.

"No, Ma, that's all right. It was man-to-man stuff," he said, puberty making his voice come in varying levels.

"Well, excuse me, Mr. Man," she teased. "I'll . . . um . . . I'll tell him to call you when he gets home, okay?"

" 'Kay. Bye, Mama."

"Bye, baby boy," she said softly, reverting back to the nickname she'd given him as a toddler.

She glanced at her Gucci watch. Just after three P.M. The day was moving in such slow motion. Usually the men got back from their deep-sea fishing trips around seven or eight. She would go crazy waiting another four or five hours to see which of the three men came home or for Jackson's cell phone to be in range.

She had cleaned until every bit of the house gleamed like a showcase. There was nothing left for her to do but go crazy. Sighing, she walked out of the living room and into their study, where there was a twin set of desks for a couple who both had demanding jobs that meant working at home.

It was perhaps in this room where the tension in their marriage was felt most. She couldn't remember one time when they'd used the office together. He would leave if she went in to work at her desk. Now, if she went in for other things, well, that was just fine. They'd had many a freak-fest in the office—before and after she went to work.

Renee strode over to his desk and instantly noticed the group photo sitting there among the various photos of their children. She frowned a bit as she picked it up. Just last month, Aria and Kingston had charted a yacht and invited them all onboard for a day of cruising.

And the group picture taken with Kingston's tripod had perfectly captured the bright sun, the bluish waters, and seven friends just having a damn good time. But now in hindsight Renee wondered if it revealed just a little something more. Starting from the left to the right, her gaze touched upon each smiling face.

Jaime, Eric, herself, Aria, Kingston, and *then* Jessa snuggled next to Jackson. His arm was around her shoulder while her arm was loosely wrapped around his waist. They looked slightly distant from the rest of the group, and if someone focused their eyes just the right way, they could block out the group and focus on Jessa and Jackson.

Jessa's long hair was blowing in the wind. Her face was free of shades and the sun gave her natural golden tone even more shine. The white sundress she wore clung to her curves.

Had this been Jackson's clever way of having Jessa with him right under her nose?

Renee turned and threw the picture against the far wall with all her angry might. It shattered . . . right along with her heart.

JESSA

I was satisfied. The bedroom was at least ready for my man when he got home. The bed was made up with satin sheets that were so divinely made to be fucked upon. That thought made me laugh a little as I took a handful of rose petals and threw them atop the sheets before making a trail with them from the bed and down the stairs to the front door.

I could hardly wait for our first night—all night—together. I was excited like a child waiting for a sleepover—but there would be no sleeping. Not tonight. I was going to fuck my man all night long. Come hell or high water, he best be prepared for the ride . . . and if he wasn't physically prepared, I was ready to slip his ass a Cialis/ecstasy cocktail. I would do that and whatever it took to make tonight a freakfest all night long. Just a little something to reassure him that he made the right decision to make that very first move that night.

That first time our hands brushed and we looked up to lock eyes, I knew we had a connection. I fought it as long as I could, and it was hard. I hadn't felt anything that strong since my own husband. For so long I had to sit back and smile and pretend that I didn't want him—and that I didn't know he wanted me. Anytime we were near each other it might have appeared innocent, but the pull between us was there and it was getting stronger with each passing day. All we could share were long looks that spoke volumes about the forbidden passion we had for one another.

Months passed before he made the first move. Right there in the middle of a party as we danced he said, "I want you, Jessa. I know that I shouldn't but I dream about you. Your soft skin. Your body. Your smell. And the more I see you and can't have you, the more I want you."

His wife was just feet away and it made his admission all the more delectable to me. All the more enticing.

My body was warm beneath the innocent touch of his hand on my back, and my nipples hardened into tight and aching buds as his words pumped more life into my soul and my heart and my core than I had felt in years.

For a moment I thought of my friend and the hurt we might cause her. I thought of the betrayal. I thought of the loss of loyalty. I thought of what I would do if one of them had danced with the devil with my own husband.

I said nothing. Absolutely nothing. But my desire must have been in my eyes or in my stance because he looked around before he slowly but surely rocked us off the dance floor and into their kitchen. We had barely gotten into the empty room before he pressed my body against the wall and kissed me.

I released a moan that was filled with hunger and my anguish and I brought my hands up to clutch his face as he sucked my tongue hotly and sweetly. "Yes," I sighed into his open mouth.

His strong hands eased up my skirt and I shivered as he pulled my panties to the side and stroked my clit like a guitarist before he plunged one finger inside me.

We jumped apart at the sound of footsteps.

I pretended to look for something in the fridge while he quickly moved across the room to the pantry.

She smiled as she breezed into the kitchen, not suspecting a thing, as I shared one more heated glance with my lover as he sucked my pussy juices from his finger.

From then on I knew I had to have him. I had to.

And once we decided that sex was not enough, I knew taking him from her meant cutting ties with all three of my friends. But for him, I'm absolutely fine with that.

CHAPTER 12

Jaime had another secret. One that she'd never shared with anyone. And she knew that particular secret was safe because it remained locked in her innermost thoughts. She used it to help her get through the hell of her marriage and particularly the shame and disappointment of her sex life with her husband. She knew she was wrong. She knew she had to release her secret obsession.

She found it harder and harder to do.

Sex with Eric had become torture over pleasure. Jaime couldn't remember the last time he made her cum. It had become all about him humiliating her. It brought stress instead of relieving it.

But in truth, Eric had never, ever brought her to heights that her romp with Pleasure had. Playing the role of the pearl-clutching virgin had led to her marrying a man that she'd never been intimate with. She'd made the mistake of thinking his lukewarm kisses would pick up vigor once they were able to take things all the way.

She had been wrong.

And the lack of the passion she secretly craved had led to her monthly visits to see Pleasure. True, she had been wrong to cheat on her husband, but Eric had opened the door with his shortcomings. He couldn't compare to Pleasure in size or skill. Compared to the exotic dancer, her husband resembled a schoolboy.

When he left their marital bed, Eric had no clue that his punishment had left open the door for her dreams to wander.

One night, after Eric had sent her from his bedroom with her naked buttocks still sore from his whip and her pride destroyed by his words, Jaime had walked up the stairs in the darkness feeling emotionally and physically numb. The sessions with her husband were slowly killing something inside her.

But that night she was determined to reclaim her sexuality and she eventually found just the *thing* to do it.

Jaime locked her bedroom door and slowly walked to her adjoining bathroom for a scalding shower to try to wash away the memories just like that night. It didn't work.

Still damp from her shower, Jaime searched beneath her mattress for a small key and used it to unlock the chest at the foot of her bed. From beneath the folded quilts she removed a shoe box. Her hands were already shaking in anticipation as she removed the lid.

Nestled atop black velvet was a long and thick black phallus that was nearly the size, shape, and color of Pleasure's—she'd meant to buy a near replica of him. She had derived pleasure from using the debit card to her secret account to order a replica of Pleasure's dick from the Web site she discovered Eric used to order the whips and things he used on her.

Next to her shiny new dick was the business card Pleasure gave her.

"Pleasure's Principles," she read in a whisper. "For all your exotic needs. Humph. nine-seven-three-five-five-five-UCUM."

Jaime held it to her nose and inhaled deeply of the scent of him still clinging to the card. She fought the urge to lick it.

He had filled her dreams nearly every night since she had a taste of him.

Tonight it was time to make the dreams as much of a reality as she could.

Jaime wrapped her hands around the dildo as she closed her eyes and thought of the sharply defined muscles of Pleasure's body and his shaved crotch, square buttocks, and strong thighs. She imagined that the cold molded dick in her hand held his heat, but for now the hardness would have to suffice.

Crawling on the bed, she lay down on her back and spread her legs wide as she drew the thick top from the base of her pussy up to circle around her clit.

Biting her lip, she jerked her hips at the feel of it and arched her back with a deep, guttural moan.

"Pleasure," she moaned with a shiver.

Gone was the shame and humiliation she felt on the floor of the club when he requested payment for his sex.

Gone was the guilt she felt for hurting Eric.

Gone was her good-girl demeanor as she gave in to a primal instinct for sexual satisfaction.

Gone was the drama of Jessa, her mystery lover, and their text message.

Nothing existed in this moment but how alive she felt.

In her mind, Pleasure's clever mouth was on her hard nipples. His hands on her body. His dick inside her. His skin and flesh pressed against hers.

"Whoo," she sighed as goose bumps raced across her skin.

She opened her legs wider and slid the dildo between her thick lips and deeply inside her, inch by inch.

"Pleasure," she gasped again, twirling the rod so that it hit her walls and stroked her clit.

She was adamant to never cheat on Eric again. She put up with his crap in the hopes that their marriage would get back on track. But she could have the sexy stripper in her dreams. She needed him there.

If only it could be the real thing. . . .

———⟨⟩———

"I knew you would be back."

Jaime paused as she walked through the door of the crowded strip club. Pleasure was standing there waiting for her. Dick hard. Body gleaming. Dressed in nothing but a mask and a black thong.

In a blink she was naked.

She said nothing as he stepped forward and scooped her up to straddle his hips. She pressed her swaying breasts against his chest and licked a trail from his broad shoulder up to his ear. "Why can't I get enough of you?" she moaned in his ear as his hands massaged her bare buttocks before he slipped his thumb inside her.

"Aahh!" she gasped.

He turned and walked them to the stage. The audience applauded them as Pleasure laid her down upon it. "Because your husband ain't giving you what you need, is he?" he asked roughly as he dropped his thong and stroked the oiled length of his curving dick.

"Don't say that," she begged as she brought one hand up to tease her nipple and the other down to stroke the base of his dick and his swinging dark brown nuts.

"Why not? It's true or you wouldn't be here."

"But I love him."

He laughed as he squatted to tap the thick and hot tip of his dick against her pussy. "But you love this more. Don't you?"

"Yes," she admitted. "Yes."

The women watching them closely roared and Jaime had to admit that it turned her on that people watched them.

Pleasure grabbed her legs and sucked one of Jaime's toes

into his mouth hotly as he thumbed her clit and finger fucked her all at once.

Eric never had a fighting chance. Never.

Jaime shivered like a fiend and arched her back off the cool black floor of the stage as a fire started to build deep inside her. She was filled with a building anticipation.

"Let me see you play with that pussy," he ordered, grabbing both her ankles and spreading her legs wide.

"Do it! Do it! Do it!" the audience chanted.

They broke into thunderous applause and catcalls as Jaime locked her eyes with his and eased her hands down to play in the wet, throbbing folds of her pussy.

"Make that pussy cum."

She gripped her inner thigh with one hand and massaged it deeply as she thrust her hips forward and used two fingers to massage her wet and throbbing clit. "Oooh," she moaned, absolutely loving it. Loving it. "Oooh, I'm gone cum. Fuck me, Pleasure. Fuck me right now!"

"Fuck her! Fuck her!" the audience chanted just as the colorful light above the stage began to flicker.

"It's my pleasure," he said, pushing her legs down so that her ass was high up in the air.

She gasped when he dived his dick deep inside of her just as her pussy walls began to spasm with her release. She hollered out roughly, her hands slapping against the floor and her nails clawing the floor.

The crowd roared. . . .

Jaime came crashing back to reality as she free-fell through wave after wave of her climax. "Pleasure," she gasped, her nipples hardened and thrusting as she worked her wrist to slide the dildo up and down along her walls.

"Good God, I needed that," she sighed in between pants as her heart thudded wildly.

Jaime's body slumped with pleasure-filled fatigue.

As her walls continued to contract and release the rubber dick still deeply implanted within her, Jaime rolled over onto her side and clutched the pillow tightly before she fell asleep.

Renee's chin dropped to her chest. She jerked her head up and looked around wildly at her surroundings. "Huh? What?"

She was sitting on the living room sofa with a bottle of Windex in one hand and paper towel in the other, dozing off. She shook her head at herself as she set the items on the table before rising to her feet.

She had intended to complete her goal of cleaning her house, but the last thing she remembered was sitting down to free the glass insets of her wooden coffee table from fingerprints.

Hard to do when she was drunk.

Thankfully the nap had helped her. Renee leaned back. She had plenty she could be doing, but at that moment the big comfy sofa felt damn good.

To hell with the chores.

To hell with the report she had due.

To hell with her BlackBerry and waiting on calls/e-mails/texts that might or might not come through.

To hell with preparing for a fish fry that might not happen because one of the bastards was leaving his wife.

"No, not one of them. Me," Renee said, remembering the look in Jackson's eyes that morning.

"We need to talk. We *have* to talk."

Renee knew she should be plundering Jackson's things looking for clues, but she was afraid of what she would find.

Ding-dong.

Renee rose to her feet and made her way to the front door. She raked her fingertips through the short curly locks of her hair as she opened the door. "Hello, Arnie," she greeted their tall white mailman of the last five years.

"Howdy there, Mrs. Clinton," he said, his voice amplified like he had a mic. "Got a package for you."

Renee stepped back as he set it on the floor just inside the house. "Thanks, Arnie," she said, eyeing the large cardboard box. "It must be the clothes I ordered for my son."

"They never stop growing, do they?"

"No, they sure don't."

"Okay, have a good one," he said with a brief wave before he turned and made his way down the walkway.

"Um, Arnie," Renee called out, following an impulse.

"Mrs. Bell moved to—today," she began as he turned around to face her.

"Yes, ma'am, we got her change of address form weeks ago," he said, using one bent finger to push his glasses up on his nose.

Weeks ago, Renee's brain screamed although she kept her face calm. She nodded. "Jessa always plans ahead. We're going to miss her around here, but I know she's going to love her new house. I can't wait to visit her."

"Yeah, Saddle River is a really nice town," he said.

Renee's heart soared to pick even that much info from the unsuspecting postal carrier. *Thank God for living in a small town,* she thought as she plotted a way to get her address.

"I know when we went to visit her I was just blown by the whole area," she said.

"I'm not really familiar with the residential part, but my wife loves the mall there," he said, placing his hands on his hips.

"Oh my goodness! It makes Richmond Hills look like the projects . . . especially Jessa's house!" Renee exclaimed, hoping she didn't overdo it.

"Well, I'm happy for Mrs. Bell," he said. "I better get going."

Damn. "Okay, thanks, Arnie," she called out to him, even as she grappled with the disappointment of not getting Jessa's new address from him and feeling some relief because it would have meant deciding whether to hunt Jessa down.

Renee closed the front door, leaving the box in the foyer, and she made her way to the bar. She eyed the dozens of bottles as she lightly bit down on the side of her thumb.

Jessa Bell had moved to Saddle River, which was just thirty minutes away. The whore hadn't run very far. In fact, it was close enough that they might run into each other at the right social events.

Renee couldn't imagine attending an event and having to sit by while her husband was there with another woman. Just as she knew she would *never* allow her children to go play "happy family" with their father and his mistress. N-E-V-E-R.

Renee dropped her head into her hands because she wasn't an ignorant twenty-year-old looking to give out baby mama drama, and she firmly understood that after a divorce she had no right to dictate to Jackson about where he took his children.

She looked up at her reflection in the mirror behind the bar. "Surely Jackson wouldn't try to take Aunt Jessa and make her Stepmama Jessa?"

And that's why she had so much more to lose and to deal with if Jackson was Jessa's lover.

Renee felt anxiety flood her. How embarrassing would that be, to stand at the doorstop and watch her teenage children climb into Jessa's flashy car to head to their father's love shack in Saddle River? "Oh, hell to the no," she said, walking behind the bar to grab a bottle of Cîroc vodka.

Renee carried that and a shot glass up the stairs to the bathroom. She poured and then downed two shots out of the never-opened bottle as she drew a bath. Stripping off her clothes, Renee sipped another shot as she studied her own reflection in the full-length mirror.

"Not half bad for a mother of two teens," she said with another sip as she turned and studied her tall and solid frame. She loved that the effects of her workout regime were evident in her toned arms, legs, and relatively flat abdomen.

She jiggled her still firm and high breasts and circled her hips like a belly dancer. "Humph. I remember when all this had a Negro running," she told herself, doing a little two steps as she sipped away.

And she knew if Darren wasn't gay that she could've whipped some of her skills on him and had that young man's nose wide open.

Darren.

At times she forgot or belittled that she almost had an affair of her own.

At times she forgot or diminished that Darren had turned her on from the first day he walked into her office for the interview.

At times she forgot or blocked out that the *only* thing that saved her pussy from Darren was his homosexuality.

Darren had been so fine and so much Renee's type that she never wanted Jackson to meet him because she knew if he flat-out asked her about him that she might blush from head to toe.

And so, knowing that as much as she loved Jackson, another man had drawn her attention and sparked her fire, then how could she not believe that another woman could do that for him?

And how did that affect her ability to forgive him?

Renee tipped her head back and swallowed the liquor with a wince. She was sick of all the questions. Sick of all the uncertainty.

And as she caught a glimpse of herself in the mirror

with the shot glass still to her lips and filled with memories of lusting for her younger assistant, Renee was feeling particularly sick of herself.

——————⟨≈≈≈⟩——————

Aria stepped out of the bathroom stall and danced to the music thumping against the walls. She washed her hands in the stylish and modern bowl sink as she checked to make sure her hair and make-up were still on point.

A night out on the town was just what she and Kingston needed. Usually he resisted her urgings to dine at a trendy New York eatery and then find an upscale and vibrant spot to have drinks and a few dances. But not this Friday night.

Aria even planned on blogging about her night out with her hubbie. With one last wink at herself, Aria walked through the blacked-out revolving glass door.

"Long time no see."

Aria looked up at the sound of the voice and she paused at the stranger standing before her.

"Do I know you?" she asked with a polite but decidedly distant smile as she took in the short, obese, freckled man standing in the darkness of the corner.

"Oh sthit you know me," he said with a lisp, his tongue seeming to be attached to his full bottom lip as he spoke.

And then Aria remembered. He was one of her tricks from those crazy-ass summers with her country cousin Jontae. But she covered it well, still feigning ignorance even though she clearly remembered that she and Jontae had run a double on him, slipped him some X and then bounced with his jewelry, his loot, and his leather coat when he fell asleep.

"I'm sorry, but I think you have me confused with someone," she said in her best "black girl who clearly went to an Ivy League college" voice. "Have a good night, though."

Aria's heart was straight pounding as she turned to walk

away. She gasped and closed her eyes when his pudgy hands closed around her upper arm. She snatched her arm away. "Do I have to call security? I said I do not know you," she said, being sure to maintain her Valley Girl accent.

She was trying not to go ghetto on his ass, but she couldn't hold it back much longer. If he didn't release her, she was going to crack his nuts and bust his damn jaw. Straight up. One thing about Club Visions, there was a metal detector at the door. So it was just her and him, and Aria swore she could take the fat fucker.

He shoved his hands into the pockets of his dark denims. Her eyes dropped to watch him closely.

"Onceth a shtrick always a shtrick," he said snidely with his heavy tongue before he started to make his money fly up and rain in her face.

Aria's eyes flashed, but she kept her anger in check because her husband—her future—was waiting for her and this clown—her past—wasn't worth fucking up her happy home because she wanted to flip and whip his fat, high-yellow ass.

She turned away and he grabbed her arm again. "Hell no, bitch, you gone give me money or some ass. Choice is yours."

Aria snatched away again and roughly pushed his chest, repulsed by the feel of his jellylike breasts beneath her hands. He stumbled backwards.

"What the fuck is going on?"

Aria flew to Kingston standing at the end of the hall. "I don't know if he's drunk or high, but I told him he has me confused with someone else."

Kingston took her and pushed her securely behind him. "Man, you put your hands on my wife," he said in a cold roar, his eyes filled with rage before he took two steps forward and two-pieced the man's fat jowls.

Bad-dap.

The man fell back in the corner, his fat tongue truly

hanging out of his mouth now. Aria, feeling somewhat guilty, stepped forward and grabbed Kingston's arm to hold him back from striking the man again.

"Kingston, your hands! Don't hurt your hands," she exclaimed, knowing his love for his medical profession wouldn't let him risk injuring his moneymakers.

With one last glare at the man struggling to rise to his feet, Kingston locked his hand with hers and pulled her through the growing crowd and out the door.

Thank God, Aria thought, because she was acutely aware of the eyes on them.

She was glad when the valet brought their car around and they were snuggled safely inside on the plush butter-soft leather seats.

"Are you okay?" he asked, reaching over to clasp her hand and massage her wrist with his thumb.

"I'm fine," she told him, her heart still racing.

"I wonder who the hell he thought you were?" he asked as he steered with one hand.

She shrugged. "I guess it's true everyone has a twin out there in the world," she said lightly. "But I'm cool. And you handled business. So let's forget about it, baby. We can go somewhere else or we can head home and get into some other things."

Kingston shifted his hand down to squeeze her thigh through the silk jersey of her charcoal gray wrap dress.

She still felt that nervous anxiety from the close call, but she was glad she had changed his focus.

"So now that we're married for a couple of months we have to keep all the sex at home?" he asked, pulling to a stop to look over at her.

Aria laughed huskily as Kingston leaned over to kiss her. "So what you saying?" she asked softly as he licked her bottom lip.

"I still want my lady in the street and my freak wherever the mood hits, you know."

Aria brought her hands up to grasp the sides of his handsome face. "What did I do to deserve you?" she asked in total honesty as her past seemed to chase her.

"Just being you . . . and the promise to give me some beautiful babies with your face and my eyes."

Aria opened her mouth and then closed it. In that moment she wanted so badly to tell him the truth, more than ever before. Maybe it was the trust and love she saw in his eyes. Maybe it was the fear that she should reveal more about her past before someone else did. Who knew?

She just didn't want the secret between them any longer, and she knew that ultimately it wasn't fair to him. . . .

———— ⊷ ————

Aria sighed as she moved away from the window of their laundry room. She hadn't found the courage that night to reveal her secrets to him, and with her fears that Jessa had used those secrets to destroy the foundation of what she hoped was a solid marriage, her worst fears had come true.

She moved back to the hamper with Kingston's dirty clothes and began to check the pockets of all of her husband's clothes. She had no guilt or qualms over her chore because it wasn't her first time.

In truth, in the beginning of their relationship Aria had done it all in her quest to catch Kingston. As the years went by and her searching and snooping became futile, she had eased up considerably—but she had never forgotten her tricks.

And rule number one was to not let him know he was a suspect, because then he would tighten up his shit and make it that much harder to catch him.

She'd checked cell phone bills for unusual numbers or long phone calls.

She'd checked his boxers for sex stains.

She'd played like she was giving him head just to smell his crotch.

She even used to check his mileage and gas usage.

She'd fucked the shit out of him when he came in late, and he'd better be ready, very willing, and all the way able.

She'd dropped by his office randomly.

She'd done it all except use a tracking device on his car, buy one of those home DNA infidelity test kits to find traces of semen in his boxers, or buy any spy equipment.

Aria had done it all, and not once had she caught him doing anything. Not once.

Shouldn't I trust my husband? Hasn't he proven himself worthy?

Sighing, she dug into his pockets looking for anything and everything to claim or disclaim Jessa as his lover.

She just couldn't help herself.

CHAPTER 13

Jaime would admit to no one that she dialed not only her husband's cell phone number but the cell phones of the other two husbands as well every ten minutes—at least. She also tried to remember the name of the charter company and then searched for a receipt, but came up empty. She was sure the captain of the boat had a way of calling ashore, but she had no way of knowing how to get a call put through to the boat.

And so the wait continued.

Needing a distraction, Jaime walked out onto the front porch. She wondered if Jessa's lover knew about her message. Did he put her up to it or would he be just as shocked by its delivery as Jaime and her friends?

Squinting her eyes against the sun, Jaime looked out at Richmond Hills. She had absolutely loved the subdivision from the very first day Eric had carried her across the threshold. It spoke of everything she cherished.

Everything she had ever hoped and dreamed for as she thought out her life plan. Education. Pledge a sorority. Meet and marry the successful husband. Move into the perfect house. Live the perfect white picket dream with two kids, two vehicles, a timeshare in Florida, and a dog.

She knew that her actions had been the fatal blow to the foundation they'd built, but now, brick by brick, he was tearing them down and doing far more damage than she felt she had.

"Afternoon, Jaime."

She turned her head and focused on her next-door neighbor. Mrs. Killinger knelt down beside her flower garden on the side of her house. "Hello, Mrs. Killinger," she called over with a wave, eyeing the short and plump woman who reminded her of a Munchkin.

"Oh shit," she muttered as Mrs. Killinger made her way over. She really just wanted to wrestle with her thoughts and not have idle chatter or gossip.

"Jessa moved, huh?" Mrs. Killinger asked, her skin as dark and smooth as onyx and her eyes bright and sparkling.

Jaime's heart pounded. "Yes, ma'am."

"Didn't see that coming, but I guess you girls are all so close that you all knew about it, huh?" Mrs. Killinger asked, placing a gloved hand on her hip as she looked up at Jaime, who leaned against the large white post of her porch.

And this is what life will be like in the aftermath of Jessa's betrayal, Jaime thought, keeping a forced smile on her face. *Questions on top of questions and lies on top of lies.*

"We didn't keep many secrets from each other," Jaime said, wishing the woman and her nosiness would go the hell back in her own yard.

Mrs. Killinger smiled, showing off what had to be false teeth. "There is nothing like a good friend."

"Yes, ma'am," Jaime said, hoping the shortness of answers would clue the woman in that she didn't feel like talking—especially about that undercover trick Jessa Bell.

"I was so shocked to see that moving truck this morning."

Jaime just nodded.

"Surprised none of you are at the new house helping her unpack, as close as you all were."

Jaime just shrugged.

"Oh. Humph," Mrs. Killinger said, turning to look down the street. Her face fixed with a frown.

Jaime turned and followed her line of vision to see Jasper Wiggins and Kelly Ortiz talking across the white picket fence separating their homes. Their conversation looked innocent enough. "Something wrong, Mrs. K?" she asked.

"Humph. They do a lot of talking across that fence," she said, her disapproval clear.

Jaime's eyes shifted back to them. "They're just talking."

Mrs. Killinger sucked air between her teeth. "Humph," was all that she said.

Jaime wondered if Jessa and her lover had been the talk of the neighborhood. Did an overly observant neighbor notice signs that Jaime, Aria, and Renee had all missed?

"Them two gone get enough of thinking their spouses are stupid. People dying these days behind these affairs and shit."

Jaime was surprised by the older woman's profanity. "So they're messing around, Mrs. Killinger?"

Mrs. Killinger shot Jaime a hard stare. "They stay in one another's pants, but you ain't heard that from me," she spat.

Jaime again was surprised, this time by the woman's obvious anger.

"You okay, Mrs. K?" she asked.

"I just hate a liar and a cheat," she said, removing her gloves to ram them in the back pocket of her jeans.

Jaime thought of Jessa and her unmasked lover and said, "Me too."

But then she thought of her own explosive sexcapades and flushed with guilt and shame.

"They gone get enough of that Motel Six. That I know."

Jaime started in surprise. "How do you know that?"

"Humph. This old woman know a lot of shit," Mrs. Killinger said, leveling her eyes on Jaime.

Her stomach fell so low she was sure she could shit it out with ease. Jaime's brows lowered over her eyes a bit. "Is there something you know that I should know, Mrs. K?" she asked, hating to reveal even one glimmer of insecurity about her marriage.

"Oh, goodness no. Eric adores you," Mrs. Killinger said with a dismissive wave of her hand.

Jaime took that assurance with a grain of salt because Mrs. Killinger was wrong about what Eric felt toward her and she could also be wrong about Eric's fidelity. Eric fronted like he adored her, but deep down Jaime was sure he hated her and wanted to punish her.

"I better get back to my garden," Mrs. K said, shooting one more angry stare at Jasper and Kelly before she turned and walked toward her house.

"Mrs. Killinger," Jaime called out behind her.

She stopped and turned. "Yes, Jaime?"

"What did you do about your husband?" Jaime asked, curiosity getting the better of her.

"Well, it wasn't just about my husband. It's about the marriage overall. You know what I mean?"

Jaime nodded in understanding.

"I had to weigh the good versus the bad and, baby, the bad was winning," she said with a chuckle.

"So you left?" Jaime asked, not being able to even imagine leaving Eric.

"No, I put my foot down and told that whoring Negro that he had to shape up or ship out. Mind you, my knee was in his chest and a box cutter to his throat at the time—but he got the point."

Jaime frowned a bit as Mrs. Killinger laughed as if that was the funniest thing she ever heard.

"Seriously, baby, I was in a rut with that fine man. I was spinning in one spot not knowing what to do. And I knew if I didn't do something I'd keep spinning in that one spot like a fool-ass screw and run myself in the ground."

Mrs. Killinger winked at Jaime. "I got tired of getting screwed by him and being screwed by the situation. So I handled it."

"You handled it, huh?" Jaime asked, imagining a younger and more vibrant Mrs. Killinger wielding a knife and a knee.

Mrs. Killinger just laughed.

She waved Jaime off as she walked over to one of the rocking chairs on her porch. She put her foot up on the chair and wrapped her arms around her leg.

For so long Jaime had gone along with Eric punishing her, but she had pulled one good piece of advice from her elderly neighbor with the bright smile. It wasn't just about the affair. It was about the marriage. And long before today, Jaime's marriage had lost its shine.

How much more of Eric's cold and punishing treatment could she take? How much more could she pretend to the world that her husband didn't treat her like shit on his shoes?

Tears filled her eyes. She was so tired of being so lonely in her marriage.

Only the sporadic clink of utensils on plates echoed in the dining room. Jaime looked across the table at Eric as he ate their meal of meat loaf, mashed potatoes, and string beans in total silence . . . just like always.

"How was work, Eric?" she asked with hesitance, trying to stop the widening gap between them.

Silence.

She pressed on even as her hurt feelings nearly choked her.

"My mother came over today and helped me bake a red velvet cake," she told him, knowing it was his favorite.

More silence.

"Ooh, how could I forget," she said, forcing excitement into her voice. *"Today the Martins had it out on their front lawn. She egged his new BMW and slashed the tires. It felt like watching a soap opera live."*

He looked up at her pointedly, tore a chunk from the garlic bread he held before he shoved it into his mouth. He eyed her with hostility as he chewed but he said nothing. Absolutely nothing.

Jaime was the first to look away and she knew he relished that he'd won yet another small and insignificant battle.

"Eric, this is ridiculous," Jaime snapped, her emotions causing the outburst. *"If you're going to ignore me, why even come to the dinner table? If you're going to ignore me, why do you even come home? If you are going to ignore me, why are we together?"* she asked, hating the anguish she felt soaking her words.

She watched him with pain-filled eyes as he pushed his plate away and pushed his chair back to rise to his feet as he wiped his mouth with a cloth napkin. *"Be in my room in an hour,"* he said shortly, dropping his napkin atop his plate before turning to walk out of the dining room.

Jaime closed her eyes as a wave of revulsion caused her to shiver. She didn't think there was any woman who detested her marital bed. Their sex had been lackluster before, and she had wished for some inventiveness. She would give both her legs to go back to the ho-hum sex of the past.

After she washed the dishes and took a quick shower, Jaime locked up the house and then made her way to Eric's room naked as the day she was born. The door was open—yet another sign that she could enter only to satisfy his perverse sexual appetites. With every step she wondered why she allowed him to treat her this way, and with every step she knew her answer. Guilt and shame.

He was standing nude beside the bed removing his spec-

tacles. The room was brightly lit—another variation from their sex life pre-affair. Her eyes shifted to his penis. It was slender and not very long, resting above his nuts. Even when it hardened, he only picked up another inch—maybe two.

She recalled Pleasure's long, curving, thick dick heavily hanging away from his body like a muscled arm and she shivered, knowing she was wrong to think of him. Wrong to compare him to her husband.

Wrong to still desire him.

"Put it on," *he ordered, pointing to a red patent leather contraption on the foot of the bed.*

She stepped forward and picked up the teddy, releasing a heavy breath as she stepped into it and pulled the studded straps onto her shoulders. Her breasts were pushed through two studded holes and the crotchless plastic stuck to her pussy lips. The g-string was way too far up her ass.

"This is what a no-good whore like you should wear," *he said.*

So it begins, *she thought.* "Eric, stop this," *she begged.* "When are you going to forgive me?"

His eyes raked her from head to toe as he reached into his drawer and pulled out a small whip. Her eyes widened. She held out her hand. "No, Eric!" *she said forcefully as she pointed her finger at him.*

He slapped the whip softly against his own thigh as he circled her. "Every time I listen to that voice mail, it sounds like your stripper lover is whipping something on you, and since my dick can't be enough for you I decided to buy a little help."

She felt his hand at the back of her neck and he pushed down until she was bent over.

Whap.

She gasped at the first feel of the whip against her fleshy buttocks. It wasn't painful but it stung—just the way he wanted it to.

Whap.

He walked around her with his dick in one hand and the whip in another. "Did you suck his dick?" *he asked as he tapped the slender tip of his dick against her lips.*

Same questions. Same humiliation.

"Did you, slut?" *he asked again, angry.*

Whap.

Jaime raised her hands and pushed him, one of her hands landing against his testicles, and she rose and stepped back. "That's enough, Eric," *she shouted at him, tears streaming from her eyes as he hollered out and grabbed his nuts.* "I don't deserve this shit!"

He limped over to her and pushed her shoulders roughly until her body was pressed against the wall. "You deserve this and much more. I have always taken care of you and loved you and respected you. And now I know that you never did the same for me, up in some motherfucking strip-club fucking a stripper. You lucky I don't kill you, Jaime, because* that's *what your ass deserves.*"

Jaime was frozen with fear at the look of rage in Eric's eyes.

"So unless you want me to throw your cheating ass out on the street to see if you can fuck your way back into the beautiful home, nice car, and nice clothes that I gave you, then you will do what the fuck I tell you to do or get the fuck out."

Jaime vaguely noted that the plastic of the teddy was sticking to the wall as she felt the fire of Eric's anger. "I am sorry. I made a mistake. One mistake, but I love you, Eric, and I want you back. I want my marriage, I want to be happy again," *she confessed to him softly, barely able to hear herself over the hard pounding of her heart.*

"I said all I have to say to you, Jaime," *he told her roughly, pushing her against the wall before he stepped back.* "You made our marriage this way."

"But I love you," *she whispered.*

"Love this dick," Eric told her coldly with a cruel twist to his lips as he pointed the whip at it.

As she dropped to her knees, closing her eyes and taking Eric's limp and short dick in her mouth, the tears flowed but Jaime knew she couldn't—wouldn't—admit that her marriage was over. She refused to believe that this would be the footnote of the years they'd shared.

His dick hardened against her tongue and he roughly grabbed her hair and thrust his hips forward as her lips cupped him. "Suck it, you no-good bitch. Suck it, slut."

And she absolutely refused to admit to her inner circle that her marriage was over, especially since she was the one who had the affair. She couldn't chance that getting out. The whispers behind her back and to her face? The scorn of the church and her sorors?

She still thought those things were far worse to face than the constant humiliation that Eric put her through.

Jaime was pulled from her memories, sure that Eric was more than angry at her. He hated her. He had to. What else could fuel the way he demeaned her?

And who knew that such rage existed in him? Such a mean streak? Such vindictiveness? Perhaps he was truly enjoying it and just was looking for a reason to break loose with his unreasonable ways.

Seriously, Jaime was starting to think—in her best Aria imitation—that motherfucker was straight crazy.

She dropped her head in her hands but not before she saw Mrs. Wiggins drive by in her white Volvo station wagon. She glanced up the street and all of the chitchat at the fence was done. One of them must have spotted her car as well.

"You see that?" Mrs. Killinger called over.

But Jaime didn't answer. She didn't even look in

Mrs. Killinger's direction and she made herself focus her eyes away from that white picket fence down the street. She had drama of her own to deal with. Maybe she had swept around so many other doors that she missed the dirty drama going on in her own house.

Jaime smiled a bit as she thought of their wedding day. Her parents had made it the fairy tale she always dreamed of, all the way down to her arriving to the church in a white horse-drawn carriage. When she walked down the aisle she honestly thought her prince was waiting for her at the altar.

But now?

Now her life, day in and day out, was a nightmare. The dream had long since faded. The only bright spots in her day was her friends and her family, but even that was growing on her because in truth she was tiring of the facade.

Tired of the humiliation.

The punishment.

The degradation.

She wanted to hear "I love you."

I forgive you.

I need you.

Jaime released a heavy breath as she rose to her feet and walked back inside the home she cherished. This was her showplace. Her domain. She'd imagined many happy years here. Years filled with love and family.

Not pain and torture.

She held herself close because they'd plotted out their lives, but all of their plans were fading into nothing with time. Next year they were going to start a family. And Jaime was ready to be a mother, but how would she get pregnant if her own husband wouldn't fuck her without a condom anymore?

Truth be told? It was all too much.

Stay with Eric and risk living this lonely and phony life that was beginning to look bleaker without children to love.

Leave Eric and risk the shame and ridicule from her parents and friends for sleeping with a stripper and cheating on her husband. Plus start over. Plus leave her dream home and give up her status and financially comfortable life.

Face the humiliation of her husband leaving her for one of her best friends.

All of it came flooding into her like a series of emotional body blows.

Shame.

Humiliation.

Fear.

The pressure of a rock and a hard place nearly squeezed the life from her.

It was too much.

"I don't know what to do," she said softly, clutching at her chest as she began to hyperventilate.

Jaime raced up the stairs to her bedroom suite, shivering as she struggled to calm herself. She made her way to the bathroom and tightly grasped the edges of the sink and stared at her reflection. Searching for herself. Looking for a sign of some happiness. Needing some peace.

It was all too much.

As one tear raced down her cheek, Jaime screamed from the pit of her tortured soul and raised her fists to slam against the mirror.

It shattered.

She gasped as shards cut her hands, piercing her flesh, slashing her hands and arms. Her blood flowed in tiny streams, dropping into the sink.

She didn't care because even then, with the pain of her injuries, she looked at the hundred different reflections and the pain in her eyes—the pain reflected from her soul—was far worse.

Jaime slid to the floor and cried gut-wrenching tears that echoed in the bathroom. The tears of a broken spirit.

I wish the glass had slit my wrists, she thought.

And that thought scared her.

"I'd rather die than face my marriage and fix my life?" she asked herself aloud in a haunted whisper as blood continued to stream from her hands and arms onto the floor and her clothes.

Jaime closed her eyes and forced herself to breathe. Forced herself to find the calm. Forced herself to fight through the darkness that had been her private hell for months. Forced herself to look beyond the facade she presented that she had begun to fool herself with. Forced herself to get to the real.

Her marriage couldn't continue like this.

Jessa Bell or not.

"Lord, I plead with You, Heavenly Father, to forgive my sins. Forgive my lies. Cleanse me, Father. Make me whole again. Lead me down the right path. I'm afraid of living in truth, but I am more afraid of taking my own life. And I know that I need You now more than ever. I am calling on You to strengthen me and help me fight to live a better life. I am calling on You to help me strengthen myself."

Jaime left bloody handprints on the plush carpeting as she worked her way to her feet to try and stand on solid ground—physically and emotionally.

She cried silently, and with each passing second she prayed for the strength not to give up or give in.

She picked up the shards of glass and prayed for the will to pick up the pieces of herself.

As she made her way over to the phone, she prayed for the power to change her life step by step, one day at a time.

She dialed her parents.

"Hello."

Jaime opened her mouth to speak but stopped herself as she looked at the blood drying on her hands.

"Jaime? Are you there?"

Jaime balled up her fist and banged it against the wall.

"Hey . . . hey, Mama," she said finally, her heart pounding terribly as she fought back the tears.

"Is something wrong, Jaime?"

"Mama, I . . . Eric . . . we . . . we are having some serious problems . . . and I don't know what to do," she admitted in a soft voice filled with her emotions. The pain. The anger. The regret. The confusion. The fear.

The line went quiet and the silence shook Jaime because she realized in that moment that she had no idea what her mother would say or which way her mother would go.

"What's going on, Jaime?" she asked.

"I'm not happy," was all that she said, not at all prepared to reveal her affair. Not yet. "Mama, sometimes I sit in the house all day and I cry, Mama, I ache, I hurt and I don't tell a soul but, Mama, I'm tired."

"Why are you unhappy? You have a beautiful home, a good husband, a good life. Some women would kill to be in your shoes."

Jaime laughed bitterly through her tears as she thought of Eric and his whip. "No, they wouldn't, Mama," she insisted softly as she slumped down on the edge of her perfectly made bed.

"Did he have an affair? The Bible speaks of forgiveness and a woman standing by her husband until death. You knew that when you went to that altar."

"It wasn't Eric, Mama, it was me," she said, surprising herself.

Some of the weight on her shoulders lifted even as her mother gasped in horror. Some of the veil was lifted and she didn't know the repercussions of her admission . . . and she was quickly learning not to care. Not even if it meant living or dying.

"The truth is the light, Mama, and I'm sick of the dark," Jaime said, ready to wash the guilty blood from her hands.

CHAPTER 14

"Girl, you are beaming. Do I smell new dick in your life?"

Aria's brows furrowed and her fingertips paused on the keys of her laptop as she'd remembered the innocent question she'd asked Jessa just a few weeks before. She was trying her very best to focus on her column but was failing miserably. It was hard to pretend that Jessa Bell had never sent that message. It was hard to pretend that she was waiting to see if she was the victim of a betrayal.

Aria typed the word "betray" into the dictionary search box for her computer. Of the four definitions listed, she found that one truly suited her best:

> **be·tray** [bi-'trā] **go against promise:**
> to act in a way that is
> contrary to a promise made

On their wedding day, Kingston had promised her fidelity, but those summers she'd shared with her crazy-ass cousin had taught her men were not to be trusted. Although Aria had always lived waiting for the other shoe to fall with some cheating bs she still was caught off guard by this ish.

When she graduated from high school, Aria was hellbent and determined to get her shit together. Her goal was to become the exact opposite of the trick she made herself into during those long hot summers.

Her school grades never really suffered, and during her senior year she excelled once she put true effort into her studies.

She pushed her laptop off her lap and rose to her feet, knowing she had no hopes of getting any work done. Not when her mind was so preoccupied.

"*Girl, you are beaming. Do I smell new dick in your life?*"

Aria shook her head at being played for a dang-on fool. . . .

"*Damn, she fine as hell.*"

Aria smiled a bit as she looked over at the table of suit-clad men sitting beside her. The smile faded as she saw the eyes were not on her. She followed their line of vision. Jessa stood at the door looking around the crowded restaurant. She fought not to roll her eyes.

She should be used to Jessa getting all of the attention when they were together. Her friend's light caramel complexion, long hair, and endless curves stroked the hot spots of most men.

Easing out of her chair, Aria smoothed her stretchy turtleneck and fitted black jeans over her own curves as she stood up and made a big gesture of waving Jessa over. Out the corner of her eye she saw the men eyeing her as well. Humph, I thought so.

Jessa waved as she eased her wide hips through the crowd to reach her. "Hey, Aria, I'm glad you got a table. It is packed in here," she said, sliding onto the chair as she sat her monogrammed denim Louis Vuitton on the seat next to Aria's Coach tote.

Aria eyed her friend. The brightness of her eyes and slight flush in her cheeks. There seemed to be an excited air surrounding her. "Girl, you are beaming. Do I smell new dick in your life?"

Jessa looked at her over the rim of the leather-bound menu. "Huh?" she asked, just the hint of a smile at her peach gloss-covered lips.

Aria's mouth formed into an O as she reached across the table to grasp Jessa's hand. "You heard me. Don't play, Jessa."

"I don't really want to talk about it," she said lightly.

Aria gasped. "So you are seeing someone," she said in wonder as she released Jessa's hand and reached for her goblet of white wine.

Jessa shrugged, closing the menu to sit beside her plate. "Yes," she admitted.

Aria saw her reluctance. "Jessa, don't feel guilty for moving on. Just because Marc passed on doesn't mean your life had to be put on pause," she assured her. "It's been years, and you deserve to be loved on, loved up, and just purely loved again."

Jessa smiled but it didn't quite reach her eyes.

Aria eyed her over the rim of her goblet. "When do we get to meet him?" she asked.

"Um . . . we're taking things real slow, so the whole meeting of the family and friends thing won't be happening . . . anytime soon," Jessa said, opening the menu again to cover her face.

Aria lifted up in her chair to pull the menu back down. "Tell me about him, and I want it all. Men are like plans . . . it's all in the details."

Jessa cast her eyes out the window and a soft smile curved her lips. "I'll just say this. He's an amazing man. An amazing friend. And an amazing lover," she admitted, actually dropping her head as she blushed.

Aria smiled. "You're already in the sex zone? This thing has been going on for a while, then," Aria said assuredly, knowing her friend.

Jessa just shrugged.

"Why the secrecy?"

"It's just different because he isn't Marc and all of my friends were Marc's friends. I don't know. It all just kinda happened and I just want to hold on to it and cherish it a little before we let the world in."

"Aww," Aria sighed playfully.

"Girl, hush," Jessa said, pointedly picking up her menu. "I am starving and in the mood for seafood."

"Where did you meet him?"

"Um . . . through a mutual friend."

"Who? Someone I know?"

"Not really," Jessa said vaguely.

"Wow, you really are keeping him under wraps, huh?"

Jessa reached for her sweating goblet of water.

"Is he good to you?" Aria asked, truly wanting her friend to be happy.

Jessa locked her eyes with Aria's. "Yes," she answered with a light in her eyes. "It is nothing that I expected but everything I never knew I wanted."

Aria nodded as she leaned back to allow the waiter to set a goblet of ice water down in front of her. She lightly touched the sleeve of his crisp white shirt. "Please bring us a bottle of champagne," she ordered politely.

Jessa looked surprised.

"We are going to celebrate your new Boo," Aria said, feeling—and ignoring—the eyes of the men at the neighboring table.

"I must admit that he is worth celebrating," Jessa said.

"Humph. That good, huh?" Aria teased.

Jessa laughed a bit. "Yes, but it's more than that now. It's really good, you know, and hopefully . . . hopefully *we'll be able to take it to the next level. I know that I want to and he says he wants to."*

"Well, I can't wait to meet him and add him to our little circle and get to know him," Aria said, completely curious about Jessa's mystery man.

Jessa smiled as she met Aria's stare. "Yeah . . . one day everyone will know just who he is. Just wait . . . you'll see. You'll all see."

Aria shook her head as anger consumed her at the thought that Jessa had been talking about Kingston—her husband— the whole time. Jessa had played her like a fool with her vague answers cleverly cloaking her betrayal of a friend. The same way she was playing the hell out of them now.

Aria would give anything to see Jessa. She was a mature, self-confident woman who knew how to effectively use brain over brawn . . . but she would love to whip Jessa Bell's ass six ways 'til Sunday. And not a bitchy and whiny slapfest, but she wanted to land some hardcore gut punches and vicious roundhouse kicks.

But whupping Jessa's ass wouldn't change the fact that only a marriage without a solid foundation could crumble at the hands of an outside person. Jessa or any other woman shouldn't have ever been an issue.

And she shouldn't feel so assured that her husband— the man she loved and cherished—was the culprit.

Not once since they received the infamous message had the thought crossed Aria's mind that it *wasn't* Kingston. Not once. What did that say about the state of her marriage? Where was her faith in him and why was it so easily lacking?

She thought of her past, her secrets, her shame.

"My marriage might be over," she said aloud as she

walked to her office windows and looked out at the street below.

Her dulled eyes landed on the house across the street. Vaguely she noticed Jasper Wiggins and Kelly Ortiz talking across their fence. Aria's eyebrows arched at the look of intimacy between them. They weren't touching or even standing that close together, but there was an air of familiarity between them that went far beyond "Howdy, neighbor."

Had the concept of fidelity completely flown out the window?

Suddenly Jasper and Kelly both moved away from that fence. That whole scene made Aria frown. Jasper and Kelly were on their respective porches walking into their homes. She'd never seen roaches scurry away that fast. Moments later Victoria Wiggins drove up in her Volvo wagon and pulled into the driveway. Of course it could be a coincidence, but in light of Jessa's betrayal, Aria was even more suspect of everything. Aria's eyes shifted to Victoria, who just stood by the car with her head shifting back and forth between the two houses.

"Humph, that's right, Vicky, don't sleep on it," Aria said aloud. "Follow your gut, Boo, because they up to no good."

Damn, is everybody double dipping?

Just like Jessa and Kingston.

She'd hidden her scandalous past and even lied about a vital part of their future, but not once had she reverted to her old ways and cheated on Kingston. Today her anger and pain had her flirt dangerously close to the idea of sexing Malcolm, but even then she couldn't quite push herself to grab the dick and go for a ride.

Once she met and then fell in love with Kingston, she knew that his heart and his dick was all that she needed. The day they got married she felt like she had finally outrun her past and was claiming a better future. She had

MESSAGE FROM A MISTRESS / 185

vowed to be a good wife: the lover, the friend, the caregiver, the whole nine yards.

And now all of that could slip through her fingers just
like that?

The thought of that scared the shit out of her.

Being angry was easy.

Wanting to fight Jessa and kill Kingston was a breeze.

"So now what?" she wondered aloud as she glanced
down at her watch. Four hours and counting.

Surely Kingston or any of the men wouldn't leave without saying a word, offering an explanation?

"Humph." Then again, maybe Kingston was smart, because if he dared to tell her he was leaving her she would've
immediately gone into kick-ass mode.

Especially when he *promised* that he would never leave
her. . . .

---

*Aria stepped out onto the spacious balcony of the hotel's
ballroom terrace, smiling up at the stars with love and
laughter in her heart and her eyes. She looked over her bare
shoulder at her tuxedo-clad husband before she twirled in
her wedding gown with her arms splayed wide. "Mrs.
Kingston Livewell," she said with a soft smile of pure satisfaction.*

"Any regrets?" he asked.

*"About us? Never. But I wish I had taken my grown-
girl pill and called to invite Jessa. It's been years since we
fell out, but we used to daydream about being in each other's
weddings."*

"I won't say I told you so."

Aria side-eyed him. "Thanks."

*"After our honeymoon, you make the first step to re-
connect. But for now," he said, walking up behind her to*

wrap his strong arms around her, "today is the first day of the rest of our *lives together.*"

Aria tilted her head back against his shoulder. "Yes," she sighed, truly feeling like she had found her prince.

Aria thought of her past and what all she had overcome to better herself, to stop being a trick and a thief, to be the woman her mother raised her to be. And she had. Now, not too many years later, here she was a college graduate and married to a handsome doctor who made her feel like he adored her.

For a moment, Aria thought about her past and her secrets. Things she knew she could never share with this man . . . her man.

The men.

The wild sex.

The weed and liquor.

The stealing.

All of it.

What woman wanted to tell a man that she was fucking out of both pants legs and even had a train or two run on her?

What woman wanted to 'fess up that all of the sexual tricks she used on him she learned before she was sixteen?

Pushing aside memories of a line of sweat-funky teenaged boys humping away between her thighs one after the other, Aria forced a smile to her lips as she turned in her husband's embrace. "I had no idea when I interviewed you for the alumni column that we would wind up married."

"Even though you were throwing me sexy eyes?" he teased.

"I did not," Aria protested, lightly pounding on his broad shoulders. "You weren't my type . . . or so I thought."

"Oh, really? So what was your type, because I know I am the S-H-I-T forever more."

"Yes, you are," Aria agreed, even as she shifted her eyes

*away from him. Back when making money and hustling
was paramount she had no type. Anything with a pulse
and a dick was fair game back then.*

"To be honest, since my senior year in high school my
education was my focus," she admitted with honesty. "I
had swore off men and you were the first man who made
me even want to give relationships another try."

And that *was* the truth.

"Found out knuckleheads and deadbeats weren't working out?"

Aria playfully nudged him upside his head. "Who knew
a nerd could fuck so well?"

Kingston lifted Aria up in the air against the length of
his body. "Now you know it so well, don't you?"

Aria sighed in anticipated pleasure as she arched her
breasts higher in her strapless gown. "I cannot wait for our
honeymoon to begin."

Kingston looked over his shoulder before looking back
up into his wife's beautiful face. "Why wait?"

Aria yelped as Kingston twirled them toward a dark
corner of the balcony to one of the cement benches along
the balcony railing. "Kingston, we can't do the nasty out
here," she weakly protested even as she hitched the front lay-
ers of her wedding gown higher as she wrapped her legs
around his waist. She was grateful for her thigh-high stock-
ings and barely there white silk thong as her strong and
sexy husband settled her on his lap.

With the back of her gown's skirts falling to the floor
and covering his knees, they were shielded as he unbut-
toned and unzipped his tailored tuxedo pants before lifting up to ease them down to his thighs.

Aria reached between them to wrap her hands around
the length of him and in just a heated second her seductive
touch had his dick hard. She licked her lips as she looked
down at him, dark as chocolate, thick and weighty in her

hands. "I wish I could suck this big dick," she told him, knowing her husband loved it when she talked dirty.

Kingston tilted his chin up to suck her lips. "You do?" he asked thickly as he reached underneath the voluminous skirts to tightly massage her fleshy ass cheeks.

Aria raised up and held his hard dick with one hand as she slid her throbbing and moist pussy down onto him. "Hmmmmm," she moaned, arching her back as she adjusted to the feel of him pressing against her pussy walls.

"You got all this dick up in you," he told her hotly as he locked his eyes on her face intently.

"Stick out your tongue," Aria ordered him softly as she settled her arms around his neck and brought her face close to his. She flickered her tongue in rapid motions against the tip of his and she felt his dick harden even more inside her before she sucked his tongue deeply into her mouth. "I want to feel that dick against my tongue, Kingston."

He lightly slapped her ass as Aria began to roll her hips, her pussy walls tightly gripping and releasing him as she did. "You like sucking that dick, don't you?"

Aria nodded, sucking his whole mouth before she whispered against his lips. "Until it cums in my mouth, Kingston."

"You like sucking up all that nut, don't you?"

"Every. Last. Drop."

Aria gasped as Kingston sucked the exposed tops of her breasts as she continued to fuck him like she was trying to complete a mission. "Shit, you big-dick motherfucker," she moaned as electricity shimmied over her body and her heart beat wildly.

"Damn, you got some good pussy."

Aria released a husky laugh into the air as she leaned back in his lap, still working her hips in a wicked clockwise and then counterclockwise motion.

"There you two are!"

At the sound of Aria's mother's loud voice, Aria sat up straight and Kingston froze. They both were glad for the cover of her skirts.

"Your reception is going on and y'all out here?" Heather Goines said, her short and plump frame covered by her lavender dress and matching capacious hat tilted to the side. She walked up on her silver heels to stand right beside them. "What are you two doing?"

"Just talking, Mama Goines," Kingston lied with a charming smile.

Aria giggled before she buried her face in Kingston's warm neck.

"We're coming, Mama Goines," Kingston told her. He coughed suddenly.

Aria giggled some more as she worked her pussy walls against his dick, obviously shocking him.

"Aria, get your pretty dress off this dirty floor." Mrs. Goines bent down to pick up the dress.

"No!" Aria and Kingston yelled out.

She dropped the hem and stepped back to eye them oddly. "Hurry up and get inside, you two," she warned them and walked away. They burst out laughing.

"My parents are the stereotypical bourgeois upper-middle-class black folks, but even my mom would've known what we were doing," Kingston told her even as Aria began to plant kisses along his warm neck.

"I told you my mom walks to the beat of her own drum . . . but she just gave us some great advice."

"What's that?"

Aria began to ride his softening dick until his strength and length returned full force. "Hurry up and get back in-side," she whispered into the heat between them.

Aria threw her hips into overdrive as Kingston released one of her breasts from the top of the strapless gown to suck her nipple deeply. She shivered and moaned, enjoying *the rapid-fire motion of her pussy sliding up and down the length of him. "Coming in . . . five . . . four . . . three . . . two . . ."*

Kingston flung his head back and bit his bottom lip to keep from hollering out as his dick shot round after round of cum inside of his wife's pussy just as she released a tiny yelp that was but a small representation of the pleasure she derived from cumming on his dick.

They clutched each other tightly in the aftermath, both weak and spent but completely sated.

"Do you have any idea how much you mean to me? How special you are to me?" she asked in a soft voice filled with her emotions as she leaned back to look down at him. "You are the man of my dreams, and I know now that every step in my life—good and bad—was meant to be so that I could find my soul mate."

Kingston's eyes locked with hers as she brought her hands up to stroke the sides of his handsome face. "I had no idea some college kid with a chip on her shoulder would get me so caught up," he admitted, his eyes so intense. "And I am caught up, Aria. You are everything to me and I know that today is just the first day of the rest of our lives together. I will honor everything I said at that altar, Aria, I will never hurt you, disrespect or dishonor you, or leave you. This right here is forever. I promise you that."

Aria smiled softly and kissed her husband just as one lone emotional tear ran down her cheek.

"Big bunch of bullshit," Aria muttered, trying to rub a tension headache away with her fingertips to her temples. But then she thought that she couldn't—shouldn't—live the next few hours blaming and hating her husband when there were two other possible culprits. She had to start to at least leave some glimmer of hope that everything Kingston promised her, he would continue to deliver.

If not, there were problems in her marriage that had nothing to do with Jessa Bell or any other Jezebel.

The thought of that was scary as hell.

CHAPTER 15

How does one sin compare to the other?

Renee wished she knew the answer to that as she stared down into the amber liquor in her glass. Drinking had become her best friend today. "Fuck that," she muttered, her voice slightly echoing inside the glass as she took a sip that scorched its way down her throat to burn her belly.

She turned another page in her wedding photo album. Flipping through time, reliving good memories. With manicured fingertips she touched her husband's handsome face. She felt like a fool sitting there, but for the life of her she couldn't close that album. She couldn't remove herself from the past. She couldn't stop wishing she had done things differently. Renee knew it was time for a hardcore, no-holds-barred look at her life and her marriage. And she felt like her plate was full.

Truth: She was seven successfully hard inches from having her own affair.

Should she forgive Jackson an affair because of her own secret dalliance? How could she cast the first stone? How could she really jump all in Jackson's ass (to copy Aria) when she had let their problems and a few drinks lead her into bed with another man?

Another sip of her fiery drink. A deep one that caused Renee to belch lightly.

"Fuck it," she said again, looking down at a photo of Jackson swinging her up into his arms.

Her heart swelled with love for him.

Truth: She had almost cheated and her love for Jackson had never wavered.

Could she allow herself to believe that Jackson had cheated with his dick but never . . . *never* with his heart?

Boom-boom-boom-boom.

Ding-dong. Ding-dong. Ding-dong.

Renee frowned deeply at the ruckus coming from her front door. Thinking it was Jackson and he'd forgotten his keys, Renee jumped to her feet—while she guzzled down the rest of her drink.

She gagged and her eyes bugged out comically as she pressed one of her hands to her throat. "Have mer-cy," she mouthed, feeling as if the liquor took away her voice.

Renee rushed around the sofa to the front door, snatching it open. She frowned at her neighbor from across the street, Kelly Ortiz, nervously looking over her shoulder with her fist still raised to bang down Renee's front door. "Kelly, is something wrong?"

"She's crazy. Help me."

Renee frowned as Kelly pushed past her and stormed into her house, jerking her back to slam the door closed. The liquor definitely had her moving in slow motion. "Hold up. What the hell is going on?" she screamed as she watched the short and curvy Latin woman take a cell phone from the back pocket of her tailored jeans and start dialing.

Boom-boom-boom-boom.

Renee swirled to eye her door.

"Bring your no-good behind out here, Kelly."

Renee's brows raised at the sound of Victoria Wiggins's voice screeching through her door.

"Yes, I need the police."

Renee swirled back to look at Kelly. "Hold on. What

the hell is going on?" she yelled, the alcohol making her slightly unsteady on her feet.

Boom-boom-boom-boom-boom.

"What kind of ghetto-ass shit am I in the middle of?" Renee asked herself, turning to open the door and set whoever was banging on her door straight.

"Noooooo!" Kelly yelled out from behind her.

Renee felt herself spin like the Tasmanian Devil as Victoria breezed past her into the house and straight dead on Kelly's ass. Her mouth fell open as she watched the two women fall atop her sofa, pulling hair and clawing at each other.

"Victoria! Stop!"

Renee's head whipped from left to right as she watched Jasper zip past her to grab his thrashing wife by the waist. She gasped when Victoria twisted enough in his grasp to double slap him like she was a professional pimp.

Jasper roared but he didn't release her as she thrashed like a wildcat.

"I'm going to teach your ass to stay the hell away from my husband," Victoria roared over Jasper's shoulder, pointing her finger and shooting daggers at her nemesis across the room.

Huh? Say what? Say who? Another *Jezebel?* Renee thought, crossing her arms over her chest as Kelly raced past her to close the front door securely.

Renee frowned at the woman and all the animosity she had for Jessa Bell leveled on her. "Oh, hell no. There's no safe haven in here. I've had enough of no-good mistresses for the day," she said, striding to Kelly and grabbing her arm with one hand and the door with the other.

"Renee!" Kelly gasped with her heavy Spanish accent. "She's trying to kill me!"

"Bitch, puh-leeze. I don't blame her," Renee snapped, walking across the room to snatch up the cell phone Kelly dropped during the melee. She strode over to her, pressed it into her hands, and shoved Kelly's little ass right on out the door. Renee took way too much pleasure in slamming and locking it in the woman's shocked, dazed, and amazed face.

With the sound of Kelly knocking wildly on her door as her backdrop, Renee calmly picked up her glass of liquor, sat on the edge of the chair, and looked out the window at Victoria digging Jasper's eyes out and then racing across the yard as soon as he released her to grab Kelly by her throat with one hand and slap her silly across the face with the other.

Normally Renee abhorred violence and public acts of foolishness, but in light of her own drama she felt the distraction to be pure damn entertainment. *Jerry Springer* and *Maury* wrapped all up into one. Hell with it. In fact, she raised her glass in toast to the coonery.

As Jasper fought to separate his wife and his *alleged* mistress, the threesome got tangled up as the women fought around him, trampling through her garden. Fuck it. She didn't care at that moment because the yard was Jackson's domain, and if he was leaving, the flowers would die right along with her soul anyway. She bit her lip as her heart ached terribly.

A crowd of neighbors began to gather in the street enjoying the show just like Renee. Her eyes searched the growing crowd for her friends. She didn't see them. She shifted to look at their respective porches. Jaime's was empty, but Aria sat alone on hers watching the drama unfold. Even from a distance Renee could see the same pain, lost, confusion, and anxiety that had her stomach twisted in knots.

Why on earth are we going through this drama alone?

Renee rose and grabbed her keys from the foyer table before she slammed out of the house. She took a moment to watch one of Kelly's fleshy titties pop out as Victoria tore away the front of her shirt. A collective gasp went through the crowd. Renee kept it moving, waving to her neighbors as she made her way across the street like there wasn't a catfight going on in her front yard.

"Can somebody help me?" Jasper roared, sounding out of breath and aggravated.

Renee turned on her heels and eyed Jasper with daggers. "No one was there to help you get yourself into this mess, motherfucker, now get *yourself* out of it," she snapped. "You're lucky all of us wives don't jump on you and help Victoria whup both of your asses."

As she turned and continued on to Aria's house, Renee heard the sound of police sirens in the distance. She'd barely stepped onto the sidewalk before Aria hopped to her feet and came down the stairs. "Can you believe that mess?" she asked, turning to watch as a police car came to a screeching halt in front of her home.

"I know how Victoria feels," Aria said.

"Right now, we all do," Renee said, looking over her shoulder as the police officers finally tore Victoria off Kelly.

"Damn right."

They fell silent.

"I was going crazy sitting in that damned house all alone," Renee admitted, still feeling a bit light-headed from the alcohol.

"I know what you mean. All kind of crazy shit been running through my mind," Aria said, holding her hand up over her eyes to shield the sun.

Renee nodded as she watched the police place Victoria in the back of one of the patrol cars. "I wonder if whupping Kelly's ass was worth it to her now that she's headed to a police station."

"Oh, it was worth it," Aria assured her.

Renee said nothing else for a while and their silence was filled with the "elephant in the room." She frowned as she watched Kelly pointing in her direction and the police officer's head swinging to lock his eyes on her. Nerves hit her.

"Um, Aria, can I get in trouble for putting someone out my house and sitting back to watch someone else whup they ass?" she asked as one of the police officers made his way to her.

"You . . . *didn't?*" Aria asked in total disbelief.

"Mrs. Clinton?"

Renee was tall but she had to tilt her head back to look up into the face of the officer. "Yes."

"My name is Officer Junton and I just needed to take a statement on what you saw of the altercation."

Renee and Aria looked at each other and shared a glance. "Officer Junton, to be honest, I have drama of my own I'm trying to wrap my mind around and I was drinking. All three were in my house but I have no clue who hit who or what was what. I'm sorry," she lied.

Dark eyes leveled on her. "You appear sober enough now," he said.

Renee sighed. "Watching a catfight in your petunias has a way of being very sobering."

"Yes, ma'am." He turned and nodded in the direction of her house. "Did you want to press charges for trespassing?"

Renee shook her head. "No, sir. I needed the entertainment."

His eyes became amused before he tipped his cap. "Good day, ladies," he said before walking away.

They watched silently as the police car whizzed past with Victoria handcuffed in the rear, turned around in the seat to watch Jasper closely as he climbed into their Lexus SUV and followed the police car out of Richmond Hills. Kelly avoided the eyes of her neighbors as she scurried across the street into her home.

"I wonder what she's going to tell her husband when he gets home," Renee said as the homeowners of Richmond Hills began to head back to their respective homes.

"I'm more concerned about mine coming home at all," Aria drawled, showing just a hint of her usual spunk and humor.

Renee released a heavy breath. "I'm so sick of this shit already. Part of me wants this day to be over and part of me is afraid to find out the truth," she admitted, raising her hands to rake her fingers through her short, jet-black curls.

"At least you're honest," Aria said, turning to climb the stairs back onto her porch.

Renee turned and shifted her eyes down the street to Jaime's home, knowing that's who Aria was referring to. "Maybe she doesn't have a reason to worry."

Aria sucked air between her teeth. "Why not? She got the text just like *we* did."

Renee just shrugged.

"Shee-it. Her husband has a dick just like *ours* do," Aria added.

"Aria—"

"What? She thinks she has sparks in her pussy or some shit?" Aria waved her hand dismissively. "I am so sick of Jaime and her total perfection crap."

Renee dropped her head in her hands. "Aria, please, I have a lot on my mind and I need someone to take my mind off the fact that I might have to explain to my children why their father left."

Aria's pretty mocha face shaped with a sympathetic expression.

"This does mean more for you, doesn't it?" Aria asked.

"Yes, it does," she stressed.

"I'm sorry, Renee. I wasn't thinking. I know you're right but I feel like I'm mad at the world right now and I was lashing out."

Renee just nodded in understanding as she settled onto one of the chocolate wicker chairs on the porch.

"I've done some shit in my day but I have never cheated— or even thought about cheating—on Kingston. Never."

Renee had a vision of herself naked in bed with her gay assistant and his flaccid dick. She bit her bottom lip. "I did—"

Aria gasped in surprise as she grabbed Renee's wrist tightly. "No!"

Renee rolled her eyes upward in exasperation. "Well, almost. If I had the pussy power to make a gay man convert, I would've slept with my assistant."

Aria looked defeated.

Renee was surprised by that. She'd expected a flip comment or shock at her revelation. The look of defeat confused her.

"No offense, Renee, but damn, is everybody dipping and diving on some new sex? Is anybody faithful?"

Renee felt offended. "I didn't go through with it, Aria. So save your holier-than-thou judgments."

Aria released a heavy breath. "I'm not judging you, Renee. My ass is afraid, because if you and Jackson can be married all these years facing this bullshit now, then when does the happily ever after begin? When can you trust that the man or the woman you love will not stray? I just want to be happy *in* my marriage *with* my husband."

"I want the same thing, Aria," Renee stressed.

Aria said nothing else, but the weight of their silence was heavy.

"I'm going to check on Jaime," Renee said, looking for a diversion as she removed her BlackBerry from the clip and dialed.

Renee ignored her as she listened to the steady ringing of the phone line in her ear. "She's not answering."

Aria hopped to her feet. "I'll go check on her."

Renee followed her younger and brasher friend with her eyes. She couldn't help but feel that in the one instant during her confession, something between them had changed.

But Renee didn't have time to ponder that. Her marriage hung in the balance.

She'd almost had an affair (a clear sign that there was trouble).

He might be leaving her for one of her closest friends (a clear sign that their marriage was over).

How did one sin compare to the other?

If Jackson came home tonight and confessed to the affair but begged her forgiveness, could she give it to him?

Even if he wasn't the culprit, when he came home tonight, could they ever heal the gap between them?

"Are we crazy to have spent most of the day doubting our marriages?" Renee asked herself aloud, squinting her eyes as she looked off at nothing in the distance. "Damn you, Jessa."

Renee reached for her cell phone again. She quickly typed away on the mini-keypad before she hit Send with authority.

Aria walked back up the street slowly with her hands pushed deeply into the back pockets of her jeans. "She's not answering or she's not home."

Renee eyed Jaime's house. "Maybe she went to her mother's or church or something. I don't know."

"Do you think the no-good, cheating, ass-lying mother-fucker isn't even fishing?" Aria asked, locking her bright eyes on Renee. "Who knows if he even went fishing at all."

"You're right. He might be with . . . he might be with Jessa right now." Renee felt deeply pained as she again imagined her Jackson making love to Jessa. "How long has this been going on? How long have they been sneaking around right under our noses? Like seriously, have they fucked in my house? In my bed?"

Aria's eyes flashed. "This is the reason why that show *Snapped* is still on the air—because of liars and cheaters."

Renee noticed that Aria shifted her eyes away. She felt

202 / Niobia Bryant

the unseen divide between them widen. "The one you always watch about women killing their boyfriends and husbands?" Renee asked, diverting her attention back to the show of which Aria spoke.

Aria nodded and framed her fingers like a gun, pointing it to the sky. "Pow-pow."

Renee shook her head. "And what would murder prove? He'll be dead and you'll be in jail."

"I have nothing else to say for fear of incriminating myself," Aria said, climbing the stairs, and headed straight for her front door.

Renee felt dismissed. The divide widened in her eyes. "You tried to reach Jessa?" she asked as she climbed to her feet to head home.

"I sure did, and that bitch ain't answering, but I left her *plenty* to grow on in those messages I left."

Renee could only imagine. "I'm headed back home. I guess we'll talk later."

Aria nodded solemnly before she stepped inside her house and closed the door.

Renee shifted her eyes up to the summer sun, hating how restless and lost she felt. When she woke this morning she never thought it would end like this. She had some choices to make about her life, her career, and her marriage. Tough choices that she avoided in the past, but she now knew what she had to settle down and face—especially after today.

"My marriage is in trouble," she whispered aloud to herself.

Now the question of whether her career was worth losing her marriage over was completely different in light of even the remote possibility that Jackson had left her for Jessa Bell.

She didn't want there to be another Jessa Bell.

She didn't want her family destroyed.

She didn't want to lose her husband.

As Renee walked up to her home, she knew she couldn't envision it without Jackson and their children in it.

She knew that she would fight for Jackson. Come hell or high water, the Clinton family was staying just the way it was. Period.

JESSA

Bzzzzzz.

I slipped from beneath the silky depths of my bath water to pick up my cell phone, and I sighed with pure boredom at Renee's number. I knew the fallout would not be easy and I knew my little text didn't help things . . . but I could not resist. I didn't hate her or any of my ex-friends. I was just ready to move on with life with him and without them. Once I took the plunge headfirst into happiness and love, I decided to put myself and my heart first.

Releasing a deep breath that caused the lit votives around the edge of the bathtub to flutter, I picked up my cell phone, pushing aside any nervous feelings. Any guilt. Any regrets.

> Jessa, you pulled the wool over our eyes and I for one will never forgive you for this no matter which husband it is.

I rolled my eyes at Renee's pathetic text. I couldn't care less if I had Renee's forgiveness. Fuck them all. Love was a conqueror and I loved him. He loved me. Sometimes life was just a bitch. Sometimes two people were meant to be.

Sometimes you had to throw caution to the wind and go for what you know and what you want.

I saw the icon telling me I had voice mail messages. Now what, I thought as I called my voice mail box and placed the phone on speaker.

Beep.

Beep.

"*You know, Jessa, you're smarter than I thought, because you know I would have dragged your ass all up and down Richmond Hills. You know I would have put my foot so deep in your ass that you would be shitting shoes for days. You know that your ass woulda been mine. How dare you pull a stunt like this and not be woman enough to stand and stake your claim your supposed prize, you slick, no-good, heartless bitch. I will see you one day and I don't give a flying fuck if it's years later, I'm gone fuck you up. Trust and believe that, you punk bitch.*"

I sighed at Aria's Brick City brash bullshit. Our entire friendship was based on competition. One-upmanship. But in times of crisis we always pulled together. Would I miss her friendship? Of course. But I had many years of love and passion and happiness ahead of me to replace all of my friends.

Beep.

"*Remember that you reap what you sow, Jessa Bell. Nothing good will come of this and you know it. We were friends. We trusted you. And for you to treat this like a game shows me that we never knew you, not the real you. You should be ashamed of yourself, Jessa.*"

I pushed aside any feelings of guilt I felt at the sadness in Jaime's voice. I could tell that she had been crying . . . but fuck that. Shame? Humph. I lost my shame nearly a year ago when the affair first began. It went right out the window with regrets and guilt.

"*I should be ashamed? Humph. Bitch, please. A reformed ho who can't have children, a slick bitch stealing her hus-*

band's money, and a workaholic trick fucking her young-ass assistant. Yeah . . . what the hell ever."

Closing my phone, I dropped it to the floor before I sank lower into the water. I was glad for the warmth because in that moment I felt cold . . . almost as frozen as I felt in the days after my husband's tragic death.

My friends could never understand that it was so hard for me to be with them when their marriages were a constant reminder of what I was terribly missing in my life. I thought I would never feel anything again. I thought that no man could compare or replace or make me forget.

But then we shared that stare and then that first intimate touch in their kitchen . . . and then the random calls just to say hello and then, in time, to say more . . . meeting in distant places where we hoped to remain unseen . . . and in just weeks since we crossed that invisible but still distinguishable line of impropriety, a night filled with more fiery heat than I had ever known.

And then I realized that I was wrong. So very wrong.

In his arms, his bed, and his life I discovered far more than I had lost, and soon I craved it like a drug. We craved it. Whenever, wherever, and definitely whatever. Until finally we knew that we had to be together. It was time for all or nothing. . . .

———— ⊸⊸⊱ ————

"Bring my pussy to me."

Click.

It was just the call I was waiting for. No other words were needed. I knew who it was and where I was to bring it. I snapped my cell phone closed and rose to my feet. We didn't have much time. We never did.

"Bathroom break," I said, eyeing my three friends where we sat playing whist at a portable card table in the center of my den.

"Hurry back, Jessa, we are whipping their ass," Aria told me as she rearranged her cards.

"Just the luck of the deal," Renee assured her partner Jaime, who was biting the MAC lip gloss from her lips in concentration.

I left them with a smile, picking up the pace of my steps to him as soon as I was out of their line of vision. Into the kitchen and out of the double doors of the deck. I nearly ran in anticipation. Across the deck and the yard, almost slipping into the underground kidney-shaped pool, to the double-car garage in the rear of my property.

As soon as I stepped into the darkness of the garage through the side door, he pulled my body against his and I melted at his very touch, pressing my lips to the spicy, lightly sweaty curve of his neck as his all-too-familiar hands rushed to lift the edges of the floor-length print skirt I wore.

"Damn, no panties, huh?" he asked in his deep tones as he reached between my thighs to stroke his index finger across my pussy lips.

"Kills time. We have to hurry," I whispered before I licked his earlobe with a gasp as my fingers clutched his shoulders. "Your wife and the girls are inside waiting on me."

He lowered his head to press his mouth to mine. I loved it when we kissed. It was always soft and sensual. A soul kiss. I moaned in pleasure when he sucked my tongue deep into his mouth as his hands massaged the soft fullness of my buttocks. "I can't get enough of you, Jessa. I love you," he whispered into my mouth, bringing emotional tears to my eyes.

"Shh, baby, don't cry," he whispered as he planted soft kisses from my forehead to my chin.

But that only made me cry harder. "I love you so much."

"I know you do, Jessa, and this is getting harder and harder for me because I know you deserve better," he said near my ear as his hands cupped my buttocks and pressed me against his hard, stirring dick.

Hunger for him filled me. Emotional and physical.

Time was of the essence. We had to rush. There was no time for words. Not in that moment. It had been almost a full week since we were able to snatch time to be together and I was more than ready for these heated moments with my man, but each time I wanted more and more of him.

I kissed him again, the taste now familiar to me, as he freed his dick from the zipper. I stroked the curving length of him, sure I could point my dick out in a lineup. Each vein and curve was familiar to me.

"Damn, your hand feels good on my dick," he moaned, flinging his head back as he massaged his hands over my naked ass like a blind man reading Braille.

"Better than hers?" I asked, unable to help myself. Jealousy and insecurity claim everyone.

"Don't bring her up."

I dropped down to squat, holding his dick before me like a microphone as I cut my eyes up to him. "I hate having to sit there and listen to her brag about how good you fuck," I told him before I tried to swallow every single inch of him.

His hips bucked and he bit his bottom lip.

"Especially when I know we make love better. Don't we?" I asked him in whispers against the throbbing tip of his dick.

"You're the best I ever had, Jessa," he swore.

I sucked him deep and wet for that. "And you love me?"

He grabbed my face and forced me to look up at him in the barely lit shadow of the garage. "I love the hell out of you," he told me fiercely.

My heart swelled with love for him as I rose to my feet. "Then why can't we be together? Why are we doing this to each other? To her?"

He hugged my body close to his and I buried my face in his neck. "I do need you. All of you," he whispered to me as his heart pounded against my chest.

I leaned back and looked up at him. "Then have all of me. I'm yours. Neither one of us wanted this to happen, but here it is. Now what are we going to do with it?"

With just enough light from the backyard, we looked deeply into each other's eyes, and I knew in that moment that we both thought of the repercussions. It was a lot to take on for us to be together . . . but I was ready, willing, and able. Was he?

"I have to tell her that I'm leaving. I owe her that much," he finally said.

I released a breath that was filled with relief and love.

We kissed with all of the passion and love we felt for one another. And when he used his strength to lift me high enough to then lower my quivering pussy onto his hardness, I had never felt so complete in all my life. I knew that every step in my life had led me to this amazing man whom I was meant to love and to be with.

He turned and pressed my body against the wall as we ground together, our hearts pounding. Our senses filled. Our bodies in unison as our chemistry cloaked us like a blanket.

"Jessa!"

We paused and swallowed hard as one of the ladies called my name in the backyard. "Damn," he swore, even as his dick continued to throb against my walls.

"I got to get this nut, baby," he whispered against my lips before he began to work his dick inside me again.

"Jessa . . . you out here?"

It was Renee. I recognized her voice.

"Hurry, baby. She might come back here," I whispered to him, feeling an illicit thrill to be fucking him with someone just feet away.

He stroked away until his grunts filled the air as his nut sprayed against my quivering walls. "Damn, I love fucking you," he moaned against my throat.

I laughed huskily until I opened my eyes just in time to see the top of Renee's head as she made her way back to the garage. "She's coming!" I screeched in a whisper, pushing him away before I dropped down to my feet, sending my skirt floating back down.

"Shit," he swore, rushing to fling his now-flaccid dick back inside his pants before he zipped up.

"Hide," I ordered him, ignoring the wetness and soreness of my core as I grabbed a rake and rushed out the door.

I nearly walked into Renee. "Hey, girl. What you doing out here?" I asked nervously, knowing that I was smiling like a fool.

"Shit, what are you doing out here . . . with the rake?" Renee asked, looking beyond my shoulder into the garage.

I eased the door closed behind me. "I glanced out the window and I thought I saw something floating in the pool. I was going to use the rake to get it out," I lied.

Renee glanced over her shoulder. "I don't see anything in the pool," she said with a frown.

I shrugged and opened the door quickly to slide the rake back inside. I caught a glimpse of my lover stooping behind my dead husband's motorcycle. I quickly shut the door. "Maybe it was a shadow or an animal that crawled back out."

Renee and I made our way back to the house. She was talking about cards and other things that were very trivial to me because my thoughts and my heart were filled with happiness.

Finally we would be together. The love of my life would finally be mine and mine alone.

As we reentered the house and I offered my lame excuses for my disappearance, I looked at each of my friends, knowing that to have him I would lose them and all that they had brought into my life over the years: Aria's humor. Renee's wisdom. Jaime's sense of style.

I knew that although I was claiming my own happiness, I was about to destroy one of their lives. My happiness completely overwhelmed any regret, guilt, or shame.

CHAPTER 16

Jaime didn't know when exactly she fell asleep or how long. As she stretched atop her bed, she did know for sure that listening to her mother drone on about her disappointment and rage had pushed her to mentally shut down. Even now, hours later, her words of contempt echoed.

Flopping over onto her back, she looked up at the shadows created on the ceiling from the street lamps as her mother's words floated back to her, still heavy with her disappointment.

"Your father and I worked hard to instill values and a sense of propriety in you, Jaime Lee."

And contempt.

"How dare you degrade this family, your husband, and yourself by being little more than a slut."

And disgrace.

"I am ashamed of you."

And threats.

"You better fix it, because your mess better not come back to embarrass this family in any way, Jaime. And I mean it."

Still, she didn't regret telling her mother the truth. She was sick of the lies. Sick of pretending. Sick of acting out her life to someone else's script. No matter how sweetly she wrapped lies up in a pretty, perfect package, her years of being everything that everyone else wanted her to be and nothing at all of what she used to want to be was a bunch of bullshit. Perfectly covered in designer clothes, hair, and jewelry—but bullshit nonetheless.

Sighing, Jaime sat up on the side of the bed and reached to turn on the lamp sitting on the nightstand. It was then she saw the blood still staining her hands. The sight of it reminded her of the Shakespeare play *Macbeth* that she read first in high school and then again in college. How could she forget the scene of Lady Macbeth washing imaginary blood from her hands, manifesting the guilt she felt over horrible things she and her husband had done?

Her crime of having one illicit affair hardly reached the level of murder, but her guilt had manifested and eaten away at her all the same. Made her hate herself. Made her feel as if she deserved the humiliation and punishment her husband had put her through every day since the affair. Made her think and think and overthink every little detail of her life.

But even beyond the guilt, Jaime knew she had long ago lost herself until she doubted that she even knew what she really wanted or thought. Everything in her life had become about the "right" everything. Being the stereotypical "good girl" and the "perfect wife."

Jaime made her way to the bathroom and washed her hands. She flipped her disarrayed weave back from her face as she studied her reflection. Her brows furrowed in concentration. "Who are you?" she asked her reflection.

She honestly didn't know anymore.

Maybe it was time to find out.

Jaime brushed the tangles from her weave and then for the first time in years pulled it all up into a ponytail. She took a quick shower, making it a point to skip her designer bath gels, skipped her make-up, and changed into a velour sweatsuit and flip-flops.

She shook her head thinking how she never let Eric see her without make-up . . . or passed gas in his presence . . . or took a crap when he was in the house . . . and how she'd get up in the middle of the night to brush her teeth to cure morning breath.

He never asked her to do it. He never even hinted. It had been her choice to be a Stepford wife.

Enough was enough.

Jaime looked around their spacious and stylish bedroom suite. The memories that flooded her were more bad than good. How many nights and days had she spent crying, feeling degraded, feeling foolish? She'd lost count, and she refused to add any more.

Things were going to change. They had to.

Jaime walked out of the bedroom. She paused, looking over the banister of the balcony as the front door opened and Eric walked in. He looked up at her briefly before he reached back to close the front door and stroll into his bedroom.

It's funny. Jaime had almost forgotten about the whole text message and worrying if her husband was coming home or not. It almost didn't matter anymore. She had bigger fish to fry than who Eric was fucking.

Jogging down the stairs, Jaime felt a freedom like she had never felt before. She did hate the natural urge to knock on his door before she entered, but Jaime pushed that aside as she turned the knob and pushed the door wide open.

Eric was undressing and turned to look over his bare shoulder at her. "I didn't call for you," he said in that cold voice that was now a familiarity in their marriage.

"You know, Eric, after the day I had—no, after the last six or seven months I've had, I don't really give a *shit* if you sent for me," Jaime said, actually relishing the way the curse word flowed from her lips with ease.

Eric's eyes widened a little bit as he stared at her. "Having one-night stands with strippers and cursing. What's next, slut?" he said snidely.

"Nothing much, jackass," she countered, reaching in the pocket of her ruffled velour jacket for her cell phone.

"That's enough of your disrespect," he said in a low voice still filled with chilling anger.

Jaime laughed as she sauntered farther into his room. "No, disrespect is receiving a text from your husband's mistress," she told him.

"My what?"

Jaime gave him a disparaging look. "'Life has many forks in the road and today I've decided to travel down the path leading your husband straight to my waiting and open arms.'"

Jaime looked up as Eric frowned and walked over to her.

"'I can't lie and say I have regrets. I love him more than you and I need him more,'" she continued to read, raising her voice as he neared her.

"Who sent you that?" he asked.

"Jessa, your whore, Mr. Goody Two-Shoes."

"*You're* calling someone else a whore? Please."

Jaime shook her head at him. "Are you defending your mistress to me?"

Eric stepped closer until his forehead nearly touched hers. "I don't even need to address or defend anything to you. You lost your right to question me when you opened your legs to another man."

Jaime didn't back down from him like she normally would. In fact, she stepped even closer to him until their breaths mingled in the small inch between them. She raised her phone. "'You saw him for the last time this morning. Tonight he comes home to me. He's my man now,'" she read. "So I'm real surprised to see you."

"Not that I care what you think, but those are lies.

Hell, you're probably making it up because of your own trash. Jessa wouldn't lie on me like that."

Jaime laughed bitterly. "Maybe the trick ain't lying. Maybe you two have been messing around behind my back all this time."

"After having to listen to my wife having sex over the phone, I really don't care if I brought a woman home and screwed her in our—your bed."

"Have you?" Jaime countered.

"Get the hell out of my room, and next time knock and wait for me to permit you to come in," he said, walking over to hold the bedroom door open.

"Why are you with me?" she asked, her voice incredulous as she looked over at his boyishly handsome face, which was filled with the lines of coldness and bordering on dislike.

"Get out of my room, Jaime," Eric said again. "And take your lies with you, slut."

Jaime sauntered over to the door, feeling her empowerment rise. "You know, Eric, for an educated businessman, you do a lot of childish name calling."

"Go to hell, Jaime."

She stopped and stared up into the face of this man that she'd honestly married for better or for worse. His handsome face, which used to be filled with charm and smiles all the time, was constantly twisted with anger and dislike whenever they were alone. She was married to a stranger.

"I've been living in hell these last six months with your punishing my one mistake—"

He snorted in derision.

"I have apologized. I have punished myself and I have allowed you to punish me. But no more, Eric. No more," she told him in a voice that was stern.

"What do you mean by that?" he asked.

Jaime just cocked a brow before she walked out of the room and continued up the stairs. She felt liberated. She felt free. Free of the shame and guilt she lived with all these months. Free of the charade of being happy only in public. Free of the masks she lived with all her life.

She heard his feet on the steps but she was still surprised when his hand closed around her upper arm to precariously spin her on the step to face him.

"I asked you what you meant by that," he said, his voice and face arctic.

Jaime snatched her arm away as she shook her head. "Since I was a little girl I worried about being perfect. I never got dirty. I always got good grades. I always did what was right. I wanted my parents' approval so badly that it mattered more than my own happiness," she told him, emotions tightening her throat as she pointed her finger at her chest. "I was a little girl worrying about my own parents not loving me or wanting me or even thinking they would send me away if I wasn't perfect."

"And?" he snapped sarcastically.

"And I continued that pattern of being afraid of not being liked all through high school and college and in *our marriage*, Eric." Jaime released a shaky breath. "I don't know if I've ever been happy, and I'm not blaming you. I'm blaming myself because I didn't try to do things or say things or even think things that suited me and made me feel whole. I put everybody else first and it was strangling me, Eric."

"So your affair was done for me too, right. Man, please." Eric shook his head as he looked away from her.

Jaime swallowed back the irritation and annoyance she felt at him completely overlooking her words of explanation. "This isn't about that, Eric, and our marriage shouldn't have become all about it either," she told him, sounding as emotionally weary as she felt.

"Then you shouldn't have stooped so low and done it."

"And you shouldn't have stooped so low to degrade and belittle me every chance you got," she yelled before she took a deep calming breath and looked upward as her heart pounded in her chest. "I was so worried about what people thought that I let you treat me like shit, worse than shit, these last six months. I didn't want to admit that my marriage was—no, it is over."

She looked down at him, and the look of surprise in his face gave her pleasure. She was ready to claim her life. Enough was enough.

"Jaime—"

"No, Eric," she said, holding up her hand before her. "I'm done. Done talking. Done explaining. Done begging forgiveness. Done being treated like a whore in my own home. Done with this marriage and you. You and Jessa have a wonderful life together. I wish you both the *very* best."

"I'm not having an affair with Jessa, so don't push your guilt on me."

Jaime sighed and shrugged. "It really doesn't matter, Eric," she told him before turning to continue up the stairs and into her bedroom. She grabbed her suitcases from the closet and dropped them onto the bed.

As Jaime pulled her perfectly folded clothes from the drawers and packed them she felt like imaginary wings were growing out of her back, giving her the ability to finally fly and thus flee the entire situation.

"You're not going anywhere, Jaime."

She glanced at him briefly as he filled her doorway before she walked in the closet and began removing hanging items. "I'm done, Eric. Why keep punishing ourselves? It's not healthy."

"So you think I cheated and you leave?" he asked sarcastically.

Jaime was sick of his judgments of her. She had to admit that she was surprised that he gave a damn. "And I cheated and you've treated me like your in-house slave."

"I didn't leave our marriage."

Jaime paused in putting her shoes in the suitcase to look

up at him. "No, you just made our marriage as horrible for me as you possibly could."

"No, I treated you like the slut you acted like when you slept with some stripper you didn't even know!" he shouted across the room.

"Well, this slut is tired, okay?" she told him sardonically.

Eric came across the room to grab her wrist.

Jaime snatched away as she looked into his eyes. "I'm sorry that I cheated and I know that I hurt you, but I'm also sorry that my issues run so deep that I allowed myself to live like this," she told him before breezing past him to begin picking up her dozen or so perfume bottles from her dressing table.

"I don't believe in divorce, Jaime, and you know that."

"Neither did I until I saw just how miserable marriage could be." Jaime zipped up her suitcases.

"What is your mother going to say?" he threw at her, clutching for straws.

Jaime laughed bitterly as she sat the suitcases on the floor and pulled up the handles to roll them. "Don't worry. I told her about my affair and she concurs with you that I am an embarrassing slut," she told him over her shoulder as she walked out of the bedroom, rolling her cases behind her.

Eric followed behind. "How are you going to take care of yourself? You need me. Did you think about that?"

Jaime noisily banged the suitcases against the stairs as she made her way down. "Well, let you and my mother tell it, I'm sitting on a gold mine, so maybe I'll put it to work," she snapped sarcastically.

Jaime yelped when Eric grabbed her neck and turned her to slam her against the front door. His eyes were filled with rage and his nostrils flared like a charging bull. "Let. Me. Go."

His grip tightened and he lifted her by her neck until her feet floated above the floor.

"Successful businessman found guilty in the choking murder of his adulterous wife," Jaime said. "I'm sure all of your colleagues will find this little news article amusing. Don't you?"

Their eyes remained locked for a long time but Jaime felt his grip loosening. As soon as he dropped her to her feet, Jaime used both of her hands to push him away from her before massaging the tenderness of her neck.

"You know, I'm realizing that you are sick in the head. You get off on belittling me. For months you made me feel like you hated me. Whipped me. Made me do things to you that I didn't want to do. Perverted things. And now that I'm leaving, you think I'm going to listen to you and stay, you sick bastard? I don't know if it makes your dick hard to be a perverted son of a bitch, but you are."

Jaime grabbed her purse and her keys from the foyer as Eric slumped down to sit on the bottom step of the staircase.

"Maybe you have masks too, Eric. Maybe you've always been an S-and-M freak and this was just your opportunity to have your freaky sex dreams come to life."

He said nothing as she jerked the front door and the smell of suburbia filtered in. And then it hit her. She was leaving her marriage and her dream home in Richmond Hills. She didn't even have a plan on where to go, but the debit card to her secret account nestled in her wallet would help.

Taking a deep breath, she grabbed the handles of her suitcases and walked out on her life as she knew it, not even bothering to close the front door behind her.

She loaded her suitcases into her trunk and closed it. Hopped into the driver's seat. As she passed the houses of her friends, she decided it would be best to update them on her new status. They might have their own drama to deal with as the day came to an end.

Jessa Bell.

Jaime realized she hadn't even asked Eric which of the men—if any—hadn't returned from the trip. He'd denied a relationship with Jessa and Jaime didn't know if she believed him, but she did know that right now she didn't care one damn bit.

For once it was all about her.

Her wants.

Her needs.

Her desires.

As she eased the car through the open gates of Richmond Hills, Jaime felt the solace inside the vehicle. The old Jaime would hold all of this in and not dare let anyone behind the velvet rope of her private thoughts and feelings. But she was trying to leave that part of her behind. She wanted to talk it over with someone and get it all off her chest.

Jaime reached in her purse for her cigarette case and soon she was inhaling deeply on a cigarette. She pulled to a stop at a red light.

The only person she felt she could confide in without judgment was Renee, but Jaime wasn't going to lump her drama onto her friend's lap, especially not today.

Needing a distraction and afraid thoughts that she made the wrong decision would surface, Jaime turned on her satellite radio and hummed along to the slow jams being played.

As she drove through the streets she knew she had a lot to do in preparation for her life. She could have insisted Eric leave, but Jaime honestly didn't want the memories attached to the home she once loved. She wanted a fresh start. New life. New home. New environment. New everything. But all of the decisions she had to make about her life would have to wait for tomorrow. There was not a thing she could accomplish tonight.

Well, almost nothing.

Jaime couldn't really identify the exact moment she decided this was what she needed. But she was weak and wet with anticipation by the time she pulled her Volvo into the parking lot of the strip club. It had been months since she gave in to her monthly fix, but nothing about it had changed. Same brick building with neon flashing lights. Same steady thump of the music's bass against the walls.

She eyed the door, knowing that all she had to do was walk inside and Pleasure could be all hers—for a little while, anyway. The familiarity of shame started to creep on her but she pushed it aside. She remembered how badly she felt lying on that floor, pussy still sore from his sex when he asked to be paid.

But goodness, she had never ever cum so much in all her life. Truth be told, sex that good was worth every red cent.

Over the months she hadn't forgotten it, even when she felt guilt over hurting Eric and shame over paying for sex.

"What am I doing here?" she asked herself out loud, already putting her still-running car in reverse to back out of the parking spot.

"Whaddup, stranger?"

Jaime slammed on her brakes and looked out the driver's side window at the man, the stripper, the walking sex himself standing there, looking down at her like he was ready, willing, and able to give her just the pleasure she craved . . . for a price. She took a deep breath of her cigarette as the heat infused her body. Six months and he only looked better. The black sleeveless shirt he wore showed off his muscled arms and clung to the rippled muscles of his chest and abdomen. Although his sweats were thick and baggy, his penis bulged against the material.

"Haven't seen you in a while," he said, hitching the Nike bookbag up higher on his shoulder.

Jaime had never really conversed with him before and she didn't know what to say. "Just been really busy, you know," she said weakly, putting out the cigarette and instantly hating how lame she sounded.

224 / Niobia Bryant

Pleasure smiled, his white teeth flashing against his chocolate skin as he bent down until they were eye level. "You
came here for me, didn't you?" he asked in a low voice
that Jaime found sexy as shit.

She licked her suddenly dry lips and nodded, unable to
look away from him.

"You don't want to go back in that club, do you?"

She shook her head.

"And you want me to fuck the shit out of you . . .
again . . . don't you?" he asked her cockily.

Jaime shivered and pursed her lips at the very thought
of his body and his dick on her . . . in her. She didn't answer him but the look in his eyes let her know she didn't
have to.

He stood up and pulled a card out of his pocket. "Get a
room and call me. I should be there by twelve," he told
her.

Am I really about to do this? she thought as she took
the card from his hand and shivered from the touch of his
skin breezing across hers.

He smiled and licked his lips, showing off deep dimples
she wanted to bury her tongue in, before turning to walk
toward the rear of the club.

"Pleasure," she called.

He stopped and locked intense eyes on hers.

"How much?" she asked, hardly believing she was so-
liciting sex outside a seedy strip club. *Maybe Eric isn't the
only pervert.*

"How long?" he countered.

That forgotten bud between her legs swelled to life and
called out for attention and satisfaction. "The rest of the
night . . . if you can," she said, feeling shy as butterflies
claimed her stomach.

He nodded. "Five bills. Midnight," he said, waving briefly
before he disappeared around the back of the building.

Knock-knock-knock.

Jaime walked to the door of the hotel suite as naked as the day she was born in a pair of sequined Gucci heels. She had pushed aside thoughts of her failed marriage, Jessa's text, and anything else beside enjoying herself.

As she stepped back to allow Pleasure inside the suite lit with candles, she eyed him and promised herself that this was the absolute last time. *Just once more,* she thought as he stopped and scooped her naked body up into his arms, pushing the door closed with his foot.

Just once more.

CHAPTER 17

In the few hours that had passed since she left Aria's house, Renee had busied herself settling back into her role as full-time housewife. She finished cleaning the entire house, including the kids' bedrooms. She made red rice and sausage, a garden salad, and homemade hush puppies to go along with the fish he caught—and just in case they were still having friends over. She lit scented candles, put on subtle and inviting lighting, and took a leisurely bath.

It was time to get back to basics.

Once she settled onto the corner of the club chair by the window, she picked up her cordless phone and dialed Jackson, waiting for his voice mail to come on.

Beep.

She closed her eyes and spoke from her heart. "This morning you said that we needed to talk, and I will admit that those words can be the scariest thing a wife is ever told by her husband. They are words that can make a smart woman pause and reflect. For the first time in our marriage, those words introduced me to the fear of our marriage coming to an end."

Renee paused and pressed the phone to her ear as she bit her bottom lip and closed her troubled eyes. "Of course, I could be assuming the worst, but that is what the end of this marriage is for me—the absolute worst. I love you and you are my heart. Our family is the most important thing to me and . . . and I am willing to work and fight for it."

She took a deep breath, completely aware that the next words out her mouth meant giving up everything she had worked so hard for. "If my working means losing you, then . . . then . . . then I won't work anymore. I just want things between us to be the way they used to be. I need things between us—"

Beep . . . beep . . . beep.

Renee ended the call and placed the phone back on the charger. She had reached the end of the allotted time for a message, but that was fine—she had said all that she wanted to say. Hopefully it was enough.

Renee sat there snuggled in the corner of her chair and witnessed the slow descent of night. She watched the cars slowly passing by on the street and the families arriving and leaving home, lost in her thoughts, wondering which road she was traveling on—and just how long she had been lost.

There was one thing she knew for sure.

She wasn't giving Jackson up without a fight. No way in hell.

Her BlackBerry lit up in the darkness and vibrated in her lap. Renee dropped her eyes down at the screen. It was their daughter Kieran calling. Renee picked it up but she didn't answer it. Her kids were safe and secure at their grandparents'. Right now she didn't feel like stepping into the role of mother. She wasn't up to random questions about clothes, or boys, or curfews. Renee loved her daughter, but right now Mama was going through something she hoped Kieran would never experience.

Tonight she would find the truth about her marriage. She wanted to know it all, regardless of whether Jessa was a spoke in the wheel or not. It was time to see just what cards they held.

Her main focus was her role of wife—a role that she was ready to step into 100 percent. No more half-stepping. She had all day to weigh her options and it hit her hard that she couldn't lose Jackson for anything or anyone . . . not even her career. Not anymore. For her, it was time to save their family.

She'd almost cheated.

Jackson might have cheated.

When they'd wed she wouldn't have ever guessed that either of them would stray. Never.

Sighing, she rubbed her hands over her eyes and fought the urge to rush to their bar and pour a huge drink for herself. She had long since sobered up from earlier, and alcohol would only numb the truth—not make it disappear.

The lights from a vehicle flashed against the window and Renee sat up a bit straighter. She relaxed again when she saw it was a car and not Jackson's pickup truck. Her eyes stayed locked on the car as it neared her house. It was Jasper and Victoria's Lexus SUV, and although Jasper had left in the SUV it was Victoria and Victoria alone who pulled up and parked in their driveway. Renee vaguely wondered just where Victoria had left her husband.

When Victoria climbed out of the SUV and paused to look up at the dark and unlit house of the woman sleeping with her husband, Renee felt an affinity for her betrayed neighbor. Kelly's house was dark and Renee wondered if she was home.

Her eyes shifted back to Victoria lit by the street lamp. When she angrily wiped her face, Renee knew the woman was crying. Moments later she turned and walked into her house. Although there were many feet between them, Renee felt every bit of the emotions Victoria had to be suffering with. Every single one.

Closing her eyes, Renee released a heavy breath and rubbed them. She glanced at her watch. It was just after seven. Usually by now on a fishing day, Jackson would have called to say he was on his way home. She picked up her BlackBerry and dialed his cell phone.

"If you want him, Kelly, he is allllll yours!"

Renee frowned and looked out the window just as Victoria heaved an armload of clothes over the white picket fence and onto Kelly's lawn. They resembled awkward, oversized snowflakes or confetti floating to the ground. Renee watched as Victoria stormed into her house and back several times to send what she assumed was Jasper's clothing over the fence.

As Victoria made her fourth trip inside her house, Renee spotted Kelly peeking out a second-story window. *Poor child is afraid,* she thought.

The slamming shut of a car door made Renee's head whirl and her heart nearly leapt to her throat to see Jackson climbing out of the truck and walking around to reach into the bed. She'd been so busy in Victoria's drama that she completely missed her husband's arrival.

"He's home."

That fact alone made her shiver with excitement, but it was far from time to celebrate. *Maybe he's just home to tell me I am no longer the woman he loves and needs in person. How big of him, realizing that a text message from his mistress just didn't have the same . . . class.*

Renee released a little laugh that clearly showed that she truly felt there wasn't a damn thing funny at all.

As he made his way up the asphalt walkway, Renee rose to her bare feet and smoothed the white cotton maxi dress she wore. She placed a smile on her face and turned just as Jackson walked through the door. Even as she struggled with the possibility of his betrayal, Renee thought her husband looked handsome even in jeans, navy T-shirt, and boots.

The years had been good to Jackson, she thought, crossing her arms over her chest as she took in his tall and square build, the slight touches of silver at his temples, and just the hint of crow's feet at his eyes. He was aging like a fine wine, and Renee didn't want anyone else to sip from him. Period.

He stopped in surprise at the sight of her standing there. "Hey," he said briefly, tossing his keys onto the end table before he pushed his large, beefy hands into his pockets.

Renee uncrossed her arms and walked over to him. "Had a good day?" she asked, surprised by the normalcy in her voice as she came to a stop before him.

He nodded briefly before he brushed past her. "I need a shower," he said.

Renee stiffened and clutched her hand into a fist as a shot of pain and disappointment radiated through her chest. Each sound of his feet landing on the wooden steps echoed inside her.

She didn't know what she expected of his arrival home, but it all seemed anticlimactic. Pacing, Renee bit the gloss from her lips. She wrestled with whether she should confront him about Jessa Bell's accusation or not. She wrestled even more with whether she wanted to know or not.

She paused at the foot of the stairs.

Jackson was home, but for how long?

Renee jogged up the stairs and into their bedroom. There was a trail of fish-smelling clothes leading to the closed double doors of their bathroom. She eyed his jeans lying at the foot of the bed.

Her hands itched to rummage through the pockets, but she stepped over them instead. She wasn't at all prepared for what she might find. Not at all.

Opening both the doors, Renee stepped into the bathroom. She frowned to see Jackson sitting nude on the commode on his cell phone. He looked up in surprise at her sudden appearance.

"I'll call you back," he stammered, closing the cell phone.

Was it Jessa?

"Is everyone still coming over to play cards?" she asked, deciding to play it cool.

Jackson nodded. "Far as I know."

Renee licked her lips and arched her brow. "Eric and Kingston?" she asked, walking over to the glass shower stall to start it for him.

"Did one of the ladies say different, because the fellas said they were still coming when I dropped them off at home."

All three came home? Had Jessa lied, or was her lover at home breaking his wife's heart at this very moment. . . .

Renee shifted her eyes to look at Jackson through the open glass door of their shower.

Ask him, Renee. Ask your husband if he's fucking your best friend. Ask him!

Jackson flushed the commode.

Ask him was he or is he going to leave you and his family to live with an undercover slut.

But she said nothing as he walked past her again to step into the glass shower stall.

This is ridiculous. Did he get my message? What does he think? He said he wanted to talk. About what? And when? Why is he stalling? And why am I letting him?

Renee walked over to the sink. She frowned. His cell phone was sitting on the edge but it was powered off. *What the hell?*

She looked up at her reflection in the mirror. She didn't like the woman she saw. This afraid to talk, skirting a major issue, pretending nothing was wrong wife was not her at all. But fear of losing him had the real Renee completely paralyzed.

Her eyes shifted down to the cell phone, but she turned and rushed from the bathroom instead. Flying out the room and down the stairs to the bar, she poured herself a shot of tequila and downed it quickly before she poured another. Her hand gripped the glass tightly as anger consumed her. Anger at herself.

I should boil some grits and do an Al Green on his ass right in that goddamn shower.

Instead she swallowed down another shot, and it burned like fire on her empty stomach. In one day she had drunk more alcohol than she had in years. Shit.

Renee cupped the glass like a ball and hurled it across the room. It slammed into the side of the lamp, knocking it over and shattering the lightbulb. The living room darkened just a little bit as Renee turned and slid down the side of the bar to the floor. She pulled her knees to her chest and hugged them tightly as she lightly hiccupped and then belched.

Renee giggled a bit as she craved the days when marijuana made everything in her life seem funny. In this moment she could use a joint, blunt, or whatever they called it these days. She'd even hit the medicinal kind. *Humph, it's supposed to be for glaucoma or some shit. My ass been blind to some shit. Help me see shit clearer, Mary Jane.*

"Renee?" Jackson called out.

She dropped her head on her arms as she listened to his feet slapping against the wood of their stairs.

"Renee?" he called out again.

She knew he was nearing her because the tiny, fine hairs on the back of her neck and her arms stood on end. Jackson's presence had always seemed to electrify her.

"Do you want a divorce, Jackson?" she asked, unable to take the cat-and-mouse game he was playing.

She looked up as he stood beside her still damp from his shower with nothing but a towel loosely wrapped around his waist, his heavy dick pressing through the thick material like a mighty fist.

"Do you?" he asked.

"Hell no, Jackson. No, I don't want a divorce," she cried out, tears of desperation filling her eyes. "Did you get my message?"

He nodded, his handsome and square face solemn. "I got it."

Renee clumsily shifted to her knees as tears filled her eyes and streamed down her face. "What else do I have to do to prove that I want my marriage, then, Jackson? Do you want me to beg you? Then fine, here I am on my damn knees begging."

"Get up, Renee," he said, reaching down to grab her shoulders tightly.

"Please don't leave me," she wept without shame as he pulled her to her feet.

Renee wrapped her arms around his neck, holding him close as she closed her eyes and inhaled deeply of the familiar scent of him. "Jackson, please don't give up on us," she whispered into his ear.

"Renee."

"Fuck that job. Fuck my career," she pleaded, aware that his arms didn't surround her body to hold her close.

"Renee!"

"I love you. I need you. You're the best thing to ever happen to me—"

"Renee," he shouted, pulling her arms from around his neck and stepping back from her to shake her a little bit. "Listen to me. Damn!"

Renee breathed deeply and tried her very best to calm herself as she swiped the track of her tears from her face. She felt ashamed that she had begged this man who was supposed to love her. Supposed to cherish and keep her. Honor her. All of it. Until death.

And even after all her pleading, not once had he assured her that he wasn't going to leave her and the kids. Not once.

"I don't care about anything that happened in the past,

Jackson," she told him as he steered her over to the sofa. "I just want to know that we can move forward."

Jackson sat down on the wooden coffee table, his face solemn as he took both her shaking hands in his. He looked at her long and hard and then looked away at something . . . anything . . . but her eyes. "If I could leave the past in the past, I would."

Renee pulled her hands out of his.

"I'm so sorry, Renee."

"For?" she asked softly, looking down at her wedding ring on her left hand.

Jackson swiped his hand over his mouth. "I love you, Renee . . ."

She flinched. "But," she added, feeling like it was about to drop from his mouth anyway.

He risked another look at her and Renee saw the regret, the shame, and the guilt in his face before he even opened his mouth. She gasped a little as her heart clutched tightly. *No. No. No.*

The tears that filled his eyes scared her more than anything, and when the words finally left his lips it seemed as if those words and his actions were in slow motion. "I had a one-night stand . . ."

Boom.

"And she's pregnant."

Boom.

Renee looked at this man, her husband, like she didn't know him, like she couldn't believe what he'd said, like she had been hurt far more than anything she'd ever imagined today.

She felt cold and numb as she stared at him with eyes wide with shock. Another woman was pregnant with her husband's baby.

"Renee, I am so sorry. I never meant for this to happen," he said, taking her quivering hands in his to lower his head and place kisses on them.

Renee looked down at his hands and hers, but she really didn't feel his touch or his kiss. She felt absolutely nothing—and maybe it was good that she didn't.

"Jessa is having your baby?" she asked, her face incredulous as some of the pain fought through her simulated fugue state.

He looked up in shock, his face in a frown. "Jessa? Hell no. What makes you think that?" he asked.

As Renee saw—and believed—the complete confusion in his eyes, that's when she knew she had to get away from him. All day long her mind had been fixated on Jessa, when her husband wanted to 'fess up to fucking another bitch and getting her pregnant. And she'd begged him like a junkie needing a hit not to leave her.

Her eyes shifted from his face to the bottle of tequila sitting on the bar. Her mouth literally watered for it.

"Renee, say something," he said, massaging her hands.

She pulled her hands from his as she rose to her feet. Another woman was having her husband's baby. What kind of cruel fate was this? *What have I done to deserve this?*

She had been willing to fall back into the monotony of being a suburban housewife.

She had been willing to give up her high-powered and completely fulfilling career.

She had been willing to fight for her family for the sake of her children.

She had been willing to not even ask about the affair with Jessa and move forward with her marriage and her life.

Things had changed.

Renee brushed past him and raced into the office, using the key hidden under the flowerpot to unlock the top drawer.

Jackson's presence soon filled the doorway and Renee lifted her hand with his 9mm gun in it—pointed dead at him.

"Renee—"

She shook her head and steadied her hand. Although her heart ached, Renee took a deep breath, gathered herself, and found her strength and her voice as she stiffened her spine. "I really need you to pack a bag and leave. Give me space and time and . . ."

Renee dropped her chin to her chest as she struggled to find the words.

The hairs on her body stood on end and she jerked her head up to find him coming closer to her.

Click.

Renee cocked the gun. "I would advise you to get the fuck out of my sight, Jackson. I mean it. I swear to God. I. Mean. It."

"Renee, I don't want to lose you—"

"Get the fuck out, Jackson!" she screamed at the top of her lungs until her eyes were bugged and the veins in her throat strained to what seemed the breaking point.

He held up his hands and backed out of the room. Renee stood there with the gun still pointed at the spot where he'd stood. She stayed that way until the front door shut behind him and the sound of his truck starting echoed from outside.

In time, Renee calmly sat the gun on the desk and covered her face with her hands as she bent over and released hysterical cries that left her nearly out of breath.

Maybe tomorrow she could face the who, what, when, where, and why of Jackson's affair, his mistress and his child . . . but for now she knew that her husband had just saved his own life by leaving just like she told him.

CHAPTER 18

Aria felt physically and emotionally exhausted from the day's events and it wasn't over yet. Not by a long shot. The sun had fled and the skies were ebony. Richmond Hills was more quiet than usual. Gone—if not forgotten—was the incident on Renee's lawn earlier. For most of the residents normalcy had returned.

But Aria wondered if she would ever be the same again.

Any attempts to finish her column failed.

Any calls from friends and family were ignored.

Her plate was filled and she couldn't take on any more.

She had always been the one to doubt fidelity, to question the existence of morality and to side-eye any woman who came within one foot of her husband. And now? Her husband might have been cheating on her. He might be leaving her.

Aria always felt like Jackson was the bad guy in Renee's marriage. That he made Renee suffer because of his outdated thoughts on women working. That he wasn't supportive or understanding. That he could be a pompous ass. In her eyes, Renee was the sufferer and Jackson was completely wrong. But then Renee admitted that *she* almost cheated on him. That *she* stepped outside the marriage with someone she worked with. That she had fucked up. That completely blew Aria's mind, and now everything looked different. Was different. Truth? Aria lost respect for Renee in the moments after her confession. As wild as her past was, Aria didn't understand or abide by cheating. To her, infidelity was easy and cowardly; putting in the time and effort to remain committed was the real challenge, and she was up to it. She thought Renee was too. She'd thought her friend was made up of more substance than that.

Sighing, she rolled over onto her side in the middle of the bed as she picked up her cordless and dialed Kingston's cell phone. Her heart stopped when it began to ring. The men were finally out of the water. She sat up straight in the bed, pressing the phone closer to her ear.

But her heart and stomach plummeted when he didn't answer and the call went to voice mail. "Shit," she swore, hanging up the phone just to call him again.

And again.

And again.

"Damn it, Kingston. Answer, motherfucker. You better answer."

But he didn't.

Aria let out a frustrated roar and flung the phone against the wall to shatter. She dropped her head into her hands, feeling like she could literally pull out every last strand of her hair from her own head.

Why wasn't he answering?

Her gut clenched and she felt ill at an image of him walking into Jessa's open arms. This madness, this crazy merry-go-round of emotions had to come to an end. She couldn't take any more.

Aria flopped back down on the bed, curling her body into a fetal position as tears flooded the pillow she clutched tightly. But she swallowed back the tears. She wouldn't shed another tear. Either it wasn't him and she had no reason to cry, or it was and that meant the cheating bastard wasn't worth the damn tears.

Aria began to punch the pillow with each ache of her

heart until soon she was up on her knees and punching it harder and harder as she visualized his face on it. And she worked up a sweat giving that poor pillow all the frustration built up inside her.

"Damn you, Kingston," she muttered as she gave the pillow a vicious one-two. *Boom. Pow!*

"What the hell did I do?"

Aria froze at the sound of his voice before she looked wildly over her shoulder. Kingston stood in the doorway, tall and handsome and rugged in his jeans and T-shirt . . . looking at her like she had lost her damn mind. Aria released the pillow, weak with relief. *Fuck it, maybe I have,* she thought as she rushed from the bed to approach him.

He's home. He's here. It's not me. It's not us. She felt so pathetic to be so damn happy about that.

Aria wrapped her arms around his strong chocolate neck as she pressed her mouth to his with a moan filled with happiness, pleasure, and the sweetness of relief. As she sucked his bottom lip into her mouth, Aria pressed her soft and curvy body against the entire hard length of his six-foot-three muscular frame.

"Damn, I should go fishing more often," he mused into her open mouth as his hands came up to grab her buttocks and hoist her up.

Aria gladly wrapped her legs around his waist as she snuggled her face into the warm curve of his neck and her pussy thumped with a life all its own. In that moment the mix of his sweat, the remnants of his cologne, and the faint odor of fish smelt like heaven to her.

"Damn, your heart beating fast, Aria," Kingston said with a laugh.

Aria placed moist kisses along his sweaty collarbone. "Strip," she ordered him, just knowing that she needed to be with her husband.

"Aria, I need to wash—"

She deeply kissed away the rest of his protests before

she lowered her feet to the carpet and began to strip him herself. And she heard nothing but the wild pounding of her heart and the rustle of his clothes as she removed them.

She felt desperate to fuck her husband. She wanted to take it back to the basics—fuck the hell out of him and make him cum so hard his mouth twisted.

"Damn, Aria," Kingston said as she dropped to her knees and took his hard dick into her hands to stroke fast and furiously.

She wanted to remind him that he would never have a need or desire for another woman.

Closing her eyes, she guided the thick tip into her open mouth, ignoring the faint scent of sweat as she swiped her tongue against the smoothness of it.

"Ooh," Kingston moaned as his hips bucked.

Aria drew him into her mouth, wetting him with her spit as she drew on the skills she learned from her tricking days. She felt a delicious thrill when his hands twisted in her hair and his strong muscled thighs quivered as she sucked him like she was trying to get paid.

Kingston fell back against the door and Aria moved forward on her knees, his dick still implanted in her mouth. She was relentless in her pursuit of his sexual happiness. She was on a mission.

Fuck it.

"Damn, you gone make me cum," he said, sounding as weak as his knees felt.

A small shot of his cum drizzled from the tip and she licked every drop with a moan before she released his dick from her mouth. "Get on the floor," she ordered as she stripped off her shirt and worked her pants down her hips and beyond her knees to fling over her shoulder.

Kingston looked surprised but he obliged. "Doctor's orders?" he teased with a double-dimpled smile.

Aria smiled, feeling love for him fill every bit of her. "Doctor's wife's order."

As soon as he dropped to his ass on the floor, with his back against the side of their mahogany dresser, she climbed across him and onto his dick with one swift slide of her hips downward.

They gasped in unison at the hot feel of one another.

"Right here in the door, huh?" Kingston asked, tilting his chin up to hotly lick her mouth.

"That's right, Doc." Aria arched her back as she began twirling her hips to ride his dick like a jockey with the finish line in sight.

"This has to be a quickie, baby, don't forget we're meeting everybody at Jackson's," he told her as his fingers dug into her hips.

Aria froze. So Jackson was home. Kingston leaned in to suck her nipples through her lacy bra but Aria brushed him away like a fly. "Where's Eric?" she asked, thinking of Jaime.

Kingston lifted his head to stare at her in confusion. "Home. Why?" he asked in irritation, using his hands to pump her hips.

Although Aria knew Kingston hated his groove disturbed once it was started, she had other shit on her mind. "And Jackson is home too?"

"Yes," he snapped, working his buttocks as he tried to shift his dick up inside her. "Man, fuck them. No, matter of fact . . . fuck *me*."

All of the men came home?

That meant Jessa's lover was not revealed . . . yet. Aria's heart plummeted to her stomach.

Kingston looked up at her. Something in her eyes made him stiffen his stance.

He looked wary.

Smart. Real smart.

"Are you fucking Jessa?" she snapped, punching him in the chest before she grabbed his chin in her hand roughly.

"Ow. What the hell?"

244 / Niobia Bryant

"Answer me, Kingston," she ordered coldly, giving him a bona fide Aunt Esther from *Sanford and Son* stare.

"What?" Kingston looked confused.

Aria felt Kingston's dick softening inside her. "Are you fucking Jessa?" she asked again, punching his chest as her anger built. Be it unreasonable. Be it premature. Be it unnecessary. It was building by the second until her entire body felt hot.

Kingston grabbed her wrists, locking them securely in his grasp. That only made her want to fight him more. "Calm your ass down, Aria," he ordered in a cold voice, tightening his grasp on her wrists as she continued to thrash about in his lap.

But she didn't calm down. Visions egged her on.

Kingston and Jessa fucking.

Kingston's head buried between Jessa's open thighs.

His dick in her hands. Her pussy. Her mouth.

But beyond the sex, visions of her husband and her best friend sharing intimate moments, laughing together, talking with each other, dating each other, planning a life together. That hurt more than anything.

Aria fought him harder.

"Aria. Aria! *Aria!*" Kingston rose to his feet, his dick slipping out of her in the process. Still holding her wrists, he twisted her arms behind her back and pulled her body tightly against his.

Aria's chest heaved as she looked up into the eyes of her husband. *Her* husband. *Her* man. *Her* life.

Her past—the men, the conniving, the tricking—had shown and taught her more than most teenagers would ever see. She had lost count of the married men or men with significant others she'd run through. She grew up mistrusting men and even when she stepped away from that life, the doubts remained. For so long she'd lived suspecting Kingston, watching him, monitoring him, feeling like she lived with only one foot on solid ground, waiting for their world to fall out from beneath her. She thought she'd prepared herself for it. She thought she knew what she would do when—not if—it happened.

She was wrong.

Kingston stared at her intensely, his eyes never wavering from hers. "Aria, I am not sleeping with Jessa or any other woman. Where is this coming from? What's going on?"

Aria's eyes searched his and she wished she could believe him. She truly wished she could turn back the hands of time to just before they all got that stupid-ass message from Jessa. It was imprinted on her brain:

> I LOVE HIM MORE THAN YOU, AND
> I NEED HIM MORE. HE'S MY MAN
> NOW.

Aria felt weak and she let her head drop to Kingston's shoulder. "Jessa sent this stupid-ass text to Renee, Jaime, and me saying that she's been having an affair with one of our husbands and that he was leaving one of us for her . . . today."

"What?"

Aria nodded, wishing that the smell of him didn't breathe life into her. "She's moved and everything."

"Okay, listen, Aria." Kingston released her hands and reached up to lightly grasp her face to tilt her head up. "I don't know what the fuck is going on between Jessa and nobody else, but I've never fucked her and I damn sure am not leaving you for her or anybody else."

Aria kept her hands at her sides. "I wish I could believe that, but with all three of you home and Jessa having no reason to lie, one of you changed your mind or plans to leave later—but one of you has betrayed one of us. And motherfucker, I need to know if it was you."

Kingston stiffened. "And I've already told you it wasn't me, Aria. I've never done anything to make you suspect me of cheating. It really should take more than a goddamn text message to having you acting this way," he told her coldly.

Aria stiffened as well. She brought her head up to look at him. "So I should have blind trust?" she asked, stepping out of his embrace to pace across the room in nothing but her red lace bra, which contrasted sharply against her dark, smooth skin.

"In the beginning, no, but after all these years I've earned blind trust, Aria," he shot back. "You've never trusted me."

She whirled to look at him, her face incredulous. "That's not true," she lied.

Kingston laughed bitterly as he reached down and snatched up his jeans. "You track me better than a damn LoJack. I get the third degree anytime I leave this house. The whole 'who, what, when, where, and why,' and I put up with it because I understand women's insecurities—"

"Insecurities?" Aria's eyes cut to him sharply. "What the fuck I got to be insecure about?"

Kingston sighed, holding up his hands. "Men cheat and they've made it hard for women to trust their man. All I'm saying is I understand that, Aria, and I put up with all the cloak-and-dagger crap because I had nothing to hide."

"What are you supposed to say, Kingston?" she asked sarcastically. "'Yes, I was fucking with Jessa and promised that bitch I would leave you for her.' Nigga, puh-leeze."

Kingston cocked his head to the side and walked over to her with angry strides. "Don't address me as a nigga, Aria. And as a matter of fact, is it necessary for every other word out your mouth to be profanity?"

Aria made an overly animated face of surprise before she began to clap her hands. "Or what, *nig-ga?* You gone whup my *motherfucking* ass, nig-ga? You gone wash my *fucking* mouth out with *motherfucking* soap, nig-ga?"

Kingston's eyes flashed with anger as his muscled chest

heaved. "Get yourself together to talk to me like a grown woman and then come talk to me. I'm not dealing with you like this," he said, waving his hand as he turned to stalk out of the room.

And that pissed Aria off, but shit was spiraling out of control fast. As much as she wanted to run across the room and jump on his back, she took a deep breath instead. "Kingston," she called out behind him.

He paused just outside the door but he didn't turn around.

Aria eyed the strong definition of his back and the way his jeans were slung so low on his hips that the tops of his square buttocks showed. "We need to work this out now or I don't know if we can come back from this."

Kingston stood there with his back to her and Aria had to admit that she wasn't sure he was coming back. "Come back from what?" he asked with attitude, finally turning to face her. "You had some bullshit—"

"Language, Mr. Holier-Than-Thou," Aria reminded him.

Kingston shook his head as he walked over to stand before her. "Your day has been filled with a bunch of crap dumped on you by your so-called friend, but in my world I made love to my wife this morning, went fishing with our friends all day, and came home to chill. I'm sorry your world got turned upside down, but nothing has changed for me and I don't know what you're talking about, Aria."

Aria pointed at her own chest, hating the tears of insecurity, confusion, anger, and distrust that filled her eyes. "Well, everything has changed for *me*. Every conversation between you and Jessa. Every bit of time we all spent together. Every touch between you two that seemed innocent—all of it is suspect now. All of it."

Kingston dropped down onto the bed as if defeated. "So you think I'm the type of man that would not only cheat on you but cheat on you with your best friend? That's what you think of me . . . Because if it is, then you and I have a big fucking problem, Aria."

Aria thought he sounded convincing, but she'd lain in many a bed with men who were on their cell phones with their wives and girlfriends swearing they weren't up to no good. It taught her well that men knew how to lie their asses off. "And if you were planning to leave me for another woman, then we have an even bigger fucking problem," she countered, determined to either get to the truth or get satisfaction that her husband wasn't Jessa's lover.

"Go to hell, Aria," he muttered, turning his back on her.

Aria spotted the five-by-seven frame holding one of their many wedding photos sitting on the nightstand and she snatched it up to fling at him. It clipped him on the shoulder and Aria actually clasped her hand over her mouth and gasped in shock.

Kingston turned and raced at her like a running back trying to carry a football past the goal line. "Oh, hell no!" he roared.

Aria's eyes widened as she let out a little yelp and turned to run, but Kingston tackled her onto the middle of the bed. He easily used his strength to lock both her legs with his thighs and one strong hand to capture both of her wrists high above her head.

"Don't you ever get physical with me again, Aria, and I mean it," he told her in a hard voice, his angry breath blowing in her face.

Aria tried her best to raise and arch her body to get him off her. He didn't budge. Her body was just pressed more intimately against the hard length of him. "Get the hell off of me."

"No," he answered her simply.

Aria closed her eyes and counted to ten. She tried like crazy to fight him off her, but she slowly stopped when she saw that her movements were turning him on. His eyes—

the eyes she knew so well with every emotion—were clearly filling with desire.

"No, Kingston," she said simply as his gaze dropped to watch the up-and-down motion of the top of her breasts.

He used his knees to nudge her legs open so that he lay between them.

Aria didn't bother to struggle against his strength any longer at the undeniable feel of his hard dick pressed against the top of her pussy.

Kingston pressed a kiss to the side of her neck and Aria bit her lip to keep from gasping in surprise and a hot shot of pure pleasure.

"Don't, Kingston, just don't," she pleaded.

He drew a trail from her collarbone to her earlobe with the fleshy tip of his tongue and she shivered in quick response to him. "You smell good. You taste good," he whispered against her neck. "You turn me the fuck on. All I can think about is putting all this dick in you."

"Get the fuck off—"

He kissed her, deeply swirling his tongue around her reluctant one and swallowing the rest of her protest. Aria hated the way the steam immediately rose from her body in response to him. She hated that her pussy walls quivered and her clit jumped to attention. She hated that only Kingston could make her feel this way. Only him.

Kingston shifted down to plant moist and electrifying kisses to the top of her plush breasts. Aria shook her head even as goose bumps raced across her nearly nude body. "No, Kingston. No," she pleaded, but her sorry-ass protests sounded weak even to her own ears.

He shifted his body down again, still holding her wrists as he sucked her nipples through the flimsy revealing lace of her brassiere. Aria arched her back and shut her eyes as an intense wave of pleasure hit her, dead center of her pussy. His tongue felt divine, and when he tugged the cup down to expose her hard chocolate nipple she was glad the barrier—although slight—was gone.

"Kingston," she whispered in pleasure.

"That's right, baby," he moaned against her aching nipples.

Her entire body relaxed and he felt the change in her, releasing her wrists. She knew she should fight him off, get to the bottom of the ugly truths in the room, but in that moment she couldn't resist her husband's sex appeal, their chemistry, or the urgency building inside her to cum.

And he obliged.

He rose from atop her and Aria licked her lips as she watched his hard and ready dick straining against the zipper of his jeans as he unzipped them. His dick sprang free like a pumped fist and she squirmed on the bed in anticipation. She was ready, willing, and waiting.

Kingston lowered himself to the bed again and kissed her from her ankles to her thighs. "Nobody . . . nobody can mess this up, Aria. Nobody," he whispered against her heated skin.

Aria wished she could unequivocally believe him.

He continued his hot kisses and sucks and licks up to her inner thighs, and Aria's pussy flooded in anticipation. "Once I met you, I knew there was no other woman for me, Aria. I *knew* that," he told her fiercely, just before his strong, healing hands spread her legs wide and then pushed them up high so that her ass and her pussy were high in the air before him.

Aria gave in to the seduction and brought her hands up to lightly twist and tease her aching nipples as she arched her back and welcomed the first cool feel of his tongue circling her ass before he licked the split of her pussy.

"Kingston," she cried out, her head twisting back and forth on the bed as he sucked her clit between his lips and kissed life into her soul like only he could.

And this was the type of explosive and emotional connection they had all the time. Who could compete, compare, or conquer it? Who?

She looked up as he shifted to kneel between her legs and tap her swollen and wet clit with the tip of his dick. *Pat-pat-pat-pat-pat.* "Yes," Aria cried out, massaging her breasts as she used her muscles to open and close the plump lips of her pussy before him.

"Damn, baby." Kingston stared down at her pussy tricks as he sat back and began to massage the hard length of his dick with a tight grip. "Work that pussy. Shit."

Aria eased her hands down from her breasts to massage her thick thighs deeply before she slid one of her fingers deep inside her rigid pussy while she massaged her sensitive clit with her thumb.

Kingston's mouth fell open as he watched her. "Man, give me that good pussy," he told her, rising up to carefully ease his dick between her lips, mindful of his wideness and length.

Aria gasped at the hot feel of his dick against her walls. She cried out, not caring who heard her.

Kingston lowered his body onto hers and wrapped his muscular arms around her to hold her close to him as he pressed kisses along her shoulders, collarbone, and neck. He slowly ground his hips against her and she wrapped her long legs around his waist, welcoming and reveling in the feel of his dick massaging her walls in wicked circles that caused her juices to wet him until they were drizzling down her ass onto the sheets.

"I love you, Aria. No one but you. I swear," he whispered into her ear. "No one."

"Kingston," she moaned as he pulled his dick all the way out, massaged her throbbing clit with the tip, and then swooped back deep inside her in one fluid motion.

"Tell me you love me," he demanded.

And regardless of anything, Aria couldn't deny that she loved this man, her husband, with everything she had inside her. "I love you, Kingston. I love you so much," she whispered up to him. "Please don't hurt me."

Kingston leaned up to look down into her eyes. "I'll never do anything to hurt you, Aria. Never," he swore before he lowered his head to kiss her deeply. "We might make our baby tonight, huh?"

Tears flooded her eyes. Her own guilt and secrets, the texts, the betrayal, the suspicions, the long-ass day, their angry confrontation, the explosive sex. All of it was too much for her to keep up her usual barrier against her emotions. It was *all* just too damn much.

Long after he stroked his dick inside her for nearly an hour before forcefully filling her with his cum, Aria lay beside him and watched him sleep in the moonlit darkness of their bedroom. Questions plagued her until sleep was completely lost to her.

Questions she needed answers to before she and Kingston could ever get back to their happiness.

Easing from the bed, Aria searched and found her cell phone on the floor by the foot of the bed. She walked into the bathroom and closed the door securely behind her before she bathed the room with light. Quickly she typed away.

KINGSTON SAYS NOT HIM. STILL NOT SURE. WHAT DID ERIC & JACK-SON SAY???

She hit Send and hoped her friends were up and able to answer her. She knew it was wrong to hope Jackson or Eric had confessed, but she had to know the truth. Her marriage was on the line.

Bzzzzzz.

Her cell phone vibrated in her hands and Aria jumped to attention where she sat on the edge of the Jacuzzi tub.

It was Renee.

JACKSON DENIES IT. CALL U
TOMORROW.

Two down, one to go. But it didn't make her feel better
that it was Eric. He was the most doting of husbands. But
he and Jessa were friends before he even married Jaime.
Maybe the friendship had turned into something more?

Aria knew she was reaching and that she was wrong to
almost wish pain on her friend so that she could be happy
again.

Bzzzzzz.

Aria jumped to her feet and paced as she retrieved the
text from Jaime. Her stomach was filled with nerves.

ERIC SAYS IT WASN'T HIM.
DOESN'T MATTER ANYMORE. I
LEFT HIM. AT A HOTEL. NEVER FELT
SO FREE. FUCK IT.

Aria's phone nearly slipped from her hands and she had
to hustle to catch it before it dropped into the commode.
Jaime left Eric. Jaime cursing. Jaime at a hotel. *WTF?*
"What?" she gasped in shock as she dialed Jaime's cell
phone number.

Brrrnnnggg . . . brrrnnnggg . . . brrrnnnggg.

Aria hung up when the cell phone went to Jaime's voice
mail. Aria tried to call her twice more, but both times Jaime
didn't answer so Aria left her alone. She lowered the lid to
the commode and slumped down onto it, ignoring the cool
shock of the first feel of the porcelain pressed against her
ass.

All of her journalism training kicked in and the questions flooded her, overwhelming her.

Which of the husbands had cheated with Jessa?

If all three came home, was the answer none at all? But

why would Jessa lie? Or had the culprit not had the balls to follow through on their plan to be together? Would the affair continue? Would Jessa resurface now that her plans had fallen apart?

There was one thing Aria knew for sure without question.

This all was far from over.

JESSA'S OUTRO

I hardly slept last night. As I lay in my bed alone, watching the sun rising in the sky, I guessed the final laugh was on me. My lover. The man I gave up so much for never showed last night. He never even called. And when I called him, his cell phone was turned off.

Did it hurt to be rejected? Lied to? Mistreated?

I sighed as I turned over in bed, able to roll wherever I chose without interruption. I swore that last night, for the first time, I would have him in my bed—our bed for the first night of many nights.

I guess the last laugh is on me.

For all the tough talk. For all the bravado of being a mistress who couldn't care less. I'm not heartless. These women were my friends. We shared many moments together. We made many memories.

I knew what my lover and I did was as wrong as two left shoes, but how could I make them understand?

After my husband's death, the loneliness and the grief caused an ache in me that no one could understand. Nothing soothing could touch it. I felt like a huge part of me died on the inside. Life as I knew it was over.

And every day something in me—the old me—faded. The smiles that had come to my face in the past were real, but soon I was just projecting the Jessa Bell that they wanted to see.

After that first night I became consumed with him and he became the light in my life of darkness and gloom. He said and did all the right things. He made me believe we were destined to be together, regardless of what or whom. He convinced me that he was willing to walk away from it all to be with me.

I gambled on his love and lost.

Did I regret sending the message, taunting my friends, who were now most definitely foes? I didn't know. It was spiteful and childish. And the Fates had a way of making a person regret the things that they'd done. Maybe my little message was the reason I was lying in this cold bed, in my four-hundred-dollar La Perla . . . alone. I looked around the room at the candles melted down to the wick and the scattered flower petals already drying out to a crisp. Remnants of a night gone wrong.

But it was more than just a night of disappointment. I'd had plenty of those in the last year. This might just be the end of our affair.

I had some decisions to make if it was.

Flinging back the covers, I climbed from the bed and flipped my hair over my shoulder and out of my face. I walked up to the mirror on the dresser and studied my body. He claimed he couldn't get enough of this body. Only time would tell.

Brrrnnnggg.

I cut my eyes over to my black and silver BlackBerry on the nightstand. I smoothed the pale sage lace of the low-cut bikinis over my wide hips as I walked over to scoop it up.

It was him.

I licked my lips as I sent it to voice mail.

I wasn't worried because I knew he would call back.

Brrrnnnggg.

This time I answered. Even as my heart pounded I played it ever so cool and turned to lean back against the dresser. "Did you have a good night, because I didn't," I said, hating that even in the midst of my bitter disappointment, I wanted him and craved for him to rush here into my arms and tell me that he was here to stay for good.

"Why did you send that text?" he asked.

"Why did you lie about being with me?" I countered.

"That was a childish stunt you pulled sending that text, Jessa."

"Come spank me," I taunted low in my husky voice.

"This is not a joke, Jessa," he snapped darkly.

"And neither is my life and my feelings."

The line went quiet and I said nothing, leaving a gap wide open for him to slide in an explanation, an apology, a damn let-down. Something.

"I love you, Jessa, and I don't want to lose you . . . but now is not a good time for us to go public."

A let-down it is, I thought, shaking my head at the very shame of it all.

"That damn text of yours put me in a bind. It could cost me—us—big. You shouldn't have sent it."

My eyes shifted to the beside table where an eight-by-ten framed photo of us sat. We were at a black-tie dinner with the entire group but had snuck away to snap photos with our cell phones. As he continued his tirade, I kept my eyes locked on that photo as I walked around my lonesome bed toward it.

"So what are you saying, lover?" I asked in a soft voice as I tilted my head to the side and picked the picture up.

He sighed heavily into the phone. "I think we should take a little break from each other. Your little stunt really didn't give me much choice."

So it was over. That hurt. "Really?" I ask.

I plopped down onto the bed and shoved my cell phone between my ear and shoulder as I took the picture from the frame. I tore away his image, looking down into his lying face.

"Yes, Jessa. I'm sorry."

"So everything you've told me this last year has been a lie. You have used me up and now you want to throw me away?" I asked, as rage rose in me steady and fast.

"You gave me no choice."

I reached for a lighter I used for my many candles and lit the corner of the photo. The sight of the fire building and then slowly evaporating his face fascinated me to no end. "You're a liar, because you weren't even supposed to go back there. You were supposed to come straight to me. And you didn't. You had no intention of leaving her," I said in a quiet voice.

"No, you're wrong. I went home to tell her face-to-face. It's the least she deserved."

"And what do I deserve? Heartache, lies, deceit? Huh? Huh? A mortgage and rent?" I stood to drop the burning photo in the wastepaper basket. "Scorn and retribution?"

"Don't, Jessa."

I just laughed and it was filled with my bitterness and my pain. "I wouldn't do this if I was you, lover," I warned.

I was like Pandora's box, filled with secrets and costly repercussions. If he lied to me and left me high and dry with both my mortgage and the costly lease on this new home of "ours," I would definitely be the woman scorned and play my role accordingly. Believe that.

"Jessa, we need to talk face-to-face—"

"Looking for one last shot of ass for the road?" I asked, as I walked to my closet and pulled out an outfit that could only be Sunday best. "I'll call you when I get time."

I flipped the phone closed and flung it over my shoulder to land on my bed. Time to put a lying Negro on time-out, I thought as the BlackBerry rang incessantly. I ignored it as I walked into my bathroom and closed the door behind me.

I emerged nearly one hour later, body scrubbed and now oiled and smelling of my most exotic perfume. My make-up put on like I was a true professional at it. My hair pressed to perfection.

The scent of the burnt photo still hung in the air and I inhaled deeply of it as I dressed in my lingerie and the black lace suit I'd selected from my wardrobe.

Behind the wheel of my Jaguar, I thought of how my life was my own and I'd made the mistake of making decisions based on a man—and someone's man at that. Well, I was a mistress no more.

It was time to get several things straight.

I pulled my car to a stop and lowered the driver's side window.

"Mrs. Bell, I thought you moved," Lucky said, his portly red face more flushed than normal.

"I thought so too," I said, flashing him my best smile.

"Your friends were surprised you moved," he said.

Humph. "Don't worry, I'm sure they'll be . . . even more surprised to see me."

"Have a good one." Lucky stepped back into the booth to open the wrought iron gates of Richmond Hills.

"Lucky, I plan to have a great one," I told him as I pulled away from him and entered Richmond Hills.

Guess who's back.

Dear Readers,

Message from a Mistress left you with just a few cliff-hangers, huh? As a writer, I know that cliff-hangers can be hit or miss with readers, but I really had no choice because the stories of Aria, Renee, and Jaime were just beginning. Secrets still to be discovered. Questions still to be answered. Drama continuing to unfold.

Needless to say, y'all know there is a part two, currently entitled *Mistress No More*. And those questions that are running through your clever heads will be answered: Will Eric and Jaime reunite? Will Aria ever reveal to Kingston that she can't have children? And how will Renee deal with her husband fathering a child with another woman? And there is much more that these three housewives are going to experience.

But you'll have to wait to see. I promise it will be worth it.

Best,

N.

Connect with Niobia

Websites

www.niobiabryant.com
www.meeshamink.com

E-mails

niobia_bryant@yahoo.com
meeshamink@yahoo.com

MySpaces

www.myspace.com/niobiawrites
www.myspace.com/meeshamink

Facebook

www.facebook.com/InfiniteInk (Niobia Bryant & Meesha Mink)

Shelfari

www.shelfari.com/Unlimited_Ink (Niobia Bryant & Meesha Mink)

Twitter

www.twitter.com/InfiniteInk (Niobia Bryant & Meesha Mink)

Yahoo! Group

www.groups.yahoo.com/group/Niobia_Bryant_News

Right now I'm on Twitter and Facebook more than anything. Follow me. ☺